# Nurses Under Fire

## WORLD WAR TWO NOVEL

*To Polly*
*May we always*
*be free*
*Brenda*

## BRENDA JONES

Disclaimer

The persons appearing in this novel are fictitious with the exception of General Douglas MacArthur, General Wainwright, Brigadier General Raymond W. Bliss and Colonel Yoshie. The characters are a product of my imagination and were developed over several years of reading historical accounts of the nurses and the battles fought in the South Pacific.

Nurses Under Fire
Brenda Jones
Copyright 2005

ISBN 1-930052-24-2
Library of Congress Number 2005927573


Printed in the USA by
Quill Publications, Columbus, GA

Published by:

Cherokee Books
231 Meadow Ridge Pkwy
Dover, DE 19904

LET US NOT FORGET THE SACRIFICES

OF THE NURSES WHO FOUGHT

FOR OUR FREEDOM

**THIS BOOK IS DEDICATED TO MY FATHER**
**CHESTER G. AMOS**
**(1919-1994)**
*A Veteran of the South Pacific*

# Acknowledgments

Thanks to the following friends for their emotional and physical support.

Dr. Rafael Zaragoza for his willingness to share memories of the war with me, for reviewing the novel and loaning photographs to be included. Special thanks also to his wife, Claire Zaragoza, for giving me feedback from a nurses' point of view.

Dr. Venerando Maximo of Dover, Delaware and his nephews Ariel Maximo and Eric Maximo, residents of the Philippines, for giving me an excellent tour of Santo Tomas and other points of interest. Thanks also to Dr. Maximo for loaning photographs taken in his homeland.

This book could not have been completed without the dedicated proofreading, by my dear friend, Myrna Valle. Thank you.

A special appreciation goes to my husband for his patience, love and support throughout my writing career. Thanks for standing by me during all of the thrills and dis-appointments.

Kelly Hayes, my daughter, for having faith in me, and my son-in-law, Michael for coming to my aid when I encountered computer difficulties. And last but not least, a special thanks to my grandchildren, Rebecca and Jonathan, for their continuous enthusiasm.

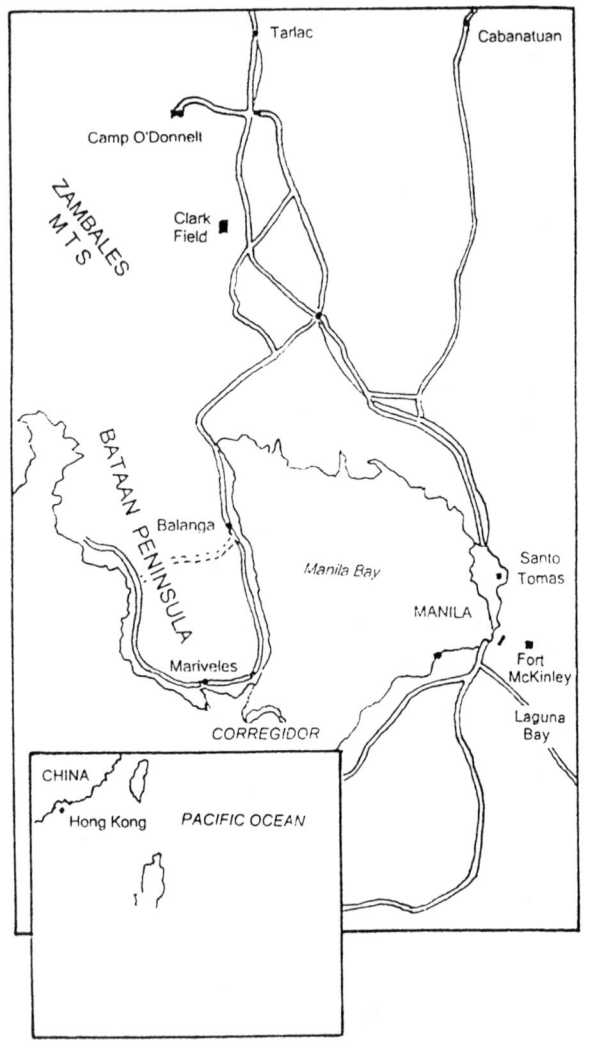

Tarlac

Cabanatuan

Camp O'Donnell

ZAMBALES MT S

Clark Field

BATAAN PENINSULA

Balanga

Manila Bay

Santo Tomas

MANILA

Mariveles

Fort McKinley

CORREGIDOR

Laguna Bay

CHINA

Hong Kong

PACIFIC OCEAN

6

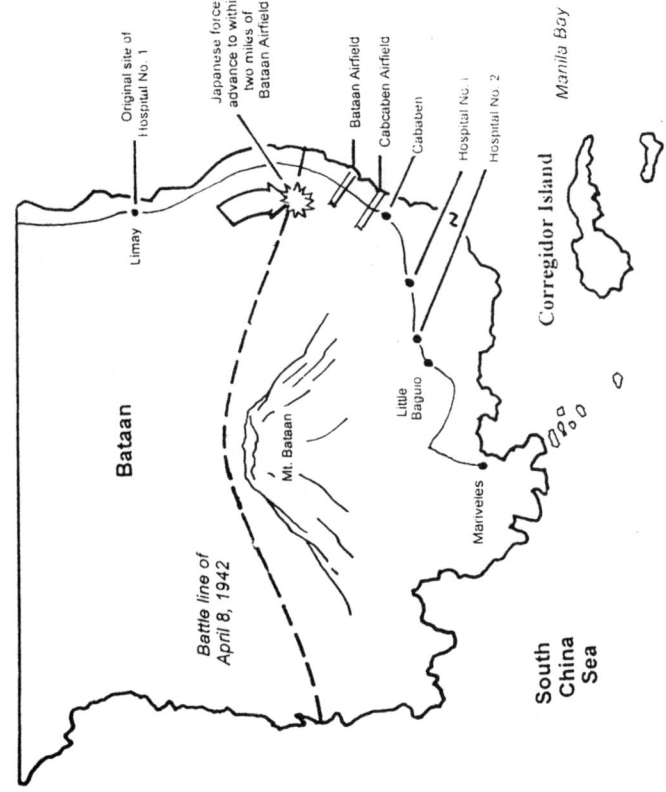

Bataan

Battle line of
April 8, 1942

Mt. Bataan

Original site of
Hospital No. 1

Limay

Japanese forces
advance to within
two miles of
Bataan Airfield

Bataan Airfield

Cabcaben Airfield

Cabcaben

Hospital No. 1

Hospital No. 2

Little
Baguio

Mariveles

Corregidor Island

Manila Bay

South
China
Sea

# Corregidor Island

Corregidor Bay

BOTTOMSIDE

South Dock

General Wainright's surrender

Stockade

North Dock

Breakwater Point

Battery Point

Power Plant & Cold Storage

MIDDLESIDE

Ramsey Battery

Service Club

Crockett Battery

James Battery

Morrison Battery

HOSPITAL

Geary Battery

Officers' Quarters

Morrison Point

Way Morter Battery

Topside Barracks

Parade Ground

Wheeler Tunnel

Hearn Battery

Smith Battery

Cheney Battery

Wheeler Tunnel

TOPSIDE

Monga Battery

Rock Point

# Chapter One

*December 10, 1941*
*The Philippines*
*Sternberg Hospital*

"What's that roar?" Knocking over her bamboo lounge chair, Cora raced to the balcony railing.

Claire quickly joined her companion. Mesmerized they stared into the sky.

"Those are Japanese Zeroes!" Cora screamed leaning over the wooden structure. Before the words fully escaped her lips the sky darkened. Silhouettes of eighty planes with large red circles on the underside of the wings formed a V formation over the Sternberg hospital in downtown Manila.

Standing helplessly under the shadow of the Zeroes the two nurses watched bombs fall on the Port of Manila. Deafening explosions thundered throughout the city, high shooting flames erupted through clouds of billowing black smoke. One by one fuel storage tanks exploded.

"We've got to get to the emergency room! Now!" Cora screamed. Forcing her body to move she grabbed Claire's arm pulling her from the balcony. Cora's world revolved in slow motion as she raced to her room in the back of the hospital complex. Her mind and body returned to their normal speed once she entered her room.

Ripping a white starched white uniform from a wire hanger, the stamped identification inside the collar, *2nd Lieutenant Cora Leigh Adams, US Army Nurse Corps,* took on a new meaning. Cora realized the responsibility she had accepted. A chill shot up her spine. *I really am serving my country.* She pulled the uniform on over green shorts and a yellow blouse. *This is no time to worry about regulations like white nylons.* She stepped into her white clinic shoes and quickly tied the strings.

Cora met 2nd Lieutenant Claire Theresa West outside her door and void of verbal communication the two twenty-three year old women sprinted down the corridor, across the lawn to the hospital's main hall and into the emergency room. Doctors, nurses and orderlies scurried about setting up extra stations with bandages and medicine. Ambulances from Clark Field were arriving with wounded that could not be treated in the small facility at Stotsenberg.

Sirens sounding across the city accompanied a steady stream of civilian and military casualties into the hospital. The wounded were carried in the arms of men, on stretchers and a few walking wounded wandered into the emergency room unaided. Within the hour the area filled with casualties, the courtyards holding the overflow. Moans and screams echoed through the long marble-floored corridor and into the congested emergency room. Off-duty nurses appearing on the scene received instructions on the procedure of separating and treating casualties.

"Separate the surgical cases from the burn cases!" Captain Jennings shouted. The short, stocky head-nurse, with a stiff white cap perched on top of gray hair resembling a used Brillo pad, scurried about the ward to the swishing sound of her well-starched uniform. Her charges normally hated her formality, especially the attention she gave to detail and regulations. Today they appreciated her leadership and World War I experiences.

"Start down that row," Captain Jennings shouted at Cora and Claire, pointing to a row of blood soaked stretchers against the wall, "Assess the wounds and if they need surgery send them upstairs!"

Screams and odors of burned flesh and mass confusion turned to panic. "Move! Now!" their supervisor shouted. "That's an order!"

Within seconds they were bending over soldiers evaluating wounds and giving words of encouragement, while attempting to hide expressions of shock. They were doing what they had trained to do. Cora leaned over an unconscious soldier who did not appear old enough to shave, and with trembling fingers she searched for a pulse. Nothing.

"Forget regulations," screamed Capt. Jennings tossing Cora a stethoscope. "It is time nurses were allowed to carry these things. Keep it with you!" Cora caught the black and silver instrument, placed the black stubby ends in her ears and found a pulse on the young man. *Oh no, I thought he was dead, I nearly kept him from receiving help.* She looked up in time to see Claire arrive with a 20cc-glass syringe; a disquieting glance passed between them before Claire medicated the casualty with 2ccs from the full syringe. Before moving to the next patient Claire said, "We have standing orders to administer a 2cc dose of morphine."

Cora stared at her with a questioning glare.

"What?" Claire asked. Not waiting for an answer she said, "Forget about changing needles, I can get ten doses out of one syringe. It saves time." They moved on to their next patient.

"Time saves lives," Cora whispered placing the stethoscope on another young man's chest.

The medical team worked feverishly through the rows of men and women screaming in pain, silent ones in shock, the unconscious and those not breathing. The nurses' terror-stricken expressions turned to concern as they moved about like robots from one stretcher case to another. Overflowing adrenaline enabled their minds and bodies to function beyond normal capacities.

Cora moved down the line of casualties that were on blood soaked stretchers, old doors and sheets of corrugated metal. Small-frightened children were held in the arms of those that could stand. The children's large, dark, round eyes expressed the terror of those around them.

*I can't believe I'm performing triage!* Cora thought as she assessed each soldier, sailor, marine and civilian while assuring them that they would be taken care of and they would be fine. "Get this man into surgery," she screamed to a young orderly while rushing to the side of another wounded kid. Glancing back at the orderly, thinking he could not hear her over all of the noise she yelled again, "Come on get moving," but the boy was in shock. With the help of Cora and a medic the orderly picked up one end of the stretcher and moved in a daze to a holding area.

"Hang on, soldier," Cora said pushing stray damp strands of her hair from her moist forehead. Forcing a smile she added, "This will stop the pain." She motioned for Claire. Claire plunged the needle through the Corporal's sleeve and into his muscular arm, his only arm. After checking the tourniquet, Cora turned her head willing the dizziness to stop. As it did she tightened the tourniquet never releasing the pressure on his open wound. *Deep breaths. Deep breaths*, she repeated to herself until she turned him over to another Filipino orderly.

"No training in the world could have prepared us for this disaster," Cora said through clenched teeth while wiping her bloody hands on her blood streaked uniform. She tried to rip another young man's sleeve but Claire plunged the needle through his shirt.

"The line of wounded is not going to get shorter any time soon," Cora said. "They are bringing more wounded in from Clark Field. I heard a medic say it was totally destroyed and the hospital at Fort Stotsenberg can't handle any more casualties, regardless of their severity."

The stifling temperature in the overcrowded emergency area intensified the stench of open wounds and charred flesh mixed with perspiration. *Thank goodness this isn't the rainy season*, Cora thought as she reached the next victim. Pushing the thoughts of the last young casualty out of her mind she focused on the new patient's needs. Placing the stethoscope on his neck she looked into his young boyish swollen face and grasped his flailing hands. "I'm 2nd Lieutenant Cora Adams. You're in Sternberg hospital and we're going to take care of you." Before the words were out of her mouth she realized shrapnel had blinded him. Hoping he could not detect the fear in her voice, she continued, "Try to stay quiet now, we are sending you into surgery." She was thankful he could not see the pity in her eyes. The medics had slowed the bleeding before moving him, but his pulse was weak. Quickly Cora packed the wound with more gauze and called for the medic to keep pressure on the wound and get him in line for surgery.

She moved on to another young boy who did not look old enough to be out of school let alone fighting in a war. His damp black curls reminded her of another man injured several years earlier, but she wouldn't allow her mind to dwell on the past. She had work to do. The sailor's legs were blown off below the knees. *Oh, this is worse than the baby raccoon I found caught in a trap with two feet cut off. That was seventeen years ago and I can't forget it.*

"Quick, Claire, over here! He needs morphine now!" *Why did I allow my mind to wander, I've lost valuable seconds.* Cora moved the stethoscope to his neck then lowering her head removed it, "Never mind, give it to someone it will help." Cora motioned for Father Arroyo to give last rites before summoning a medic. "Tag him and move him out with the other fatalities," she said refusing to allow herself to think of him as someone's brother, son, husband, dad or friend – there was no time – he was just another war casualty. Like the other medical personnel working that day she did her job putting aside personal emotions.

Ignoring her exhaustion, Cora knelt beside Claire to check the next casualty in the seemingly endless line. "Do you know if Betsy, Spencer and Flint got back from the officer's club?" Cora asked as they worked side by side. Second Lieutenant Betsy Brown, Cora and Claire became friends while sailing from San Diego to Manila on the USS Holbrook. They were assigned the same shift at the Sternberg Hospital allowing them to spend most of their free time together sightseeing, shopping and going to the

Army-Navy Club for dinner, movies, bowling and dancing.

"No, and I'm worried about them."

"Hey Antonio," Cora yelled at an orderly that she knew played cards with the doctors. "Have you seen Spencer, Flint or Betsy?"

"Yes ma'am, I got a glimpse of them running down the hall. They went straight to surgery from the tennis courts in their white outfits."

"Thanks, I was afraid to ask."

The orderly smiled and disappeared from the area.

Claire said, "I tried not to think of what might have happened to them."

Cora pictured Dr. Flint Taylor running to the surgical floor. *He is the best surgeon I've ever worked with and I'm glad he's here.*

Claire disappeared to refill her syringe. When she returned she said, "Cora, Capt. Jennings said for us to take a thirty minute break, we've been here for eight hours."

"No, we can't leave, these people need us."

"It was not a suggestion, it was an order!"

Cora stood. Placing her hands in the small of her back she stretched while rotating her head in a circular motion. "Okay, let's go have a cup of coffee and a cigarette."

"No. She said for us to eat. We're going to be here for a long time!"

A tropical breeze flowed through the open-air dining facility cooling their overheated bodies. They moved through the cafeteria line like zombies until their trays were filled with sandwiches, fruit and coffee. Seated at a table they took in the sweet aroma of the tropical flowers as a welcomed change from the odors in the emergency room. Taking a deep breath Cora said, "This is quite a contrast, isn't it?"

"Yes it is, but my body won't slow down. I think I'm tired, but I'm not sure."

"Eventually our production of adrenaline will slow down." Cora placed a piece of mango in her parched mouth, savoring the sweet juice.

"Yea, I just hope the casualties slow down at the same rate."

Cora picked up another piece of mango and examining it she asked, "Weren't we enjoying a cool mango drink on the balcony when this nightmare began?"

"Yes, and I was in the middle of a fashion article in the new copy of *Life*."

The remainder of the meal was eaten in silence, then a cigarette and second cup of coffee were enjoyed. Claire glanced back toward the emergency room. "Have you ever seen anything like this in your life?"

"Yes." Cora answered staring into the cup of hot caffeine.

"Really? I've never even imagined a catastrophe of this magnitude." Claire stared at Cora, "When? I mean where?"

Cora continued to gaze into her cup of coffee. "I grew up in a coal mining town in West Virginia and the accidents at the mines were in some ways similar to this, only on a much smaller scale."

"Did you know the people that were injured?"

"Of course, I knew them all." Cora paused. She stared at the smoke rising from the cigarette in her hand, then said, "We're lucky we don't know most of the causalities. I feel sorry for the Filipino nurses and orderlies, they know many of these victims."

"Did you ever lose anyone close to you in a mining accident?"

Cora's eyes stung from tears trying to erupt, "Yes." She tipped her cup and consumed the last of the coffee. Placing the cup on the tray she glanced at her watch. "Look at the time, we need to be getting back to the emergency room." Both women crushed their cigarettes in the glass ashtray and deposited their trays on their way out of the dining room.

Upon reentering the chaotic emergency room Cora and Claire relieved Rose Perez and Lydia Vargas, Filipino nurses that were in need of a break. Cora glanced toward the main door and thought, *is there no end to the line of wounded?* Without an answer she bent over a young soldier and started the process over again; she felt like a stuck record on a phonograph with the needle playing the same words over and over.

"Hang on, Soldier, we're going to take care of you," Cora repeated while working to stop blood spurting from a wound with a chunk of cement protruding from it. "I need help over here!" There was no one available and she worked furiously to keep the young man alive until one of the surgeons could take over. When he was taken away she stepped over another mangled body lying in a pool of blood to get to her next patient.

The burns were over fifty percent of the boy's body; charred flesh hung from him like angel hair hanging on a Christmas tree. She gave him an injection of morphine and while it took affect she spoke softly, " You are in the best hospital in the Philippines and we are going to stop your pain. Now go to sleep while I bandage your burns." *I wonder if he can hear me for the pain? So many nerve endings are exposed, and he's losing fluids fast. It is no wonder he's in shock.* Cora wasted no time in cutting away what was left of his burned uniform; it was then that she identified him as a sailor.

Claire and Cora moved from one wounded patient to the next until they had worked twelve hours. Once again they were given an order, this time it was to sleep for four hours and report back for new assignments.

"Let's stop by the dining room and get a sandwich before going to bed," Claire suggested.

"Bed? All I can think of is a hot shower, I feel like I am covered in blood and it's not mine!"

"Okay, let's get something to eat, shower then go to bed."

"That sounds great."

"Hey look who I see!" Claire said entering the dining room.

Cora turned in time to see Flint waving a napkin in the air.

"Over here," he called out.

Cora's face flushed, her lips involuntarily forming a smile as she and Claire joined Army surgeons Majors Flint Taylor and Spencer Kirby at a large round table.

"Where is Betsy?" Cora asked as she sat.

"We sent her to her room to get some rest," Flint answered.

"You two look like that's where you should be too," Spencer added.

"We're on our way, but decided to eat first," Claire said.

"Guess we won't be going to the Army Navy Club for

dinner and dancing tomorrow evening – or is it already tomorrow?" Flint sounded as exhausted as he looked.

"No, I don't think we will. You two need to get some sleep too, you look awful," Cora informed them.

"I bet you wanted to tell me that plenty of times when we were working together in West Virginia, didn't you?" Flint asked as a little twisted smile erupted.

"I don't want to hear the answer to that," Claire said. Spencer laughed as Cora squirmed.

"What makes you think I noticed how you looked?" She answered sarcastically.

Flint turned to Spencer. "She hated me. The woman hated me. Can you believe that?"

"Hey, leave me out of this," Spencer said and lifted his coffee cup to his lips.

Claire stood, "I don't want to hear this, I'm going to get us some sandwiches," she said and left.

"Cora won't admit it but I'm the reason she joined the Nurses Corps. She wanted to get away from me. She hated my looks, my personality and me. Right?" Flint asked.

"You can't prove that and I'm too tired to argue, but I will say you were different when you worked in Wheeling." Cora looked at Spencer and tipped her chin upward. "New big city doctor came to the rescue of the poor pitiful nurses at the Ohio Valley Hospital." She paused and turned to Flint. "Actually I don't think you had a personality then."

"Whoa," Spencer said. "I was right! I knew there was bad blood between you two the morning Flint and I met you, Claire and Betsy. "Were you really as disgusted at finding him here as you appeared to be?"

19

"You bet I was! But until now I thought I had done a good job of hiding it." Cora removed a cigarette from her pocket and Flint quickly produced his lighter. "I was looking forward to my assignment to Manila, 'The Pearl of the Orient,' every nurse's dream." She inhaled slowly and tipping her head upward, released the smoke. "Then he appeared; I just knew he was here to sabotage my tour."

Spencer chuckled and Flint smiled and continued watching Cora as he asked. "And have I?"

Stammering she said, "Well no, but you were so obnoxious before that . . ."

"Here is dinner," Claire announced arriving with a tray of sandwiches, fruit, cookies and coffee. Cora welcomed the interruption. "Oh good, let's eat and call it a day."

"Good idea, I'm sure we'll have more casualties coming in," Spencer said.

"We're lucky to be here after hearing what the Japanese did to Pearl Harbor, but the good thing is this war can't last. Everyone says it will be over in a day or two," he flashed a smile at Cora exposing his perfect white teeth. "Then will you have dinner with me to celebrate our victory?"

Cora could not deny she was attracted to him. The combination of wavy chestnut hair, ocean blue eyes and his display of charm and charisma made him irresistible. With her mouth full she nodded hoping he could not read her mind.

\* \* \*

Six days later there had been no celebration, the fighting continued. In Betsy's room Cora, Claire and Betsy examined their new uniforms issued by the army. "I know I'm tired, but doesn't this tag say size 44?" Cora held the tag for them to examine.

"Yes," Betsy giggled, then realizing that she too had been issued size 44 coveralls. "This drab olive-green is bad enough, but size 44!" She lifted the uniform to her shoulders.

"Oh no, this can't be right. Mine are size 44 too!" Claire announced through laughter. "At least with my blonde hair I look nice in olive green."

"We could make you two pair out of one and have material left over," Betsy said continuing to study the large ugly coveralls.

Cora, the tallest of the three, five feet and six inches, held the uniform to her shoulders while they laughed. "Oh poor Rose and Lydia, they are both a size two," she managed to say between bursts of laughter. "We will never find them."

"Listen to us, we're so tired we're silly."

"I don't know about being silly, but I'm numb and I have to report to surgery in one hour."

"I sure miss those four hour shifts we used to have," Claire said.

Standing in front of a mirror Betsy stared at her reflection. "Yea, it's been so long since I've sat on the beach that I'm losing my gorgeous tan"

"Enough complaining, come with me." Cora marched straight to her room with the two nurses following. From a mahogany chest she removed her homemade sewing basket. While she lifted the lid and took out a red pincushion, a needle and thread Claire and Betsy watched with their mouths open. Cora removed a straight pin and began pinning her coveralls for alteration.

"I didn't know you could sew," Betsy said peering over the seamstress's shoulder.

"I can't remember when I couldn't," Cora responded. "Nearly all of my clothes that needed to be patched or altered were home made or hand-me-downs from older cousins." She stopped working and lowered the coveralls into her lap. "Come to think of it I never knew any woman who couldn't sew or do some type of needlework." She raised her brow, "Until maybe now."

"My mother taught piano and I have five older brothers, so all I learned was to stay outside and play with the boys," Betsy said. "Mostly we played baseball, football, kickball and basketball. In Chicago we always had enough kids around to have two teams. No one was interested in sewing, especially me."

"All I know how to do is knit. My Aunt Irene taught me how when I moved to Maine. That's what you do during a Maine winter." Claire said.

"Well, I don't sew because I enjoy it, in fact I promised myself when I left the Appalachian region I would never make or alter my clothes again." Cora chuckled, "But right now I'm glad I know how." She stopped working and told Claire and Betsy she would do the alterations on one pair for each of them now and another pair later. "Just pin them where they need taken in and shortened. I'll do the best I can to make us presentable."

Betsy sighed, "Thanks, I don't think Capt. Jennings would appreciate me wearing them pinned with safety pins."

While Cora worked at making the coveralls fit, the threesome discussed events that had previously taken place. "It's hard to believe that just a week ago we were trying on hats not coveralls." Betsy said. "Remember? We were touring a hat factory."

"Yes, and we were silly that day too. Remember how we tried on hats and laughed? It's a wonder they didn't ask us to leave." Claire said.

"I think they were about to when we left to meet Flint, Spencer and Brice, the handsome B-17 Army Air Corp pilot, for dinner before seeing *Road to Singapore* with Bob Hope and Bing Crosby," Cora said and began humming.

"I really like the guys, especially the pilot. There is just something about a dress uniform that I can't resist," Betsy said whirling around the room.

* * *

The next seventeen days ran together like raindrops forming one giant puddle. "I'm beginning to feel like a zombie," Cora told Betsy and Claire while walking from the nurses quarters to the hospital dining room.

"Well, I'm telling you these long shifts are really messing up my social life!" Betsy announced.

"Yes, but we all know this is only temporary, the war can't last much longer." Cora said echoing the words heard daily throughout the hospital.

"It's hard to believe it's only two days until Christmas," Claire said as they entered the main dining room. After going through the buffet line they sat at a round table covered with a white linen cloth and in the center a bamboo bowl overflowed with lavender orchids. From the ceiling a crystal chandelier glistened reflecting light across the room; this was the only area of the hospital that was not a reminder of the war.

"We have too many other things to think about now besides Christmas and it's too hot to celebrate anyway," Cora responded while removing a plate of rice and fish from her tray.

"Yea you're right." Betsy answered then changed the subject. "By the way did you get orders to meet Capt. Jennings at fourteen-hundred hours?"

"Yes," they replied.

"What's it about?" Cora asked before taking a bite of fish.

"I don't know. No one seems to know." Betsy glanced at the large clock on the wall. "I've got to get back to the floor, I'll see you at the meeting."

Cora and Claire finished their meals then relaxed with a second cup of coffee and a cigarette before reporting back to their shifts.

Cora worked until fourteen hundred hours then hurried to the Army nurses' meeting. In the crowded nurses' lounge she slumped into the seat Betsy and Claire had saved for her. "Did you find out what's up?"

"No. No one seems to know anything except Manila is about to be declared an open city," Claire informed her.

"Oh no!" The lump in Cora's throat produced waves of nausea as she pictured the stories of what the Japanese did to women in Nanking.

## Chapter Two

Captain Jennings burst through the heavy door in her typical military manner, short of breath and gasping for air. Referring to papers clutched in her small hand she presented the new information to her nurses. She proceeded to call out their names and hand each one a large envelope containing their assignments. "You are being evacuated to Bataan and Corregidor." A roar of excitement filled the room while the sealed envelopes were ripped open. A wave of silence followed as they read their orders.

"You will find that the army has issued all medical personnel a set of dog tags. You are to put them on before you leave this room and they are not to be removed for any reason until you receive instructions to do so. Is that clear?" asked Capt. Jennings.

"Yes ma'am!" they answered in unison.

"Dog tags? You know what that means." Cora whispered, looking at Claire and Betsy.

"Yes, we're in danger just like the soldiers!" Claire answered.

"But a transfer means a real hospital again," Betsy said.

"I can't wait to get back into a white uniform, I feel

like a coal miner every time I step into these awful cover-alls!" Cora said.

"Where are you being sent?" Betsy asked Cora.

"Bataan. Wherever that is. You?"

"Bataan too. I leave on December 24$^{th}$. There is a Santa Claus!"

"That's tomorrow, we leave tomorrow!" Cora shouted, then she and Betsy turned to Claire. Her light complexion was colorless.

"Claire? What's wrong?"

"We're being separated. I'm staying here to prepare the wounded to be shipped out," her voice cracked as she spoke.

"But . . ." Cora couldn't speak, she feared for Claire's life.

*How can this be happening to me? I should be in Wheeling trimming a Christmas tree with a husband and baking cookies for our children. Well that dream didn't come true and I accepted it. Now I have a new life, new friends and new dreams, but it looks like that too will be shattered. What have I done to deserve this?*

"Cora! Cora! Are you okay?" Betsy asked.

"No. I mean yes. I was just thinking of the holidays."

The room buzzed with excitement as the nurses shared orders. There were cheers, tears and hugs, although no one knew anything about the new assignments hopes were flying high.

Cora and Betsy hugged Claire with tearful good-byes in case there would be no time later. "This was not the tropical tour we were expecting, but we're Americans, we're tough." Betsy held her head high. "We'll make it, the war can't last much longer, on New Years Eve we'll be celebrating our victory at the Army Navy Club!"

Cora forced a smile for Claire's benefit, knowing Betsy was doing the same. Cora reported to the ward filled with renewed hopes that the war would soon end. The new information did not affect her nursing duties as her strong determination overpowered her fear and concerns.

A few minutes after eleven, Cora left the hospital forcing her tired muscles to carry her through the courtyard to the nurses' residence. Standing quietly on one of the brightly woven rugs she admired the dark wood floor in the living room and the lush colorful sofa cushions. A warm salty ocean breeze drifted through the tall windows and over the seashells decorating the wide windowsills. Cora walked to the massive hand carved mahogany table in the center of the room and running her fingers down the sides of a tall inlaid oriental vase on the table thought, *Oh how I will miss this place.* Slowly she turned for one last look at the room filled with elegant tropical warmth.

"Beautiful isn't it?"

Her head jerked toward the voice. "Oh! I thought I was alone." Flint rose from his slouched position in a bamboo chair.

He stood. "Sorry, I didn't mean to startle you. I was half asleep myself when I heard you come in." Two days growth of stubble on his face did not affect his handsome qualities. A lock of chestnut hair fell across his forehead as he approached her.

"I'm glad to see you. Have you heard?" Cora asked stepping into Flint's open arms.

"Yes, that's why I'm here." He tightened his embrace.

*Now that I'm in an emotional turmoil he decides to show his feelings.*

"I heard about the evacuation," he whispered into her jet-black hair. "Where are you being sent?"

"Bataan." She choked out the peculiar sounding word. "Betsy and I leave in the morning, but Claire is staying here."

"Spencer is going to Bataan in a few days. I feel better already just knowing he'll be there to look after you two."

"Where are you going?" A lump the size of a golf ball formed in her throat while she waited for his answered.

"I'm staying here to prepare the wounded for transfer to Australia."

The lump began aching and her knees weakened. "So is Claire, but then what? Where will you be going?"

"I'll be sailing with them, but as soon as I can I'll get in touch with you." Flint stepped back and slid his hands down her arms and firmly gripped her hands. "From there I don't know where I'll be sent, but if we're still at war I'll get word to you as soon as I receive orders."

Flint gripped her hand and leading her to one of the bamboo sofas said, "Let's sit for a while."

While seated next to each other, he reached in his pocket and pulled out a small package wrapped in green tissue paper and a bright red ribbon tied into a bow with curly tails trailing down the sides. "Merry Christmas Cora," he said placing it in her hand.

Her fatigue was replaced with a surge of excitement, "No, wait here." She bolted from the sofa with her heart racing faster than her tired legs could move and she rushed up the stairs to her room. Minutes later she returned carrying a small gift similar to the one he had given her. She placed the box wrapped in red and white paper topped with a bright green bow in his hand. "Merry Christmas to you too, Flint."

"Open your gift first," he said.

"Okay." She methodically removed the wrapping from the box and lifted the navy blue velvet lid. The light blue lining accented a beautiful heart shaped gold locket. Cora removed the delicate gold chain and held the locket in her hand. "It's beautiful," she whispered unable to control tears puddling in her eyes.

"Allow me to open it for you." Flint slipped his fingernail in between the hearts and popped the latch open.

"Oh! When did you do this?" Cora asked staring at a picture of herself in one side of the locket and one of Flint in the other.

"It's the picture Spencer took of us at the Officers' Ball last month. I couldn't believe that our faces were the right size to fit in the locket."

"It's lovely. Oh, thank you, Flint."

"Let me help you put it on." Cora turned her back toward him and he placed the locket around her neck and secured the clasp. His soft hands brushing her neck forced Cora to wonder what her feelings toward him really were. She turned and faced him and their gazes locked.

Cora gained her composure, "Open your gift now." Rubbing the gold locket between her fingers, she eagerly watched Flint rip the paper off and lift the lid from the white box.

"Wow! Did you know I had lost mine?" he said removing the silver plated cigarette lighter from the box.

"Yes. I noticed you were using matches and Spencer told me you had lost it."

"Thanks, this is great. I've been too busy to get another one." He turned it over and saw the inscription, *To Flint From Cora 12/25/41.*

Cora enjoyed the silence of being alone with Flint, but knew she needed to be packing. She stood and he followed her lead. Staring into his tired eyes, she could detect only an ember of the sparkle. Long hours in surgery were taking their toll as well as the uncertainty of their future.

She couldn't distinguish if it were because they would be separated or if she really had feelings for him. "Well – I guess this is good-bye for now," she said.

"You take care of yourself," Flint said taking hold of her hand. "And if we should lose contact I have a plan so we can be together again after this war ends."

Cora tipped her head questioning his plan. "Oh?"

"I'll notify the Ohio Valley Hospital of my location and you do the same, okay?"

Cora lowered her gaze and nodded.

"If this war does last longer than expected, I'll meet you in Wheeling when it's over and we'll have a victory celebration." His strained words caused tears she could no longer hold back to roll down her cheeks. With a tender stroke of his thumb, Flint brushed the tears away as the grandfather clock struck twelve marking the beginning of December 24<sup>th</sup>, Christmas Eve.

"Merry Christmas, Cora," he said tipping her chin up, and ignoring regulations, they shared a kiss before going their separate ways.

Back in her room and filled with mixed emotions, Cora packed the few things she could fit in one small piece of luggage and her musette. Filled with mixed emotions, Cora packed her white clinic shoes, alabaster stockings, white starched uniforms, her white cap and her Ohio Valley Nursing School Pin. Then she put in the coveralls, personal items including makeup, several jars of Pacquins cold cream, a rhinestone choker, nail polish, two novels and personal letters and a picture. She also included a leather bound journal given to her by Dr. Warner, her mentor as well as her part-time employer before she graduated from high school.

She felt the cold dog tags sticking to her moist chest. *I can't believe all that has happened this month. War—dog tags and these ridiculous coveralls!*

Cora took a few minutes to reflect on her last visit with Doc Warner. He had spoken of his tour in World War I and expressed the importance of keeping a diary should she find herself in a war zone. She remembered his expression growing grim as he placed the stem of his curved pipe between his teeth and the conversation was over.

Cora was confused by the feelings she felt for her family and friends back home and how she suddenly missed them. Adding to her distress were the changing feelings for Flint as well. *Finally I understand the man behind the surgical mask, and now we are being separated.*

"Knock-knock, may I come in?" Claire called through the partially opened door.

"Sure come on in, I want to show you my Christmas gift from Flint." Cora pulled the locket up for Claire to inspect.

"Oh, it's lovely!" Claire shrieked stepping closer.

"Look inside," Cora said popping the clasp.

Claire studied the pictures and turned the heart over, "Oh the inscription is beautiful."

"What?"

"The inscription here on the back."

Cora pulled the locket out in order to focus on the engraved words, "All my love, Flint."

"He must think I'm awful, I didn't even see it." She looked at Claire. "I won't be able to thank him before I leave. Will you give him a thank you note from me?"

"Sure."

Cora wrote a note and when she finished Claire took it as they both walked to the door., "Take care of yourself, Claire," Cora said.

"You too, Cora." A quick hug and Claire left.

After the packing was completed Cora went to bed with thoughts of her family swirling in her head. *Everyone will go to church tomorrow night, it will be December 24th in the States, and the next day they will gather at Grandmother's house for Christmas Dinner. The house will smell like turkey and pumpkin pie and everyone will be talking at the same time.* Cora closed her eyes, squeezing them tight until she pictured the family celebration.

Placing her fingers around her new locket and feeling the tiny engraved letters, Cora vowed to not remove it until she and Flint were together again. Tears moistened her cheeks as she whispered the words, *"All my love, Flint,"* and fell asleep.

The following morning, Christmas Eve, Cora and Betsy joined eighteen American nurses and nine Filipino nurses, including Rose and Lydia, on the front steps of the nurses' quarters. Army trucks arrived to transport them to a ferry. Cora and Betsy were standing near the back of the truck when one of the nurses at the front yelled, "Has anyone heard what the hospital is like?"

"No," several nurses responded in unison, while others were quick to speculate about it being better than what they were leaving. They were all in agreement it couldn't be worse.

From the back of the truck Cora surveyed Manila as the driver maneuvered through the crowded city streets dodging water buffalo and small ponies pulling carts of household goods. Some pedestrians carried babies, others carried bags of rice and many carried personal belongings tied in bundles. It appeared that everyone was fleeing the city.

After a fifteen-minute wait on the dock in the hot morning sun Cora carried her bags aboard the ferry eager to get away from the sights of war. A somber ambiance laced with threads of excitement hovered over the group as they watched Manila disappear and the Bataan Peninsula appear.

The trip took several hours, as the ferry dodged Japanese bombs, strafing, and sunken ships. Low flying enemy planes were strafing the shoreline as the women stepped from the ferry onto Bataan. Confused, the nurses scurried to the edge of the jungle for cover under bushes. Heavy musty damp soil odors, caused by the previous night's rain intensified their awareness of the unfamiliar surroundings. When the planes left the women stepped out from hiding.

"Do you see a hospital any place?" Cora asked Betsy. The women surveyed the area as best as they could while shading their eyes from the bright sunlight and glare from the water.

"No, but someone said a medical officer is supposed to meet us here." Betsy answered.

"I think that's our transportation now," Cora said pointing toward the sounds of engines rumbling. A truck and buses came into view bumping down the dirt road toward the beach.

"I see them and none too soon. Those Japs may decide to come back." Betsy turned her attention to watch the sky.

Carrying her belongings, with Betsy close behind, Cora walked to where the nurses were gathering to board the buses. The long ride over the poorly developed road took the women deep into the jungle.

As Betsy stepped off the bus she asked the young soldier that appeared to be in charge how much farther it was to the hospital.

"This is it, ma'am. You are standing in it," he answered with his brow drawn.

"What?" Betsy asked.

The young man looked down at the ground and kicked it. "This is it."

Cora and the other nurses surveyed the area while listening to the news. They saw no building and realized the young man was serious.

"There is no hospital?" Betsy asked.

The man shook his head.

"We expected to find a hospital with polished floors and soft green walls adorned with pastoral paintings," one of the nurses announced.

"Sorry, ma'am," the young Sergeant said. "I wish I weren't the one to have to tell you."

When the nurses gained their composure, the soldier spoke to the group. "You have an important job to do and many soldiers' lives will depend on the treatment they receive here."

Captain Jennings stepped forward and faced the man, "But you are telling us there is no hospital located here?"

"That's correct, ma'am. You will find a few trashed refrigerators, some broken pieces of furniture and a jungle of bamboo, heavy vines and a variety of palm trees. The men are counting on you to make a hospital. They will be cooperative and try to make what you need."

Cora's thoughts drifted as she observed the activity surrounding them. Army engineers were clearing an area that appeared to be the beginnings of a road. Soldiers were transporting supplies to the new facility. Watching the active soldiers, Cora whispered to Betsy, "They remind me of a colony of ants building a city."

"I am wondering if they know what they are doing. Do you think they have a plan?" Betsy asked in an annoyed tone.

"We'll soon find out."

The nurses continued to listen to the medical officer. "Your mission is to set up a hospital here in the jungle, this dense canopy will protect us from the Jap planes." Swatting mosquitoes did not interrupt the officer's cadence. "This hospital will be Jungle Hospital #2. Jungle Hospital #1 is located on the east road at Camp Limay, five miles north. They are set up primarily as a surgical hospital, but can't handle all of the casualties we are expecting."

The nurses gasped as they realized the danger and work ahead of them.

"We will have a tent for surgery and one for the

records, but there will be no tents for the patients. The rainy season has ended, so that shouldn't be a problem." He paused and cleared his throat. "I know this is not an ideal situation; however supplies are on the way and we expect them to reach us soon. We will use the mosquito netting we have for the most severely wounded. A map of the hospital layout is posted at the supply area." He pointed to a makeshift lean-to on his left.

"I can't believe this. There is no real hospital here. No place to treat patients," Cora said under her breath.

The officer continued the briefing, "Report to the supply area later for your assignments and if you have not received a gas mask, steel helmet or combat boots they will be issued at that time. Wear the boots except when sleeping and keep the helmet and gas mask close to you at all times. Leave your gear here and report to the mess area for lunch then report back here at thirteen hundred hours. Dismissed!"

They all began chattering at the same time with questions and concerns.

"Well girls, we don't need to unpack our white uniforms!" someone shouted.

"It looks like overalls and combat boots will be the dress of the day here too, ladies," another nurse sarcastically called out.

When the nurses were assembled together that afternoon their orientation continued and they learned what to expect in their new surroundings. The informative medical officer began by explaining the jungle.

"Bataan is basically a wild unsettled area. There are snakes including the king cobra which hang in trees, so keep a watch above your head as well as on the ground.

The thick tropical forest is home to extinct volcanoes housing a variety of lizards. The largest is the Koto, which can be five to six feet long. The monkeys' chattering will drive you nuts the first few nights, but you will get used to them. Take your quinine tablets, I'm sure you've noticed we have a few mosquitoes. Any questions?" He paused. "You will now be shown to your new living quarters. Dismissed!"

A young private stepped up and said, "Ladies, pick up your gear and follow me!"

With their new army issued supplies in hand Cora and the other nurses followed the private down a long recently cleared winding path. The jungle's damp acidic scent and high humidity made breathing a chore. Each step became more difficult than the last.

"We look like a troop of girl scouts heading to our cabins after a day of activities," Cora said to Betsy who was following on her heels. The path did not lead to cabins, but to four Pambasco buses, their new living facility. The seats had been replaced with army cots giving the nurses a place to sleep with a roof over their heads and a floor under their cots. The outdoor living area was complete with their own latrine and a private section of a stream for bathing. The nurses each found a cot and stowed all that remained of their personal possessions underneath it.

Cora checked through her bags, reassuring herself that the letters from her mother and Doc Werner and the picture of Vince were still there. Looking at Vince's picture she thought, *I will never forget him. Memories are all I have now and I won't forget the love I once had.*

Next she checked other contents, several jars of Mum deodorant, toothpowder, toothbrush, shampoo, pencil, paper, envelopes, make-up, thread, sewing needles, a rhinestone necklace, a deck of cards and one magazine. After securing her bags under her cot, she pushed her hair back and checked her secret stash. Capt. Jennings ordered the nurses to keep a lethal dose of morphine concealed in their hair to use if captured and expecting to be tortured and killed.

After orientating themselves with the area they joined the soldiers at the mess area for dinner. Later they met with the medical officer and were told to go to their quarters and get a good night's sleep and report to their specified work areas after breakfast at zero six-hundred hours.

That evening after the women bathed they sat on their cots or logs in their new home. Cora and Betsy sat beside each other on a log smoking a cigarette and enjoying a cup of coffee made on a portable stove set up for the nurses private use. Cora subconsciously placed her hand over the unfamiliar cool locket and dog tags clinging to her chest. "Betsy do you realize that we are now combat nurses?"

"Yes, and I think we are on or close to the battlefield too." They both turned their heads as a bomb exploded off to the north of them. "I'm not sure this is any better than where we were."

"I usually welcome a challenge and I'm not afraid of hard work, but this is frightening," Cora said after the nurses discussed their work assignments.

"Well, one thing for sure, we are definitely earning our $88.60 a month."

"Yes, and working hard for it, but it's still more than we could make in a civilian hospital. That is if we could find a job."

By nightfall everyone was in bed. Cora watched the

moon pass over the jungle ceiling through the open window on the bus. Her mind raced with thoughts of wounded soldiers arriving with no place to be treated.

"Cora? Do you hear that?" Betsy whispered.

"Yes. I think it's the monkeys chattering and swinging on vines."

"How will we ever get to sleep?"

"Just try to block out all of the strange noises by mentally humming a tune and you'll get to sleep," Cora assured her.

Cora was too tired to stay awake and listen to the frightful sounds.

The next day in the mosquito-infested area seventeen doctors, thirty medics and orderlies joined the nurses to complete the Jungle #2 medical team. Captain Jennings and the army medical officers worked together in overseeing the assignments.

As soon as the soldiers cleared an area the medical team began setting up wards, the surgical area, post surgical area, malaria ward, psychiatric ward, central supply and other necessary areas. Everyone worked hard to accomplish the task of building a hospital with no floor, walls or ceiling. The sounds of bombs exploding north of them reinforced the urgency to get the hospital set up quickly.

## Chapter Three


Six nurses, including Betsy and Rose, began setting up a central drug station supplied with morphine, quinine, sulfa, various medicines and vitamins. Drugs stored on Bataan before the war, in preparation for a possible invasion, were given to the nurses to be sorted and placed in the hospital. The women buried surplus drugs in trenches to protect them from bombings.

A large number of women were assigned to the supply area. Cora and five other nurses filled mattresses with rice straw and later placed them on bamboo beds local craftsmen were making. The nurses worked from daylight until dark in the hospital area carrying out their duties without complaining.

"I heard one of the 'dogfaces' say we would bring bad luck to their outfit," a nurse working with Cora announced.

"Dogfaces? Isn't that a disgusting name to call the army soldiers? I wonder why they refer to themselves that way?" No one had an answer.

With a sense of understanding Cora said, "I can remember my dad saying it would bring bad luck to the coal miners if a woman went down into the mines. Maybe the dogfaces feel the same way about women being in a war zone."

The nurses continued stuffing mattresses and nodded as they grasped the idea of the men thinking they may be bad luck. No one knew the answer.

"They also feel a need to watch their language and actions with us present," one woman added.

Another said, "Maybe we remind them of the wives and girlfriends they left behind."

"When their mangled bodies are brought to the hospital it may be difficult not to remind them why we are here!" another one said sarcastically and they all agreed.

"They will learn soon enough that we are here to do a job just like they are, only our job is to save lives," A soft-spoken Filipino nurse said. "Not take lives!"

"The dogfaces are no different than the men back home. Together they are tough, but alone they are sensitive regular guys," Cora said.

* * *

The following days, Cora, like the other nurses, worked long hours in hot humid conditions without complaining. She noticed the men watching them complete their tasks under the same constant danger as they themselves were working. It did not take long for the nurses to earn the respect of the dogfaces and to become their comrades in arms. In Cora's eyes, the dogfaces realized the nurses' importance in their survival. Soon the men began to refer to them as the Angels of Bataan.

The nurses began to form a bond. They shared every aspect of their lives and they moved as a unit. Privacy became a thing of the past and the mess area became a place to eat and discuss the progress being made. The excitement of new experiences and a sense of urgency and survival increased their flow of adrenaline permitting them to work at an incredible rate. Most of the women joined the army looking for adventure and on Bataan they found it.

Cora and Betsy sat on the ground during lunch, "This stew is good," Betsy commented. "What do you think it is? Or do I want to know?"

"It's Slumgullion Stew, I was raised on this stuff and biscuits." Cora's thoughts drifted from the mountain in the Philippines to a mountain in West Virginia where she had eaten many meals of Slumgullion Stew. "I'll give you the recipe."

"The continuous hum of those bulldozers reminds me of my hometown," Cora said after swallowing a mouthful of stew.

"They are getting on my nerves!" Betsy said, "I don't think they will ever finish clearing away the stumps. They can't keep up with the fast bolo swinging Filipinos. Their arms must get tired, but they never stop, so the humming goes on."

"Back home when I wanted to escape the sounds of the train cars I would go up a path behind my house and sit on a big rock that jetted out from the mountain. It gave me a view of the mining town and the trains sounded far away. It was so peaceful."

"I'd like a place like that now." Betsy took another bite of the stew.

"It was nice, but then I didn't realize how nice. I would daydream, or collect rocks and bugs and sometimes

I would find Indian arrowheads to add to my collection."

"Now here you are a nurse in the middle of the Pacific Ocean in a war zone. I bet that's not what you dreamed about."

"No, but I can pretend the bulldozers are trains pulling coal cars and block out the noise the way I did at night so I could sleep." The lunch ended and they walked toward their work areas.

"How is the medicine sorting going?" Cora asked.

"Slow. We are breaking one of the first rules we learned in school."

Cora tipped her head. "How?"

"We are switching labels," Betsy answered.

"Why?" Cora asked. "How will we know what we are giving a patient?"

"We're doing it because if the Japanese capture the hospital we don't want our quinine to fall into their hands, so we are labeling it with soda bicarbonate labels. We are making sure all medical personnel know."

"That's a good idea. How near are you to finishing?"

"We may finish today, it's going well, but there isn't enough to stock a hospital that is expecting casualties from the front lines. I do know that."

"But we are going to get more supplies, they just haven't gotten through yet."

"That's what we were told, but I'm not sure they will arrive before they are needed."

They smiled and spoke to a soldier who was hanging a lister bag in the hospital and filling it with treated water. The large canvas bag hung suspended from a wooden tripod in a central area.

"I've heard there are not enough lister bags here

either, but they are to arrive with our first shipment of supplies," Cora said.

"Hey look," Betsy pointed to the wooden arrows on the trees. "They have marked the wards."

"That's a big help considering there are no doors or walls. Giving directions will be difficult, but still we are making progress faster than I expected."

"Wonder what ward we'll be assigned to when it is finished?" Betsy asked.

"I don't know, but we'll be getting our schedules soon, I'm sure."

The results of the fast working American and Filipino engineers, cooks, carpenters and sanitation crews amazed Cora. Local workers from a nearby farm were mass-producing bamboo tables and chairs for the mess tent. The talented craftsman also carved large bowls, plates and spoons. Filipino volunteer carpenters worked day and night producing beds, bedside tables, cabinets, chairs, urinals, trays, wastebaskets and other objects necessary for a functioning hospital. Nearly everyone living on Bataan wanted to be involved in winning the war and everyone was willing to work as hard and long as it took to defeat the Japanese. The nurses appreciated their determination and dedication as they worked side by side.

On the ninth day in the jungle, Cora and the other nurses were ordered to report to the officer in charge of setting up the hospital.

"Ladies, for your safety the buses are being taken to the motor pool tomorrow and your cots will be moved out under the jungle canopy." Comments and questions began flying through the air.

"Just a minute ladies," the officer raised his hand.

44

"The buses are visible from the air where they are parked now. They are providing the Japanese bombers a clear target." He paused and grinned, "We can't take a chance, you are too valuable to us."

"And they don't want to lose their buses either," the nurse standing next to Cora whispered.

"Those buses may save your life later," Capt. Jennings said and the nurses did not complain again about their new living quarters.

Later on as Cora and Betsy sat out in the open air before going to bed for the last time on the bus, Betsy asked, "Will we ever get used to the idea of working in a jungle hospital in the middle of a war?"

"No, but then I never pictured myself sleeping in a jungle either!" Cora answered.

"I heard one of the engineers say they almost have the road finished and as soon as it is opened we'll be getting casualties," Betsy said. "They will bring them in at night so they will not be spotted by the Japanese planes."

"Well, I think we've done all we can under these conditions. We are as ready as we're going to be until our supplies arrive."

Betsy crushed her cigarette in the damp soil, said goodnight and went to bed.

Cora sat on a nearby stump and with the aid of her flashlight made her first entry in her journal.

*Jungle Hospital #2*
*Bataan, The Philippines*
*January 2, 1942*
    *There was no New Years celebration here. There were many of us who didn't realize the date! I wonder if*

*there were celebrations back in the States? Today we learned that the Japanese landed on Bataan two days ago and now we can hear the ground fighting. Bombs and strafing continue to hit the Peninsula. Tonight will be my last night of sleeping under a real roof; they are moving the buses to a camouflaged area.*

*Tomorrow we will get patients transferred from Jungle Hospital #1 and all of us are eager to get back to nursing. No one has mentioned the morphine we carry in our hair. I don't know that I will be brave enough to take it should the need arise.*

*Again today I felt lonely when visions of Vince interrupted my thoughts. I miss him so much. I keep thinking that if I keep busy I will be able to forget the pain, but it still hurts.*

*I must get to bed now. It may be my last night of sleep for a while.*

Cora closed her journal and got on the bus. After placing the journal in her bag she undressed and went to bed. From her cot she stared out of the open window for the last time. A thin sliver of the moon appeared through the jungle roof; it was a familiar sight surrounded by unfamiliar sounds. Monkeys continued swinging from vine to vine, noisily chattering as if announcing that the nurses would be spending the next night in the open jungle with them, and they didn't sound any happier about the arrangements than the nurses. Cora was thankful to have Betsy with her and hoped Spencer would arrive soon. She imagined Kate Smith singing, "When the Moon Comes Over the Mountains," and drifted off to sleep.

Cora was working the receiving area the first week of

January when she received a surprise, some patients transferred from Sternberg arrived.

"How was your trip," Cora asked one of the young soldiers.

He smiled and answered, "It was free ma'am." Cora checked his papers and directed the medic to take him to ward seven. She enjoyed having contact with patients again.

"Hey Adams!" Cora jerked her head up and with her free hand shading her eyes from the bright sun, searched for the voice in the crowd. A nurse from Sternberg, she knew only as Shorty, appeared from the row of stretchers.

"What are you doing here? I thought you were leaving Manila on Christmas for Corregidor."

"We did. We've been moving these men around from Manila to Corregidor and finally here!" Shorty picked up the hand of the soldier next to her; "Lieutenant Adams, these are the bravest men I know." She smiled at the boy as Cora knelt beside him.

"We'll get rid of her and go dancing later. Okay soldier?"

"I like the dancing part, but the Captain here is all right ma'am," he said looking up at Shorty.

"I detect a southern accent. Wouldn't be from West Virginia would you?"

"Yes ma'am, Fayette County," he smiled up at Cora.

*I can't believe how great it is to hear that accent.* Cora fought to keep the wave of homesickness at bay.

"Why, we're practically neighbors, I'll make sure you're treated real good." Cora said and turned to Shorty. "Have you checked in at the nurses quarters yet?"

"No."

"Well you can't miss it." Cora pointed to her left, "Just head down the path going west. Follow the arrows with "Nurses" carved in them. When you see clothes hanging from vines and tree branches, wooden crates setting around and cots lined up under a makeshift roof you have reached your new home. "I'd give you a key, but I left it unlocked," Cora said.

"Sounds delightful, and as soon as I get settled I'll get back to you. Where will you be working later."

"Ward seventeen, the signs are posted on trees." Cora paused then called out as Shorty walked away. "Hey be careful it's a jungle up here!"

Shorty turned and smiled, "Yeah I noticed."

After Cora finished processing the new arrivals she headed toward the mess area.

"Hey Lieutenant, need an escort for dinner?"

Cora stopped nearly toppling headfirst.

"You buying?" She asked turning to greet Dr. Spencer Kirby. She could not believe another friend had arrived on Bataan.

He grabbed her and swung her around, "Sure, and I have a letter for you. That is if you're interested?" He asked.

"Thanks," Cora said taking the letter and stuffing it in her pocket, *I want to be alone when I read this and savor every word.* "Is Flint okay?"

"He was when I left Manila, but that was only two days after you left." They continued walking to the mess tent and stood in line holding their bamboo trays waiting for a bowl of beef stew and crackers. "It's hard to believe what has happened in a month and how it has affected our lives," Spencer said shaking his head.

"Yea," Cora answered looking around at their sur- roundings, then said "I'm sorry about the menu, but our food rations were cut in half last week. Few supplies have been getting through."

"I'm so hungry any amount looks good." He said.

Claire really misses you and Betsy." They carried their trays to a primitive style table and sat.

"I know. Betsy and I miss her and I know you do too," Cora took a bite of the stew before she continued. "I wish we knew where she was sent?"

"Claire is on Corregidor, she arrived before we left. I didn't get to spend much time with her, but she told me to tell you and Betsy she hoped you could be together soon.

"How is she? Is she holding up ok?"

"Yes, she's fine, overworked but she has a great atti- tude."

I'm sure we'll all be together again soon."

"You're always the positive one aren't you? Our own little Pollyanna!"

With a mouth full Cora smiled.

Spencer Kirby grew up in the Society Hill section of Philadelphia, Pennsylvania, never wanting for anything. He joined his father's medical practice until the army need- ed surgeons. In the Philippines everyone was equal. Spencer looked forward to payday the same as the others. His confident posture, stride and speech were products of his cultural background, but they did not interfere with work or fun. As an orthopedic surgeon he was one of the best and in constant demand since the bombings began.

"What's the hospital like?"

"Well, it reminds me of my parent's garden. Every spring it is planned and laid out in nice even rows, then the planting begins and there are more plants than originally planned, so in making room for the extras order is lost. That's where we are now – it's hard to distinguish the order."

"But it sounds like there is some order. That's good."

"Now who's being positive?" Cora smiled. After a few seconds of silence she said, "This war won't last much longer, at least that's what everyone says." She looked into Spencer's eyes, "What do you think?"

"I don't know what to think. They also said that World War I was a war to end all wars." He looked up from the stew with eyebrows raised.

Cora understood what he did not say. "We'll just have to make the best of what life is giving us. We're strong, healthy, red blooded Americans, we'll survive."

"Well, getting back to reality, how does the surgical unit look?" he asked.

"Not bad considering where it is and what we have to work with. The main surgical area is under a tent and there are wood floors. There is also a galvanized roof over one of the areas. The other tables are under the jungle roof. The gas gangrene patients are placed in a small isolated pavilion for surgery then isolated in a tent ward. It's primitive, but sprinkled with civilization."

"What about mosquitoes, flies and other disease carriers?" Spencer swatted at a mosquito.

"We just do the best we can with what we have. We make sure everyone takes their preventive dose of quinine, many have already contracted malaria. Some of the wounded that come to the hospital have not had quinine and they have been drinking from the streams, so we're seeing an increase in dysentery cases as well as malaria.

We've even had a few cases of cerebral malaria."

"Oh, that's not good!" Spencer said. "But I'm not surprised."

"What about sterilizing instruments? How many autoclaves do we have?"

"We have a field sterilizer."

"A? You mean as in one?"

Cora nodded.

"What about the supply of ether? I've heard it's not adequate."

"I'm not sure. Betsy could answer that for you. She has been working in the drug supply area and says we will probably run out of everything if the fighting continues more than a month." Cora took a sip of coffee, "And I can tell you that we only have one teaspoon on ward seventeen to administer meds by mouth."

"Seriously?"

"Yes."

"And how many patients?"

"About one hundred and fifty."

"Well we brought another one hundred and fifty while dodging mines and bombs all the way from Sternberg Hospital to Corregidor and now here." He looked into Cora's eyes, "Are there beds for all of them?"

"Probably not. Some patients are on the jungle floor, some on mattresses and a few on cots or beds made by local craftsman," Cora said. "We have over two thousand patients now, and counting your medical team we have forty-three army nurses, twenty-one Filipino nurses and eight civilian nurses."

"That's seventy-two nurses," he mouthed the math and said, "That's over twenty-eight patients each!"

Cora nodded and hunched her shoulders, "And grow-ing."

Spencer tipped his head and stared into space as he often did when he was thinking. "If they are on cots and the jungle floor, that means you have to bend over each patient. How do you do it?"

"We crawl. At night we hold our flashlights in our mouth and crawl on our knees from one patient to the next. We have a new perspective of backaches, not to mention sore knees."

"I bet you do. The surgical tables aren't that low are they?"

Cora chuckled. "No, they are standard height and there are lights on poles. I heard one of the dogfaces say they were building a bamboo shack close to the operating area for the surgical personnel." Cora raised her brow. "You're lucky, the monkeys, lizards and rats may not crawl over you." Spencer shivered.

His presence was like the first breath of spring on a March day. They shared an American cigarette after the meal and continued sharing their experiences since the Japanese began bombing the Philippines. Then they laughed remembering the good times in Manila and the friends they had made. It definitely was the paradise tour Cora dreamed of . . . until the war.

Spencer stood, "It's been great seeing you again Cora, and tell Betsy I'm looking forward to having dinner with her soon," Spencer turned and walked toward the surgical area.

Before Cora reached the ward she checked the enve-lope in her pocket making sure it was safe. On the ward she began changing dressings and from that completed task she moved on to the next, giving out medications, again bending, kneeling or crawling to reach each patient.

"Hello there," she said to a Lieutenant she recognized from Sternberg. "What's the idea of following the nurses here?"

The Lieutenant laughed. "You ladies saved my life so I just had to come here to personally thank you."

Cora checked his temperature and then checking the wound to his right shoulder saw the infection she suspected.

"Does your arm hurt worse now than it did a day or two ago?"

"Yes ma'am, it burns."

"Well you have an infection, I'll sprinkle sulfanil-amide powder on the area, then I'm going to leave the dressing off to allow the sunshine and air to get to it." She patted his good shoulder and added, "We're going to fix you up again, since you traveled this far to see us." Cora leaned down and whispered, "Actually, we missed you too." She turned and moved on.

The next patient was healing from a wound to his leg. The tendons were ripped apart by shrapnel.

Cora dressed his wound and said, "You're lucky, you are healing quickly and with no sign of infection."

"Yea, aren't I lucky?" his sarcastic voice trailed off.

Cora turned back quickly, "Knock off the self pity Corporal. You are one of the lucky ones! First, you are alive and second it could be the rainy season! Be thankful for what you have." She did not wait for a reply.

Little thought could be given to the letter in her pocket as she worked, but the anticipation of reading it before going to sleep gave her something to look forward to in the middle of a pit of insanity.

At the end of her eighteen hour shift, Cora stumbled to the nurses quarters where she found Betsy coming from the bathing area.

"When we were in Manila I never dreamed there could be anyplace more humid, but there is." Betsy remarked. "I've dried my clean body three times and it's still wet!"

"I don't think I will ever get used to the wet clothes, the stinging eyes or the blurred vision from perspiration." Exhausted, Cora fell on her cot. "Our job is difficult enough without all of this humidity!"

"Sometimes I think the weather here is our worst enemy."

"Oh, I nearly forgot to tell you, I had dinner with a handsome man this evening."

"Really? Anyone I know?"

"Spencer. He was with the patients from Sternberg."

"Spence is here? Here on Bataan?"

"Yes and he's anxious to see you. Claire is on Corregidor and is fine, but she misses us." Cora rambled on ignoring her tired aching body. Finally she pulled out the damp crumpled letter from her pocket and waved it in the air. "He delivered a letter from Flint."

"What's he say?"

"I don't know yet. I saved it until I would have time to digest it and that's now!" Cora studied the address: 2nd Lt. Coralee Adams, USANC. It sounded more military now than when she was working in Manila. *Flint has addressed it so if Spence didn't get it delivered it could still reach me.* The thought of knowing he had written gave her chills. *I hope these aren't chills from malaria, I have been lucky so far to avoid the jungle illness.*

Cora's heart raced as she ripped the damp envelope open.


25 December 1941
*My Dearest Cora,*

*I'm sitting in the courtyard under a Banyan tree inhaling the sweet fragrance of the frangipani and orchids and wishing you were here with me.*

*Last night I could not get my thoughts into words, funny how lack of sleep affects the mind, but after a few hours of sleep I knew what I wanted to say to you. When we worked together in Wheeling, I felt like I was suffocating when you were near, I had never experienced the feelings you caused me to have. I wasn't ready to fall in love and you were interfering with my life as I had planned it. I'm sorry for the way I treated you and hope you have forgiven me. Seeing you here in Manila stirred all the same emotions again, only this time the feelings were different – I had missed you so much that I was ready to admit I was in love with you. I did not want you going off into a war zone not knowing how I feel about you, about us. I hope you feel the same.*

*Please take care of yourself and we will be together again when this ugly war is over.*

*All my love,*
*Flint*

*P.S. Claire delivered your note. Thanks.*


Cora read the letter quickly, then slowly, then over and over until the words were imprinted on her mind. *He loves me. I promised myself that I would never love again and now he says he's in love with me – I don't know if I am happy or angry!*

\* \* \*

The jungle Chapel was set up off of the road that ended at the hospital receiving station. A sign posted on a tree at the entrance read, "Church of All Faiths." Off to the side stood another pole supporting a flag with a cross on it. Cora and most of the nurses had little time to think about religion, until one of their patients needed their help. "Could you please help me get to a Protestant service, Lieutenant Adams? I don't want to die without making my peace with God," the young blue eyed private asked.

"Of course I'll take you. Tomorrow is Sunday and I don't report for duty until noon, so I'll stop by for you at eleven-hundred hours, okay?"

"That's great, I wasn't going anyplace anyway," he said and winked.

Cora was pleased she could help the young man and get him off the ward for an hour. A change of scenery would be good for him.

\* \* \*

Sunday morning arrived and Cora kept her promise. "Here's a cane for you." She handed him a bent stick one of the Filipino carpenters had formed from a piece of mahogany, then helped the crippled man walk to the chapel. When they reached the entrance she noticed tears streaming down his face and she put aside her personal feelings. He walked up the aisle between the five rows of rough split log benches and when he reached the front row Cora helped him sit and held his cane.

"I'm sorry we're early, I didn't think you could walk that fast. Services don't start for another fifteen minutes," Cora whispered.

"That's fine," the young man said staring at two large tree limbs laced with leather shoestrings to form a crude cross standing behind the altar.

Cora sat quietly finding the solitude to be a relief from the mutilated bodies. She turned and glanced back over the makeshift pews, and saw several nurses and doctors quietly waiting for the worship service to begin.

Cora's thoughts roamed from the West Virginia Mountains to the Philippine Mountains. A bomb exploded to the north and when her patient flinched, Cora put her arm around him and patted his shoulder.

"Thanks, I'm fine," he said keeping his gaze on the cross.

The services ended and Cora studied the peaceful expression in her patient's eyes, knowing he had made peace with God.

Back at the ward, Cora met the man she had been begging to read to the other patients. "Here is a mimeographed copy of the *Jungle Newsletter*," she said handing the two pages to the young corporal. "Trust me, you'll enjoy reading it to the patients and seeing the joy it brings to them." The newsletter contained more humorous articles than news and lifted everyone's spirits. The nurses enjoyed listening to the entertainment as they went about performing their duties.

Cora lifted the syringe of morphine to eye level and

removed the air with two quick flicks of her forefinger. "Hang on, this will ease the pain," she assured the young boy. She injected the clear liquid into his vein and watched the sedating drug enter his pain-wracked body, "I'll get a new dressing on your leg while you take a nap and when you're awake I'll stop by so we can chat." She flashed a reassuring smile.

With that dressing changed, Cora moved on to the next casualty. Wiping the perspiration from her eyes, she placed her hands on her lower back and stretched. *When will this end?* She took a deep breath before crawling to the next patient and cleaning his wounded side with iodine. More canvas lister bags had not arrived and the few hanging between wards were not enough. The boiled water supply was low as was everything needed to treat the patients and keep them comfortable.

Like the rest of the nurses, Cora was tired, hot, hungry and thirsty, but she did not complain – no one did. The deeply ingrained training of following orders and healing the sick was being tested. Ignoring her aching back she bent over another frightened teenage boy, beads of perspiration covered his round cherub face while big dark brown eyes overflowed with tears, but he made no sound. "You are a brave soldier. This will ease your pain." Cora injected the morphine knowing he would not live to see tomorrow. As the liquid entered his body old memories of coal mining accidents vividly entered her mind. Screams from the next bed forced Cora to pull her thoughts back to the present and those needing her help. She crawled over to the next cot.

The Japanese continued to attack the north end of the peninsula. Each night more casualties arrived at the hospital.

"What's that noise," a blind soldier asked.

"It's the army engineers sawing and hammering. They are making more beds and instrument tables."

"Thanks, I have been wondering for a long time. It helps to drown out the screaming and moaning, but I couldn't figure out what they were doing."

"I'm sorry you had to wait so long. You look like you could use a cigarette." Cora removed a Lucky Strike from the pack in her pocket and lit it with her lighter then placed it in the patient's mouth.

"Ahh, it's a Lucky Strike isn't it?"

"Yes it is."

"The name seems ironic here doesn't it?"

"I had never thought about it, but you are alive and we have supplies on the way. You will have a reserved seat to go home on one of our supply ships, so maybe the name is appropriate."

The soldier took another puff and held the cigarette up to her, "Want a puff?"

"No, I'm on duty so it's all yours." Cora realized bonds were strengthened when comrades shared a cigarette or a cup coffee. "Sorry I have to go now but I'll catch you another time."

"Thanks again, Angel."

Cora was exhausted but continued by screwing a sterile needle onto the glass syringe then jabbing it through the rubber stopper of a bottle of morphine. In a numb automatic movement she grabbed the sponges and arrived at the next patient's side to repeat the same action and words. She would not stop. *I am the only hope and comfort they have. If only I could have helped Vince he might have lived.*

"You're lucky the medics got the bleeding stopped before they got you here. We're going to take care of that pain in your leg now," she said and again searched for an open vein like she had done so many times before. When none could be found she stabbed the needle through his shirt into the strong muscle of his upper arm and pushed the plunger.

While swatting at mosquitoes, Cora crawled through the circular designed ward. "Get off!" she shouted grabbing a lizard by the tail and slinging it away from her patient. At the foot of another bed she found a monkey jumping up and down. The brave creature made no attempt to leave as Cora approached.

"Scram, you – you pesky critter!" Cora whispered as she swung her stethoscope toward the monkey.

"Hey, he was visiting us and visiting hours aren't over for another hour," one of the patients called out. A man with a bandage around his head sat on a chair next to him, they were playing cards with a deck made from cardboard.

As the patients began to heal they amazed the nurses with their sense of humor. The ones that were well enough made puzzles or games to occupy their time while helping others pass the time. One of Cora's patients, an artist, enjoyed drawing the local varmints on pieces of cardboard for his buddy to cut into puzzles. Of course there were also puzzles of naked women, but they tried to keep them concealed from the nurses.

"How are you feeling today?" Cora said to the next patient in the line of mattresses covering the ground like a thick carpet.

"Better. Just thankful that the monkeys, rats, iguanas,

snakes and God only knows what other creatures are willing to share their homes with us."

"Share? Haven't you heard? They plan to eat us alive," a soft voice from the next mattress said. "And the mosquitoes have already started."

"Well then we'll try not to wear out our welcome." Cora smiled knowing their humor helped them survive. "Here," she said, "Your buddy five beds up from you sent these," she tossed him three comic books. "He said they would help take your mind off of the shelling."

"Thanks, I hope he's right."

Cora handed out quinine as she made her rounds, and checked for new cases of malaria. The patient she was medicating sat up, "Lieutenant are you okay?" She couldn't speak as a boa constrictor slithered down a tree behind his head.

# Chapter Four

Before Cora could react, a Filipino appeared swinging a bolo and in one swift movement cut off its head and removed the serpent from the patient area.

"It just startled me, that's all," Cora said at last. *And I thought the snakes in West Virginia were big!*

"Wow! Did anyone get a picture of that thing?" one man asked and they continued discussing the boa constrictor until Cora left the area.

Having treated all of the two hundred assigned to ward seventeen by nightfall, Cora took a break before moving on to help where she was needed. Being assigned to one of the smaller wards was a blessing, but still overwhelming.

"My back hurts so bad I'm not sure I can walk to our quarters," Cora said to one of the nurses leaving the hospital with her.

"I know, I'm not sure which is worse – my headache, backache or leg cramps," she answered.

"We know the leg cramps will only get worse if we don't get more nutritious meals or some vitamins." They talked while walking and swinging their flashlights along the path and overhead making their way to their jungle home.

At the nurses quarters, Cora found tin cans of water Betsy had placed under the legs of her army cot again. "That should keep the ants off of you tonight," Betsy said as Cora lowered herself onto the cot. "I'm so tired I don't think they would bother me, but thanks."

Betsy retrieved a cup of warm coffee from a stove made of sheet metal salvaged from a wrecked ship. "Here drink this, it's not a cold Coca-Cola but it is wet. Eat this biscuit I saved for you too. It may give you enough energy to dream!" Betsy said.

"Great! But I'd rather use my strength to keep the monkeys and wild pigs away from my cot tonight. I can dream later."

Betsy laughed. "Don't worry about them. Just think of it as a trip to the zoo at Uncle Sam's expense."

The two friends went over the day's events while Cora ate her snack, then they shared a Lucky Strike. "Betsy, don't you ever wonder about Brice? We have heard nothing from him?"

"I try not to think about him." She paused and extinguished the cigarette with the toe of her boot. "It's better that way."

Nothing more was said and they fell asleep again to the sounds of chattering monkeys swinging in the vines above their heads. Off in the distance trucks bringing more wounded could be heard rumbling down the road to the hospital.

Around noon the next day Cora lost count of the constant Japanese attacks. She spent all of her time calming patients during the bombings, leaving no time to address her own fears. She tried three times to give a shaking malaria patient his quinine before she succeeded.

"I know this liquid quinine tastes bitter but we are running out of tablets," Cora said as he swallowed it making an awful face. "I'm sorry, but you have to take it. There are seven hundred and fifty new cases of malaria every day." Cora refrained from telling him that the medical staff had stopped taking the preventive doses and they too were becoming victims of the chills. *He doesn't need to know how low the supplies are.*

Cora met Spencer at the mess for an evening meal. "Don't you wonder what is cooking over there?" Spencer asked no one in particular as he stared at the eight, fifty-gallon drums serving as gasoline stoves.

"I try not to," Cora chuckled. "Mostly I'm amazed at how five mess sergeants can prepare enough meals to feed all of us here at this hospital site!" She paused, "But then I'm constantly amazed at what is being done here with so few people."

"In a crisis with one goal there is no limit to what we Americans and our allies can do." Spencer flashed her a broad smile.

They received their ladle of weak unnamed soup and sat at one of the tables. "I hate it when I have to sit at this table," Spencer said swatting flies. "This is too close to where they bury the garbage! It can't be healthy."

"I'm not sure anyplace here is healthy and have you heard the water shortage is getting worse too," Cora said.

"Yes and I know it's causing problems in the post surgical wards. The patients can't be given nutrients intravenously because there is no equipment to filter what water we have."

\* \* \*

By March the food supply was nearly gone and the nurses' rations were cut back again, but hopes of ships arriving soon with supplies and food remained high and there were no complaints. The Filipinos could grow very little in the cleared spaces in the jungle, most of the food had to be brought to Bataan by ships from other areas. The Japanese were controlling the waters from the air and land; therefore, few ships got through the mines, artillery fire, bombings and strafing.

"I just heard that Hospital #1 took a direct hit, but everyone thinks it was an accident. They believe green pilots didn't see the large Red Cross in the yard," Cora announced to Betsy and a couple of the other nurses that were bathing in the warm jungle stream.

"I'd like to believe that, but I think the Japs are playing by their own rules." Betsy said as she and Cora walked back to the nurses' quarters.

By April malaria was at an epidemic level.

*4 April 1942— When will it end?* Cora forced herself to write regularly in her journal.

*Today I heard that we have 7,000 patients; there seems to be no end to the flow of wounded being brought here. We have eighty-eight nurses now to care for them. These last few days the patients keep asking when they will be going home or if they will live? I don't know how much longer I can smile and give them hope. It is very difficult some days. Hell couldn't be any worse than this place, but then maybe this is hell.*

*It is six weeks until the rainy season, then there will*

*be other diseases to contend with and more casualties. We can't take care of those we have now. I worry about how we will keep the patients and their wounds dry. They will be lying in muck and we will be crawling through it.*

*I worked another eighteen-hour shift today and except for weak tea my only meal was a stew at noon and I didn't ask what the meat was. We all know we are being served lizard, snake, mule, donkey and even horsemeat, but we must have protein to survive. We still get chicken occasionally from local farmers and I hope that will be the "catch of the day" tomorrow. But then most of the time I'm too tired to be hungry or concerned about the menu.*

*Some of the nurses listen to a radio station patched through Corregidor from San Francisco, but I've never had free time to listen. Maybe tomorrow I will get time to hear some music. It has been a long time since I have sung or heard music, except for the occasional outburst of a soldier singing or playing a harmonica. Hymns are sung at the chapel, which I happen to hear occasionally, but that's different than the popular tunes.*

*Tomorrow is Easter. When will the fighting end?*

Cora switched off her flashlight, tucked the journal under her pillow and in spite of her fears and the nearby bombs exploding, she slept.

Easter morning Cora heard ambulatory patients making arrangements to attend one of the several services offered throughout the day. She ignored the hustle and bustle and did her job as she did every day; this year Easter would just have to be another day filled with caring for her patients.

"Which service are you attending," Betsy asked when they took a break.

"I'm not sure I can make it this year."

"Go with me, I'm taking a couple of patients to the service at nine-hundred hours. We'll meet you outside the chapel."

"Okay, I'll be there if I get my meds passed out. I heard a couple of my patients say they would like to go to a protestant service. I'll bring them with me."

Back on ward seventeen Cora approached the two patients and offered to take them to the nine hundred-hour service. Their faces brightened with appreciation; religion offered hope to many of the men.

As the time to leave approached, Cora welcomed the change in her routine that allowed her to exploit her mother-like nurturing instinct by leading the men to the Chapel.

"Thanks Lieutenant Adams," the nineteen-year old private said as she helped him to his feet. "I can't remember ever missing an Easter Service. Our whole family got up early every Easter and went to sunrise services out at Harper's Lake." He was still babbling when they reached the second patient, a twenty-five year old medic.

"Are you sure you are up to walking to the chapel," Cora asked.

"Yes Lieutenant. I feel great today!"

Cora studied the facial expressions of the crowd sitting under the bright hot sun giving their full attention to the Chaplain while bombs exploded nearby.

An air raid interrupted the service, and when it ended the service continued. Interruptions had become a normal occurrence.

On the way back to the hospital, family traditions and

remembrances of Easter Services were exchanged. The conversation was therapeutic for those celebrating their first Easter away from home. One they would never forget.

"Thanks Lieutenant, I enjoyed the service," the older patient said to Cora.

"Yes, thanks and didn't you enjoy that singing," the private added. "I don't think I ever enjoyed singing more than I did here today."

"You are both welcome and yes the singing was beautiful."

"Angels, that's what it sounded like, yes that's it, angels!" the private said softly.

With the patients safely deposited in the ward Betsy said, "Cora, I'll meet you in the mess area at noon, there is a contest for the most original Easter bonnet."

"You entering?" Cora teased.

"No. I've not had time to shop and the stores just aren't what they used to be."

Cora chuckled, "I'll meet you there." She glanced at her watch, "Right now I'm going to attend a Chinese checkers tournament; it's the play off. One of my patients made the board and another one made the marbles out of plaster of paris and painted them."

At noon the mess area was crowded, but Cora spotted Betsy and joined her in the area where most of the nurses were gathered. They were sharing stories about Easter egg hunts, chocolate eggs, outrageous Easter bonnets and big Sunday family dinners. They also shared their best memories and for a little while everyone forgot the war and enjoyed a pleasant celebration.

Cora's thoughts were on what her life should have

been like as she remembered her last Easter with Vince and their plans to be married the following year.

"I keep wondering how my family is celebrating this year. With at least two of my brothers in the Navy, probably more serving in the military by now, and me here. I don't imagine my folks are doing much celebrating," Betsy said to Cora.

"I know what you mean, it's hard to think of our families without picturing them worrying about us."

"It's also hard for me to celebrate without a box of chocolates!" Betsy added.

The Easter Bonnet Parade started fifteen minutes late, but several nurses and men donned decorated steel helmets, baseball caps, straw hats, paper hats and homemade versions of an Easter bonnet.

"Listen," Cora said.

"What?" Betsy asked, never taking her eyes off of the hilarious parade.

"Laughter, hear the laughter? How long has it been since we have laughed like this?"

A bomb exploded several hundred yards from the hospital and the contestants all grabbed their hats, causing more laughter from the spectators. After a short parade around the tables the Master of Ceremonies announced the winner.

"The first place goes to Private Hunter, a medic from Alabama!"

Sporting a bedpan filled with grass and flowers strapped to his head, Private Hunter strutted around one more time before accepting his prize, a beautiful decorated egg donated by the mess staff.

"Our runner up is Sergeant Clark, from the great state

of North Dakota!" He wore a hat made from the hospital newsletter decorated with colorful cockatoo feathers.

"Hey, that's one of the cooks!" Someone shouted. "We probably ate that cockatoo in our soup last night!" A roar of laughter broke out.

The Master of Ceremonies handed Sergeant Clark a bouquet of wild flowers. Everyone cheered and left with a new event to add to their memories of Easter on Bataan.

The following two days were busy, more wounded arriving each night and the bombing getting closer to the hospital site. Two days later Cora made another entry in her journal.

*I wish I knew where Flint is. Is he safe? Is he alive? Yesterday ten bombs fell on Hospital #1 and this time it was no accident. Details are sketchy, but there are heavy casualties.*

*Spencer told me today that there is no nitrous oxide, sodium pentothal or curare so the anesthetists were using ether, and the whole surgical area is filled with that sweet rubbery sickening odor. Yesterday six doctors performed 420 operations, though some of the minor cases were handed over to the nurses. There is no end to the casualties.*

*Today a snake dangled from a mango tree as I walked by. I am always frightened and always hungry. Will I ever be normal again?*

The Japanese were within three miles of Hospital #2. Plans to surrender spread through the hospital like waves rolling ashore.

"All nurses are being ordered to get off Bataan. You

are to gather what personal items you can carry and report to the motor pool as fast as you can. You will then be taken to a boat that will ferry you to Corregidor." The commanding officer shouted.

"What about our patients? Shouldn't we prepare them for transport first?" Cora asked.

"No. You will follow orders, gather what you can carry and get to the buses and trucks. Get out of here now!"

"We are abandoning our patients, we can't do that. We took an oath!" Another nurse called out.

He swung around and faced her, veins at his temples bulging as he screamed. "Look lady, stop and think what will happen to you if you are here when the Japanese arrive! Didn't you hear what they did to the women in Nanking." He added a few adjectives not normally used in the presence of women, then swinging his clipboard by his side turned to leave. "That's an order!" he bellowed, and the women hustled to prepare for evacuation.

Cora remembered the horrible stories in the newspaper after the 1937 Japanese attack on the Chinese women in Nanking, but she had taken an oath. *I'm abandoning my patients, they can't survive long without medication, food and water,* Cora's thoughts raced as she ran toward her cot. Subconsciously she checked to make sure the morphine was still in her hair.

Cora joined the women who were grabbing wet clothes off the vine clothesline, "I can't believe they have ordered us to leave these men to die!" she said to Betsy as they gathered their belongings. She grabbed her toothbrush, a comb and her clothes that were draped over a stump and stuffed them into her two bags not taking time to shake out the lizards and other ugly creatures.

"Cora this is not textbook procedures, this is war!" Betsy shouted.

"Yes, but dressings need to be changed and many can't feed themselves. What will happen to them if we desert them?" Cora continued babbling.

"Stop the chatter and get moving, the Japs are so close I can smell them!" The Sergeant shouted. "Move out now!" He said frantically swinging his arms in the direction of the motor pool. "Head to the buses and don't stop for anything!" The path was lit by a frightening display of fireworks blanketing the night sky as the Americans blew up their ammunition dumps before surrendering.

The exhausted nurses ran stumbling down the path to the motor pool where fumes hovered overhead as the buses and trucks waited in lines with their engines running. Dogfaces were busy siphoning gasoline from cars and trucks to fill the buses.

The acrid smell of gunpowder burned Cora's eyes and nose as she searched through the thick dust for a bus to transport her to the docks. As soon as one bus filled it left and the next one filled and followed until all the American and Filipino nurses were taken away from their patients and the approaching Japanese soldiers.

Most of the nurses were experiencing stages of dysentery, malaria, hunger and exhaustion, but they did not complain. Their training had prepared them to put the welfare of their patients first, which they had been doing. Now they had only themselves and each other to save.

Cora found a seat next to Shorty on the stifling hot bus and sat doubled up with cramps from dysentery. She held her bags close to her chest trying to deal with her illness. *It isn't right to abandon my patients for my own survival! It's immoral!*

*Betsy? Where is Betsy?* Cora raised her head and through her dizzy state could not find Betsy. "Betsy! Betsy!" Cora called out. Betsy was not on the bus.

"Don't worry, Adams," Shorty said. "There are other buses, she's on one of them."

"No, she was right behind me. Betsy! Betsy!"

## Chapter Five

Rose and Shorty tried to comfort her but Cora turned and stared out the window. Lydia was sitting in the front of the bus, "Look at all the civilians evacuating the island! The road is jammed with trucks and soldiers, we'll never get to the docks." About that time the nurses felt the bus rock as civilians began banging on the sides begging for a ride to the docks.

"Don't look at them," Captain Jennings ordered.

Even in her current state, Cora recognized the desperate expressions of people she had worked with minutes earlier. She knew she would never forget the scene of leaving Jungle Hospital #2.

Questions flitted through Cora's mind faster and faster. *Spencer? Where is Spencer? Are the doctors staying with the patients or are they being evacuated too? No one had mentioned the doctors.*

The bus reached the wharf at Mariveles as a barge filled with nurses from the first buses was pulled out from the shore. Rushing off the bus dodging strafing from the planes overhead the nurses took cover in the trees and bushes. They waited and waited in the moonlight hoping a boat would arrive.

Many were uttering prayers or sobbing, but Cora chose to save her energy, what little she had, to get on the next boat regardless of its size or condition. The bombing continued for what seemed like hours with hits close to the bay. Suddenly a small launch appeared out of the darkness. "It's here! It's here!" the nurses shouted.

Some of the women ran, but most of them took time to help their sister nurses who were ill and could not keep up with the group. Lydia helped Cora to the launch and the stronger women pulled the weaker ones aboard.

"Come on, we can make it! We're not going to let the Japs get to us after what we've been through! We're American and Filipino nurses!" Shorty shouted as she helped her comrades aboard. All of the nurses waiting in the brush made it to the launch.

The boat maneuvered through Manila Bay like a potato bobbing about in a boiling pot of broth filled with vegetables. Cora sat on her musette on the floor of the launch looking out at the shimmering water reflecting the colors from the explosions. She became ill and placed her head between her knees to prevent herself from fainting. Gasoline and oil fumes from sinking boats filled the thick heavy air. Sounds of the dumps exploding and shrapnel zinging into the water muffled the screams of men and women when their boats were hit. It was more than Cora could stand, she held the palms of her hands tight against her ears trying to make it go away. It did not and a voice in her head kept repeating, *"You know that in that dark eerie water there are sharks waiting for their next meal and it could very well be you."* The voice faded and she could see the frightened faces of the patients left behind and her future, if captured. The spinning thoughts provoked dizziness.

After the launch dodged motor boats, rowboats and other launches it banged against the shore alerting the passengers of their safe arrival. The nurses of Bataan, or as the soldiers now referred to them, "The Angels of Bataan," embarked again on unfamiliar soil and an unknown future.

* * *

Cora – Cora!"

Second Lieutenant Cora Adams raised her head and stared into the crowd gathered to meet the launch.

"Over here!" Shouts erupted from the crowd as they waved frantically at the new arrivals.

Cora dropped her bags onto the beach and held her hand up to shield her eyes from the intense sun. Looking in the direction of the voice calling her name, she saw Claire running toward her. Cora staggered forward to meet her friend but her trembling weak body allowed her only a few steps before collapsing into Claire's arms.

"You're going to be all right." Claire held her friend and they sobbed.

When Cora could stand on her own she backed away, "Let me look at you." Claire's starched white uniform fit perfectly, she hadn't lost a pound. "You look great," Cora paused and glanced down over her own tattered dusty coveralls and combat boots two sizes too large and hunched her slumped shoulders. She removed her steel helmet exposing her damp thick black hair, "Where is Betsy?" Cora looked up the path ahead of them. "She is here isn't she?"

"I haven't seen her, when did she leave Bataan?"

"I don't know, we were separated. I thought she might already be here."

"I'll look for her later, right now we need to get you processed and settled into your new living quarters."

"All I need is a shower and a short nap, then I'll be ready to report to the hospital."

"Do you have any uniforms in here?" Claire asked, picking up the musette.

"Yes, two white uniforms and a pair of shoes and nylons and another uniform like I have on." They began walking.

"Well while you rest I'll get you something to snack on from the mess and when you feel like it we will go to the mess and get a hot meal." Claire stopped and studied Cora. "What medicine do you need?"

"I have dysentery and malaria, but I'll be fine."

"I'll get you some meds from the pharmacy."

Cora tried to smile as timid little Claire took charge. She heard her voice saying "Thanks," but her thoughts were on those left behind. The tormented feelings returned and she blurted out, "Claire, I abandoned patients starving to death and dying of thirst, I don't know if I can eat." Her shoulders shrunk as she lowered her head. "By the time we left there were twelve thousand patients and we left them there to die or be captured."

Claire spoke firmly, "Cora you have to eat, there are wounded here that need attention too. You will need your strength to care for them, accept the fact that you have no control over where you are sent but you do have control over taking care of yourself." Claire stopped so Cora could rest.

Cora raised her head. "Thanks, you're a true friend."

*I can't tell her Spencer may not have been evacuated with us. Not yet.* Cora reasoned with herself trying to remain sane.

Claire straightened her five foot two inch frame and placing her hands on her hips said, "Yea, well this is war and we have to be strong, our boys are counting on us." Cora stared at her clean neat friend whose blonde hair glistened in the sunlight, then glanced around at the worn-out women from Bataan.

Cora followed Claire and the other women into a tunnel carved deep into the rock that was Corregidor. The gray concrete complex of Malinta tunnel was divided into a series of corridors. Claire explained that they were known as laterals. They turned down a narrow passage. "This is the nurse's lateral. It contains a toilet, a sink, a shower and bunk beds."

"What was this tunnel before the war?"

"It was built as a storage facility."

"You will share my bunk," Claire insisted. "The men are getting more beds for us, but we will double up for now."

"Thanks." Cora's eyes burned when she smiled. For the first time since docking, she realized her eyes and throat were irritated from the fumes and exhaust hovering over the bay. The taste and smell of the fuel penetrated deep into her respiratory system causing her to wonder how the irritant could dissipate while she lived in a cave.

Cora's lower lip began to tremble, as her safety became a reality. "You don't know how good it is to see you Claire. Betsy and I felt miserable leaving you."

"It's good to see you too." She hugged her friend again. "Now you get settled in and as soon as I get you some food I'll go back down to the docks and see if I can locate Betsy." Claire paused and with a familiar quirky expression. "That girl never could be on time, not even when her life depended on it."

After Claire disappeared Cora studied her surroundings and noticed the familiar picture of Claire and her little sister, Courtney, on a stand next to the cot. *I've never known two sisters to be so close,* Cora thought. *Claire would give her life for that little girl.*

By the time Cora undressed and was about to shower Claire returned. "Here is something for the dysentery and some quinine."

"Cora accepted the medications, "I never knew quinine could look so good," she said studying the pill.

"I also got a couple of rolls from the bakery for you until we go to the mess."

Cora viewed the fresh baked rolls through her sunken eyes, "Are they real?"

"Yes silly. I intend to fatten you up while we're together." Cora took the bread and pinched off a bite. The aroma displaced the fumes and filled her with a forgotten sensation. She placed the morsel on her tongue before devouring it. "Ahhh," she said taking another bite, hoping it would not make her ill.

"Our food and water supply were rationed. The medicines and medical supplies were nearly exhausted," Cora informed Claire.

"Yes, but General MacArthur says help is on the way."

Cora forced a smile. *Where have I heard that before?*

True to her word, Claire appeared after Cora showered and napped. "Betsy isn't here yet, but there are small boats docking regularly. "If I know Betsy, she'll get here if she has to swim with one arm while fighting off sharks with the other."

"Thanks."

"When you are dressed we'll go to the mess. It's not far, but if you're not up to it I'll bring you something."

Cora sat on the edge of the bottom bunk. "I need to get oriented in this cave so I can get to work."

"Well it will take some time. The tunnel is seven hundred and fifty feet with twenty smaller laterals running north to south. The hospital lateral is off the lateral where you came in; there are fourteen other laterals off that main lateral. Another nine laterals and the quartermaster area is off of the fourth main lateral on the south side." Claire chuckled, "It's really just a small city underground, I like to think of it as Mole City. Some call it Tunnel Town. You'll learn your way around in no time."

"Right now it is just wonderful to have a roof over my head with no fear of monkeys jumping in bed with me."

Claire's eyes widened. "For real?"

"Oh yes, and when they weren't jumping on us their chattering nearly drove us crazy. Then there were the rats, snakes, iguanas, ants, mosquitoes and of course the Japs."

"We heard stories but I didn't think they were true. You really did sleep in the jungle? Oh how terrible."

"Trust me, they were true and probably worse than you heard. Everything was in the open except for some surgeries and our records. We bathed and did our laundry in a stream, though there wasn't much time for either. We did have a laundry setup run by Chinese men that did the hospital laundry by boiling the clothes and linens." She

80

paused. "When we had water."

The corners of Cora's mouth turned up, "Our quarters looked like a gypsy camp on the outskirts of a city. Clothes hanging from tree branches and vines, mirrors hanging from a couple of tree trunks, not that we cared how we looked, but we improvised. Her expression saddened. "I just can't stop thinking of the patients left behind," her voice quivered and tears overflowed her big brown sunken eyes again. "I wonder what has happened to them?"

"Cora, listen to me," Claire said placing her hands on Cora's shoulders and looking into her eyes, "This is war. We do what we can and never look back. Understand?"

Cora was shocked by Claire's tone but proceeded dressing as they chatted about working conditions. Cora combed her hair, "There now, I'm ready to have a tour and a real meal. Maybe Betsy will be in the mess, she's always hungry."

The day was slipping away without Betsy's arrival. The allied military personnel numbered twelve thousand on a three and a half mile long island with it's widest point being a mile and a half wide.

"After we eat I'll bring you back here to sleep and I'll report to work," Claire said.

They talked as they walked down the laterals. "How many of us are living inside this tunnel?" Cora asked.

"Ten thousand, that includes military and civilians. Amazing isn't it?"

"Yes. How many more can it accommodate?"

Claire shook her head. "It is already crowded and more wounded are being brought in every night. I'm not sure how many more it will hold."

Cora could not believe the food offered in the indoor mess hall.

"I know you should eat slowly but you have to eat more than you are." Claire said matter-of-factly.

"I know, but I can't forget my patient's faces as we were told to leave. There is no one to feed them except the ambulatory patients."

"It won't do them any good for you to starve yourself."

"I know," Cora said and picked up her fork. "Tell me about the hospital here?"

"Well, there is a beautiful modern hospital outside the tunnel, but of course it is not being utilized." Claire took a sip of coffee. "The five hundred bed tunnel hospital is located in laterals and the west entrance is wide enough for two ambulances to come in side by side."

"Do you have equipment?"

Claire stared, "Like what?"

"Thermometers, medicine cups, bedside tables, you know just things we need."

"Yes of course we have most everything any hospital has, but we are beginning to run low on bandages and medications. Of course we're expecting a shipment any day now." Claire answered then asked, "Didn't you have those things when you got to Bataan?"

"No, or at least very little. Some supplies and equipment were shipped over from Manila. We learned how to improvise and the Filipino craftsman made furniture and other necessities that could be made of wood."

After the meal of rice and fish ended, Cora enjoyed a short tour without the fear of being attacked by creatures or Japs.

They ended up at the nurse's lateral. "I am ordering bed rest for you Cora, but first I have a letter for you that Flint gave me before he left on the hospital ship."

"But how did he know we would be together again?"

"Like us, he just hoped we would." Claire removed the letter from her musette and handed it to Cora. "Is Spencer still on Bataan or did he get transferred?"

Cora sighed, "I should have told you earlier, Spencer is on Bataan. He is fine and he misses you." Cora lowered her gaze. "I don't know if he was to be evacuated after we were or not. No one seemed to know. It was real crazy there at the end. I'm sorry."

"But he was in good health when you last saw him?"

"Yes, as good as anyone at the hospital," Cora tried not to alarm Claire any more than necessary. "He told us you were on Corregidor but I didn't see him after we were given orders to evacuate." Cora shook her head. "It's all a blur, we only had a few minutes to get to our quarters, pack, and get to the motor pool for a ride to the docks. That's all, just a few minutes! Then the ride was over fifteen minutes."

"Well thanks for telling me now, he's a survivor you know." Claire turned from Cora. Both knew he could be dead and that with each hour that passed Betsy's chances of arriving diminished.

"I need to run some errands before reporting for work." She took several steps then stopped. "Yes, I'm going to try and locate Betsy first!" Claire said and left.

Cora removed her shoes and hose, propped up the pillow and sat on the bunk massaging her feet while she read Flint's letter.

*31 December 1941*
*My Dearest Cora,*

*I have a few free minutes before shipping out. I'm sitting in the dining room, remember the meals we shared here? We had some good times didn't we? Remember the tour we took in Old Manila, riding in the calesa and the pony refusing to obey the driver. I wanted to tell you how much you meant to me then, but couldn't find the words. I was afraid I'd scare you off again. Cora, I have loved you since I met you in Wheeling, and I hope you will find it in your heart to love me too.*

*I've heard reports of what you found when you arrived at Bataan and I'm praying that you will be strong and take care of yourself until this horrible war is over and we can be together. After the war I would like to take care of you.*

*I set sail tomorrow aboard the Mactan for Australia. We have prepared the 375 patients that are well enough to make the trip. Looking into the eyes of those we were leaving behind hurts so bad I can't describe the feeling. (I trust Claire with this letter knowing that she will destroy it before allowing it to fall into enemy hands.) With her going to Corregidor, I hope she will be able to somehow get this letter to you.*

*Remember West Virginia after the war! We'll celebrate at the McClure Hotel's formal dining room. I hope to hear from you soon.*

*All my love,*
*Flint*

Cora savored each word before tucking the letter into her musette with the other letter, then turned over and slept safe in the confines of the rock. She dreamed she was a black bear hibernating in the cave on the side of the mountain behind her house in West Virginia with coal dust penetrating her nostrils.

The next morning there was still no news of Betsy or six other nurses from Bataan. The earlier arrivals from Bataan that were well enough went on with their new duties leaving little time to worry about the missing nurses or the men left on Bataan.

"Hey, you are looking better. Was it the rest or the letter?" Claire jokingly asked when they met for lunch.

"Probably both."

"Did you get your schedule?"

"Yes. I start tomorrow morning in the post surgical ward."

"I'm going to check the docks and the new arrivals then get some sleep before time for my shift. What are your plans?"

"I'm going exploring in this mammoth cave and enjoy walking around free of wild creatures and strafing."

"Sounds great I'll see you later."

After a two-hour adventure through Malinta Tunnel, Cora returned to the nurses' lateral hoping to find an empty bed to sit on and write in her journal. She stopped short of the bed. "I can't believe my eyes?" she whispered. On the cot next to Claire's was Betsy curled up into a little ball, fast asleep. Her dark wet hair framed her soot-smudged face. She was a sight, but safe.

Cora found her journal and sat on the bunk next to Betsy and waited for her friend to open her eyes.

*She looks so peaceful. I hope she has been fed.* Cora's motherly instincts were taking over again. She opened her journal and began:

*9 April 1942*
*Malinta Tunnel*
*Corregidor, The Philippines*

> *I am safe on Corregidor in the Malinta Tunnel. I learned that Malinta means many leaches, but after what I've seen that isn't scary.*
>
> *Claire met me when I arrived yesterday and took care of me. Betsy is here now. We are together again. We don't know where Spencer is, but we are hoping he left before the Japanese arrived.*
>
> *I worry about the twelve thousand patients we left on Bataan. All is not bad. My stomach is full, I'm receiving quinine and I have a roof over my head.*

Betsy opened one eye and then the other before stretching then sitting only to be knocked back by Cora's welcoming hug.

"Where have you been? I've been worried sick!" Cora's voice shrieked.

"Claire said you were worried. I was right behind you, when the bus filled and the door closed. I got on the next one and shrapnel hit us. We caught rides on jeeps and trucks then had to wait until morning to get a boat over here."

"Oh Betsy! That's awful, you must have been scared to death." She hugged her tired friend again as tears rolled down her cheeks.

"Hey, all of us made it. The soldiers were right when they named us the 'Battling Bells of Bataan!' That's what we are you know. We are survivors!"

"Yes we are. By the way, doesn't Claire look great?"

"Yes, she brought me here, fed me and offered me a place to sleep then disappeared."

"I'm so glad we're together again!" Cora removed her shoes and rubbed her sore feet.

Betsy stared at Cora, "Yes, but I hope I don't look as worn out as you do – you look awful. Is the dysentery worse?"

No, they have medicine here and Claire insisted I take some, and it is helping."

The following day Betsy and Cora were working the same post-surgical ward. "I think Bataan was just a period of training for us, don't you?" Betsy asked.

"Yes, complete with live bodies being sacrificed!"

"Yea, the patients are different here but the wounds are the same."

Cora didn't answer. She enjoyed working inside the fortress. Caring for post-surgical patients was a pleasant change from dealing with battle injuries of the walking wounded and stretcher cases. Occasional laughter replaced the screams and moans she had become accustomed to hearing. Suddenly she was pulled from her thoughts as Betsy rushed to the side of a boy screaming.

"You're okay. You're okay! You are having a nightmare. It's okay now. I understand." She held him down while his nightmare tormented his unconscious mind, then she held him in her arms while he sobbed.

Cora was busy attending a patient coming out from under heavy sedation, he was agitated and fighting the restraints. She couldn't leave him until he returned to a restful state.

"He doesn't know how much we understand," Cora said to Betsy. "All of us from Bataan have nightmares."

Cora reflected on her own nightmares, awakening most nights with a rapid heartbeat and in a cold sweat. Opening her mouth to scream but nothing coming out. Watching Vince being carried up out of the coal mine. It seems real as she removes his crushed headlamp. *"Get out."* His voice is weak.

*"Vince don't try to talk."*

*"Get out of this town, like we planned."* Bright red blood trickles from the corner of his mouth. *"Promise."* Vince breathes his last breath. Cora awakens realizing her dream is real, it took place almost eight years earlier.

A soldier in the next bed begins thrashing about and Cora snaps out of her thoughts. *The noises sound so different in this tunnel. They are shallow and muffled. They are dreadful. We've gone from one bad situation to another!*

That evening Cora made another entry in her Journal.

*12 April – Corregidor*

*I just completed my first day in the post-surgical ward of the Malinta Tunnel Hospital. There are white enamel bedside tables supplied with bedpans, drinking glasses and bathing supplies. I feel like a regular nurse again but more casualties arrived today and we are at full capacity. I heard that some of the wards use metal bunk beds and they are considering placing a third bed on top.*

*The trip from Bataan is fuzzy at best, but we all made it and now Claire, Betsy and I are together again. The other good thing that happened is Claire gave me a letter from Flint. I can't believe how I miss him and not just working with him. I miss his gentle voice and words of encouragement and I can't wait to hear his deep laugh again. I don't want to love him or anyone else, but I can't control the feelings I have for him and my concern for his safety. Tomorrow when I feel better I will write to him with hopes the letter will reach him wherever he is.*

*We don't know where Brice is and we are concerned for Spencer's safety too. No one will say but we know he would be here by now unless he was captured or even worse.*

The next morning during her break, Cora walked to the west entrance to the tunnel and went out into the sun warmed fresh air to smoke a cigarette and grieve the men she left on Bataan. Claire had told her that many of the nurses came here in the evening to escape the stale dusty air and some met men for a wartime version of a date. Cora stood alone with her mind fixed on Bataan. *That's enough dwelling on the past! I've got work to do*, she thought and stomped out the cigarette. She reported back to the ward to complete an eighteen-hour shift, hoping to have little time to think of Bataan.

Cora reentered the ward and began working her way down the rows of patients. Stopping at the next bed she gasped. Cora could not believe what she was seeing.

## Chapter Six


"Brice, Brice," Cora whispered. "It's me Lieutenant Cora Adams, can you hear me?" There was no response. She grabbed his chart from the foot of the bunk and began reading it.

"I could if you'd speak up, Darlin'!" A wide grin crossed the cowboy's face as Capt. Brice T. Weatherby looked up at her."

Standing beside his bed with her hand on his shoulder she asked, "What happened? How did you break your arm? Were you shot down?"

The bomber pilot nodded. "Whoa slow down, little filly!" They laughed. "My plane was hit in the mountains, but I was lucky – a guerrilla group close by saw me go down. They set my arm and kept me with them for three days until I was conscious. They had medicine for pain too. You know they have quite an organization and we couldn't fight this war without them.

"Really?"

"Yes, there are guerrillas all over these islands. When I was well enough to travel they took me to a camouflaged boat and brought me here; that was last night, so everything is swell." Brice paused while studying his nurse.

"Hot dog! You look as pretty and fresh as a new born calf." His Oklahoma drawl changed Cora's expression of concern to joy.

"Betsy is here too." Cora paused as Brice's face brightened. "She will be so happy to find out that you are okay."

"Really? Tell me was she worried about me?"

Cora nodded. "Yes, we all were. Claire is here too."

His questioning eyes led her on to explain. "Spencer was on Bataan with Betsy and me, Claire came from Manila to Corregidor." Cora couldn't control the flow of words pouring out of her mouth. "Flint left at the same time, but we don't know where he is, all we know is he left right after Christmas with a ship full of casualties heading for Australia." She paused and drew in a deep breath. "We haven't heard from Flint since he left Manila or Spencer since Bataan was captured."

Cora placed a thermometer under his tongue and picked up his wrist. She felt his pulse and watched the second hand on her Elgin wristwatch. *I must sound like a magpie, but I'm happier than I have been since I first saw Claire at the dock.*

His pulse was rapid which she contributed to the excitement of finding his friends, she knew her heart was beating faster than normal too. Cora removed the thermometer and recorded a reading of 100 degrees.

"You get some rest now and I'll be back later with your medicine. I'm glad you're okay, Cowboy," she called back to him as she hurried down the lateral with a new spring in her step.

Cora took an early break to search for Betsy and found her on the ward filling medicine cups. "Betsy," Cora was out of breath. "I have a surprise for you."

"What? Your face is flushed, are you okay?" Betsy asked.

"I'm fine. No I'm great! Guess who I just found on my ward?"

"The Easter Bunny– I don't know Cora, just tell me, I don't have all day." Betsy closed her eyes and rubbed the middle of her forehead with two fingers.

"Brice – Brice Weatherby!"

Betsy's eyes popped open. "Brice?" She lowered her arm. "How bad is he? What happened?"

"He's not bad at all, he was shot down and has a broken arm and a bruised ego. Can you believe it? Only a broken arm! He has a fever, but he's here and he's gonna be okay."

Betsy could not contain her excitement, and bouncing up and down did not appear to be helping to calm her. "He's really here? You're not joking? He's here?"

"And you said you two were just friends. Of course we all thought otherwise." Cora tipped her head, tightened her lips and raised her brow. "Well?'

"Okay, so maybe it did mean something," Betsy admitted. "I thought we would never see each other again so I tried to forget him." A smile radiated across her face then faded. "But here we are again for now at least."

Betsy called out for someone to relieve her, "Take over here, I'm due for a break." Turning to Cora she said, "I'm going back to your ward with you."

Cora led the way to Brice. "It looks like he is asleep."

"I'll wait here until he wakes up," Betsy said loud enough to waken him.

"I'll wait with you, I have a few free minutes left." Her thoughts were on Flint not Brice. *Why isn't he sent to Corregidor? We need more surgeons and he's one of the best in the Army. Why didn't I appreciate the time we had together? I may never see him again.*

"Remember when we first met Brice?" Betsy asked

Cora chuckled. "Yes, you Claire and I were eating in the hospital dining room and making plans for our first full day in Manila when the tall, dark and handsome Captain Brice T. Weatherly introduced himself."

"He said he was meeting a couple of friends and our table was the only one with enough empty seats and he asked to join us," Betsy said. "And we fell for it."

"I'm surprised we didn't scare him away the way we all answered so quickly. Then after the introductions he looked at each of us before sitting by you."

"When I saw his insignia I made some dumb remark about him being a pilot and he told us that he flew a B-17."

"Claire and I could tell you were impressed, but that's when Spencer arrived and Claire was not very discreet in checking out his ring finger. Remember that?" Cora asked.

"Yes but she denied it. Then just as things were going well, Flint arrived and the mood changed."

"I know, but here I was with an assignment to paradise and the man I joined the Army to get away from was here! He acted so polite that I remember thinking that he should get an award for his performance. I thought he was a real hypocrite because I knew he hated me!" Cora said.

"And it was obvious that you hated him too."

Cora smiled, "Yes I guess it was."

"Well knowing what I know now, I think you both handled the situation quite well. I remember that you told us that he was one of the best surgeons you'd ever worked with. That must have been a hard compliment to give, considering."

"Well it was the truth and what could I say, Brice had figured out I had worked with Flint and he set me up!"

"The look on Flint's face when he saw you was not an act Cora. It was obvious to everyone at the table but you, he was in love with you."

"Well I had hoped to never see him again and when I did I just knew he would ruin my assignment. I thought his flirting with me was just an act to humiliate me in front of my friends."

"See how wrong you were. Flint didn't ruin your assignment, the Japs did!"

"I know that now." Cora glanced at her watch, "Oh, I've got to get busy." She left Betsy to sit alone with Brice.

The following morning, Cora awakened early feeling rested and stronger than she had in weeks. With Claire working and Betsy sleeping, she made her way through the laterals that were becoming less intimidating. She turned the corner leading into a main lateral that would take her to the mess. She was reliving the excitement of Brice's appearance when she stopped in her tracks. She squinted as she stared at the thin man leaning against the wall.

"Spencer!"

He stepped away from the wall that appeared to be keeping him from collapsing. "Cora. Oh thank God you are okay!"

"You're alive! We were so worried. When did you get here? No wait. You're starved and I'm sure you could use a cup of hot coffee. Let's get to the mess and you can tell me everything." Cora placed her arm around his waist and with her support he started walking.

"You said we were worried, does that mean that Betsy made it too?" Spencer asked.

"Yes." Cora answered, and then she explained how they had become separated.

"You are lucky," his weak voice trailed off.

"Claire met us at the docks."

"Is she okay?"

"Yes she's fine and just wait until you see her, she looks great!"

"Where is she now?"

"In surgery, but we may see her at breakfast. Yesterday Brice arrived with a broken arm, he'll be thrilled to see you too."

"Brice?"

"Yes."

"It will be good to have another old friend to talk with." He stumbled and Cora tightened her grip around his waist. "As soon as you eat, I'll see that you are taken to the hospital to be checked."

Spencer and Cora were just beginning to eat when Spencer stood, but was too weak to move. Cora turned in time to see Claire's burst of excitement. Spencer waited as Claire ran into his arms. After a brief reunion she filled a tray with food and joined them for breakfast.

"This reunion is one I shall never forget seeing," Cora said as her eyes began to puddle with tears.

"What happened after we left?"

"I was removing shrapnel from a soldier's hip hoping to save his leg when the nurses were ordered to leave. The surgical nurses took off their gloves and gowns and walked out past hundreds of wounded laying in the open jungle waiting to have surgery." Spencer bit his lip and shook his head. "I didn't have time to think about it then, but that had to have been rough on them. Anyway I completed the operation and by the time I finished the Japs had arrived. None of the doctors were ordered to evacuate, just our Angels."

Claire's big blue eyes widened. "What happened then?"

Spencer's face became pale and after several seconds and two sips of coffee he spoke. "The Japs were very disorganized. They tried to operate our vehicles with little success, then demanded we teach them. If a soldier couldn't get a truck started because it was out of fuel they would shoot him. Everything they couldn't use was destroyed." He took a bite of a biscuit followed by a drink of coffee.

He stared into Cora's frightening eyes. "They ordered us to walk." She pushed her plate away and lowered her gaze. She knew he was only telling what he wanted them to hear. Cora didn't ask about those that couldn't walk. She didn't want to hear what the Japanese had done to them.

"I walked the first day. There was a lot of confusion, the sun was hot and the Japs were still unorganized and trigger-happy. They would not allow us to get out of line for any reason and if anyone tried to help a comrade that fell or was to ill to walk both were shot. We were given no food or water."

Cora willed her food to stay down as he continued.

"How did you escape?"

"I'm not sure. I tried to stay alert and I remember

being close to the edge of the path, and the guard closest to me was busy killing two of our men. I must have stumbled to the side in fear and I found myself in a ditch. I was afraid to move because I knew they would shoot me or run a bayonet through me. My only hope was that they could not see me." He paused. "The sun had gone down, but it wasn't dark yet. I must have blacked out. I awakened at daybreak and all I could hear were birds and monkeys. I didn't know for sure where I was so I followed the sun all day, then did the same with the moon. Two days later I heard water beating against the shore. When I reached the beach I found cover and watched for a boat; after several hours a small fishing boat appeared."

"Oh Spencer, I was so worried. I'm glad you're here now," Claire said.

*Claire, there is no way you can understand what he has been through mentally or physically. I'm not sure I can.* Cora finished her coffee and stood. "I need to be going now, Spencer get some rest, you will be needed in surgery as soon as you feel up to it. Bataan was just our training ground for what is beginning to happen here!" She knew he understood but Claire's expression showed no comprehension. After breakfast Claire escorted Spencer to the medical commanding officer.

Cora's thoughts were on Flint when she reached the lateral and prepared to sleep. She removed a small dull pencil and stationary from her musette and began a letter to him. *This may be crazy. I have no idea where he is or if he will ever receive this, but I have to get it written.*

*14 April 1942*
*Dear Flint,*

*I am safe on Corregidor with Claire, Betsy, Spencer, Brice and others from Sternberg hospital. I have received both of your letters. I wish you were here so we could talk, then I realize that is being selfish so instead I hope you are in a safe location with food and water.*

*The stories you heard about Bataan were probably true and maybe worse. It was an experience I shall never forget, but I'm glad I was able to be of some help. We left our patients behind to die, and I will always remember their expressions and the pain I suffered by abandoning them. It continues to bring tears to my eyes when I think of them. There were so many and they were so young and helpless. It is a nightmare I hope to forget someday.*

*Yes, I do often think of our day in Old Manila, but it seems like years ago instead of six months ago. I still can't believe what is happening. I never dreamed anything could be worse than a coal mine disaster —- boy was I wrong. Here young men also die leaving their sweethearts alone, bitter and not understanding why it happened. In a coal mining accident you at least know why and have family to mourn with and give support.*

*I shouldn't go on like this. I'm looking forward to a nice dinner at the McClure Hotel soon. When I close my eyes I can see the white linen tablecloths, smell the food and hear the music. I do hope we can get a table by the window looking out on Market Street so we can watch the streetcars and shoppers rushing around without the worry of being bombed.*

*Please stay safe.*

*Yours truly,*
*Cora*

That evening while Cora was filling out a patient's chart before ending her shift she saw Betsy and Claire arrive to visit Brice. She quickly finished her task and joined them.

For a while they were able to forget where they were and laugh at Brice's embellished war stories. It was almost like old times and a couple of patients close to Brice appeared to enjoy the entertainment also.

"Honestly Weatherby, you are a sight for sore eyes – you're the only person I know who could find humor in being shot down by the Japs!" Spencer said when he made his presence known. A young boy in the cot above Brice laughed, "You got that right Sir," causing others around Brice to join in the laughter.

"Hey, it's good to see you too Doc." Brice tried to sit up, but Spence placed a hand on his shoulder urging him not to move.

"Lie still, you're still weak from the injury and long trip, and besides this is the first time I've been able to give you an order!"

"You know Spencer, I thought I'd died and gone to heaven when I opened my eyes and saw Cora staring down at me, I thought she was an angel of mercy, but now seeing you here, I'm not sure where I am!" Brice gave a hearty laugh with the others joining him. "Hot dog! This was worth getting shot down for, but I won't promise to do it again for a another reunion."

Cora's replacement informed the visitors that Captain Brice needed his rest and while he tried to charm her into letting them stay, they paraded out promising to return the next day.

The following morning Brice told Cora of his earlier

visit that morning from Betsy before she reported for her shift. "She brought me up to date on what the two of you have been through since leaving Manila."

"Yeah, it's hard for me to believe too and I was there."

"I told her I was going to take her dancing in a few weeks. My arm will be healed and this war will be over. It will be just like it was when the war started, maybe even better."

"What did she say?"

"Nothing until I squeezed her hand and flashed my big famous Oklahoma grin." Brice laughed. "And she said what if the war isn't over?"

"I had to think a minute for a comeback to that! But I did and I said, hey, aren't you nurses suppose to keep the patients' morale up?"

Cora laughed. "And did she agree to go dancing?"

"I think so," she smiled and said, "Touché!"

Their smiles faded as a warm understanding passed between them.

Cora checked Brice's temperature and attempted to hide her concern. His escalating fever indicated a worsening infection. An earlier examination had shown damage to his kidneys, but the doctor that had examined him hoped it was a bruise that would heal itself.

When his temperature reached 104 degrees with no sign of breaking, Spencer smuggled four bottles of beer onto the ward, in hopes of forcing Brice's kidneys to work. Within an hour after Brice consumed the liquid his temperature was down to 100 degrees.

While sponging his forehead with a cool cloth Cora said, "Serving beer to our patients is not routine, but with our water rationed and tasting terrible we've learned to improvise. I'm sure even your mama would approve of our unorthodox treatment to keep you alive."

"Maybe, but I'm not going to tell her, are you?"

Cora grinned. Even with worrying about his fever these last few days had been the best days since leaving Manila. They were all together except Flint, would he ever be with them?

* * *

Cora had not posted the two letters she had written to Flint even though she had located the tunnel post office. Military personnel were not required to pay postage, so she was not sure why she still had the letters in her possession. She reread the most recent letter several times before tucking it in her journal, with the one she had written earlier. *I need to make sure they get out if there is a way off this rock. I should write to Mother again too, I know she is worried.* Cora's thoughts were on home more now than they had been since she joined the Army.

Betsy arrived as Cora was going to bed. "I am really surprised at how the better working conditions have boosted the morale of the nurses that came here from Bataan." Betsy tipped her head and looked at Cora, "Is it just me or have you noticed it too?"

"Yes, I'm aware of it, but when you think about it we had no way to go but up! We appreciate all the things we had taken for granted," she paused and looked up at the tunnel ceiling, "like those light bulbs."

Betsy smiled and nodded. "It is nice isn't it?"

"Yes Betsy, it is. Good night." Cora turned over and

smiled.

Two hours later Cora awakened with aching muscles and chills. It's only a minor inconvenience she told herself. *I no longer suffer from dysentery and the malaria chills are not as often now.* Her thoughts shifted to the endless hours she had worked on her knees on Bataan.

\* \* \*

"Look!" Cora said to Betsy. "My uniforms fit again!"

"Mine too and to think we've only been here two weeks. I've noticed that my hair is shinier too," Betsy added.

"But I still wake up in the night thinking I am hungry and thirsty. Then I look around and know there is food and water so I slip into a peaceful state of sleep."

"Speaking of food lets go see what's being served today." They started walking and Betsy whispered, "Do you think the same thing is going to happen here that happened on Bataan?"

Cora answered in a low voice, "Yes. I try not to think about it, but when I look into the faces of the young men I am caring for I wonder if I will be ordered to abandon them too."

"I think we all wonder that, but for now all we can do is care for our patients and hope this war will soon end."

Claire joined Cora and Betsy in a rare time that they were free to eat together. "I just heard that we now have fifteen hundred patients!"

"I'm not surprised, look at how many bunks are now triple-decked," Betsy added.

"Can you reach the top patient?" Cora asked Claire.

"No, but so far I've been working with taller women and they make their rounds treating the patients on the top, I do the lower and we split the middle. I wonder how Rose and Lydia are doing, they are shorter than I am."

"My mother is short and she always said it was no disgrace to be short, but very inconvenient," Cora said.

"Well she is right about that!" Claire responded.

"Speaking of short," Betsy said. "I've done some investigating and we are running short of most of our supplies."

"I'm worried that the frustrations we experienced in the jungle will surface, only this time those of us from Bataan know what lies ahead," Cora said getting up and refilling her coffee cup.

"When the old generators failed today the surgeons were forced to do surgery by flashlight," Claire informed her friends.

Cora and Betsy looked at each other. Finally Betsy spoke up. "We were without electricity on the wards too, but I'd grown so accustomed to working in the jungle with a flashlight in my mouth that it seemed natural."

"That's what I was thinking," Cora added. "Electric lights are a real luxury here. I am just glad I don't have to crawl."

"Crawl?" Claire looked at her friends as they nodded.

"I miss the fresh air in the jungle, but feeling suffocated in here is still the best of the two choices," Betsy said.

"The ventilation system is outdated, and we depend on old generators to run the fans, so when it goes out like it did today it's horrible. The dust and humid air, mixed with the stench of medicines, illnesses and disinfectants has nowhere to go."

"It goes into my nose!" Betsy said.

"The gasoline, cordite and gangrene stench is what I can't stand. Of course the odors and dust are starting to affect our breathing which interferes with our work."

"That's probably what is causing my headache. It has hurt for so long I can't remember living without the pain." Betsy gently massaged her temples with her fingertips.

"We had better get back to the wards," Cora said and they left.

"I'll see you later," Claire said and continued to smoke a cigarette and drink her coffee.

"My head aches too," Cora said as they walked. "But it's better than having an earache like Claire has had for days. I'm afraid she's going to lose her hearing."

"She's using ear drops now and that should help."

"This stale muggy tunnel air isn't good for any of us."

"We'll all probably die of lung diseases if the Japs don't kill us first!" Cora's voice softened, "My dad died from 'Black Lung,' most of the older miners suffer from it until it kills them. I can remember Dad sitting on our front porch having coughing seizures and the blood spewing out of his mouth. It was so normal that it was either ignored or accepted. I'm not sure which."

"I've read about 'Black Lung' and it sounds like a horrible way to die. You had your share of disasters and diseases before you ever got to the Philippines didn't you?"

"Yes, I guess I did. Black Lung Disease was bad, but now I realize the victims from the coal mines die at home or in the mine, not like these boys, stuck on some far away island among strangers."

"I know, every time a boy dies in my arms I wonder

about his family. I would like for all of the families back home to know that we give the best care and compassion possible."

"This is my ward, I'll catch you later, Betsy." Cora said, leaving Betsy to continue alone.

* * *

By mid-April gas drills became a dreaded routine for the nurses and everyone in the tunnel. They hated having their work interrupted to pull out tubes, nozzle and face-masks from the bag hanging on a heavy canvas belt strapped around their waist. The masks were heavy, hot and an inconvenience, and were to be with the nurses at all times and used during drills. Getting the mask on and repackaging it took time, but the nurses did not complain or appear frightened, it was just another inconvenience.

Claire and Cora met outside the north tunnel entrance for a break. "How is Brice today? Is his temp staying down?" Claire asked.

"Yes he is much better except for boredom. I have him reading to several of the patients to occupy his time.

"Does he still talk about getting back to his squad and flying again?"

"Of course, but until now I don't think he's felt well enough to get back and he does have Betsy's visits to look forward to."

"A couple of days ago he was telling Spencer and me about his parents' ranch in Oklahoma, he got so excited I was concerned about his blood pressure shooting up. He explained how he loved rounding up cattle, building fences and anything else that required being outside. It sounded like heaven compared to this place."

"He's told me about it too and I think being in this underground fortress makes him more eager to get up in a plane and soar through the wide open skies."

The women returned to their wards in time to experience another failure of the large out dated generators. This time while they were in the dark the rock shook from heavy shelling. The generators were restored by the time Cora's shift ended and she made her way through the laterals with the aid of light bulbs hanging from wires extending from the ceiling. She was growing accustomed to having a gas mask and flashlight with her constantly.

Back in the nurses lateral she made an entry in her journal before going to sleep.

*23 April 1942*

*I am still in the confines of Malinta tunnel, which becomes more like a prison every day. The water supply was knocked out for four days and I hope to never have to drink boiled salt water again! The fruit juice quenched my thirst, but I missed pure water. They have limited our food and our wards are overflowing with patients.*

*Sometimes I feel that Bataan was a classroom to teach us how to work here. Two nights ago a shell hit the east entrance and the people standing outside and in the entrance were injured or killed by the explosion. All they wanted was a breath of fresh air, a view of the sunset and the enjoyment of a few minutes outside of the tunnel. (We all miss the sunshine and the stars.) I was ordered to report to surgery where I worked twenty hours straight.*

*The mangled bodies were worse than the casualties I saw in Manila and Bataan. We were tripping over buckets of bloody body parts setting around the surgical area. We had to snip off fingers and toes with our surgical scissors and treat wounds I never dreamed possible.*

*Since a few of the wounded were acquaintances, I didn't want to look into their faces for fear I'd see someone I knew. As we worked the red lights hanging above our heads blinked, alerting us to incoming enemy aircraft. No one back in the States would believe the conditions we are working in, they couldn't even imagine them.*

*Spencer was in surgery at the time of the attack and I assisted him and Betsy assisted Dr. Phillip Baker. Phillip was sent from Manila to Corregidor when we were ordered to Bataan. We knew him from the hospital and the club. He had asked Betsy out several times, but she was never able to go. She spent her free time with Brice.*

*I wish I could talk to Flint or Doc Warner. I need to tell Doc that I understand why he never talked about World War I.*

The following morning more casualties arrived and Cora remained in surgery working a sixteen-hour shift. The lights above the operating tables swung during her shift from the heavy shelling and strafing on Corregidor. The routine continued for a week before she was assigned back to a post-surgical ward. The population of the tunnel continued to increase and supplies continued to diminish.

"I just talked to a nurse in the mess and she said twenty nurses are going home," Claire reported to Cora and Betsy while they were sitting on their bunks enjoying a cup of weak coffee and sharing a cigarette before reporting to work.

"How can the army do that? We're shorthanded now

and there are new casualties arriving everyday," Cora stated.

"Are you sure you heard it right?" Betsy questioned after a long drag on her cigarette.

"Yes, the nurses were given a gag order. No goodbyes, but they disobeyed the order."

"Who are they?" Betsy and Cora asked in unison.

"They are all over forty-five or too ill to work."

A hush fell across the area, and the three turned toward the end of the row of beds, two young attractive nurses hurriedly packed their bags and exited the lateral.

"Old nurses, huh?" Betsy said with an eyebrow raised.

"I don't believe this, I've heard that redhead is a friend of a General back in the States. Do you think that's why she is getting to go home?" Claire questioned.

"Wouldn't we if we had the chance. Just think of the fresh air, good food, movies, new clothes and current newspapers, but most of all freedom. I can't blame anyone for leaving this place." Betsy said.

"Well I guess I can't either, but I hate to see politics deciding who leaves and who stays." Claire finished her coffee and lit another cigarette. "I know I miss my baby sister and would like to be with her but it wouldn't be fair to the wounded or the other nurses."

Cora did not express her thoughts on the evacuation. Her concerns were on the future of those staying on Corregidor. The Japanese were getting closer everyday. *Will we survive to go home?*

## Chapter Seven

On the way to their respective wards the trio learned of four more young attractive nurses that were also going home.

"We're attractive too. I wonder what other qualifications they have that we don't?" Betsy said sarcastically. Claire and Cora gave her a questioning glare, but did not answer.

"Ahhh. I see."

Word spread through the nurse's lateral and the wards that the planes would also be taking several bags of mail off of the rock.

Cora posted her letters immediately. *At last, maybe now Flint will receive my answers to his letters. I'm glad I wrote to my mother and Doc too, it could be a long time before mail gets out again.* Cora's thoughts were bittersweet.

On 29 April two navy PBY seaplanes landed on the water and taxied up close to the shoreline of Corregidor. Supplies and mailbags were unloaded before evacuating the twenty nurses. In the tunnel, the solemn mood of the nurses was short lived. There were patients to be cared for and the nurses remaining in the tunnel would be absorbing the workload of those leaving. The ever questioning thought haunted the nurses. Would they be ordered to leave their patients once again.

* * *

"Our mail got through!" One of the nurses shouted and the news spread through the laterals like dominos falling. Cora dashed toward the mailroom where she stood in line with Betsy and Claire.

"I'm so excited I can't keep my feet on the floor," Claire announced. "I'm sure Courtney is quite a little lady now."

"How old is she?" Cora asked.

"Five, she will be six on May tenth." Claire glowed with pride as she went on to explain how smart Courtney had been when she last saw her.

"So much could have happened since our last mail call," Betsy said.

"Yes, that was the first of December, five months ago." Cora added and they returned to the nurses' area and sat on their cots with the treasured letters scattered around them. Silence filled the area except for an occasional sob, scream, or chuckle. After all of the mail and newspaper clippings had been read and reread they began sharing their news.

Betsy held her five letters close to her heart, "Four are from my parents and one is from my oldest brother."

Cora stared at her four letters addressed to her. "Mine are all from my mother, except one and it is from Doc Warner."

"I got nine letters from Aunt Irene!" Claire announced after Cora and Betsy had reported. "Apparently we haven't received all that were sent, because Aunt Irene mentioned things that she had written about earlier."

"Same here, Mom gave me a health update on my grandma, and I didn't know she was ill," Betsy added.

"No one has died, or at least it wasn't mentioned," Cora said and Claire and Betsy quickly said it was the same for them.

"It's also obvious they have no idea of what is going on over here!" Betsy added.

"Maybe they just want to tell us happy things to keep us cheered up." Claire said justifying the news of Christmas celebrations and marriages.

"My mother asked me how I like the songs, *There'll Be some Changes Made* and *Chattanooga Choo Choo*." She must think we hear all the latest hits!" Betsy exclaimed.

"You're right," Cora said. "My mother asked if I was wearing my blue gown to a lot of dances! I know she and my brother listen to the news every evening, they have to know what is going on."

"Our families are refusing to believe what they surely must be hearing, or they don't want us to know how worried they are," Claire suggested and they agreed. She folded the letters and placed them under her cot.

"Something Doc wrote may help all of us," Cora said, and began to read to them. *"No matter how bad things get never stop dreaming of winning and coming home!"*

\* \* \*

New wounded arrived each day and the tunnel air grew dustier. Food and water rations were cut again and

111

longer shifts were now becoming a routine for the nurses; they slept only when too tired to function.

Cora, Claire and Betsy sat on their bunks talking late one evening as bombs exploded above the tunnel. "I'm glad my ear has stopped hurting," Claire said. "This noise would drive me crazy.

"You know, when I worked the emergency room at Cook County Hospital back in Chicago I thought I had seen every type of wound, illness and filth there is in this world." Betsy shook her head. "Boy, was I wrong!" She fumbled with a match trying to light a Chesterfield. After it was lit she inhaled then tipped her head up allowing rings of smoke to escape. "Do you think it will get worse?" Betsy asked and passed her cigarette to Claire who lit her cigarette with the burning embers and passed it back to Betsy.

After releasing several smoke rings Claire said, "Yes, I'm beginning to think it could last a lot longer than we thought. There must be millions of Japanese out there! Just listen."

No one answered for a while, then Cora said. "It's probably best if we don't think too much about it. Just take one day at a time and do as Doc suggested, think of winning and home." She removed a Lucky Strike from her pack and lit it from Betsy's cigarette. "Did you realize today is the first day of May."

"No, is it really May Day?" They asked.

"Yes and back home all the young girls go out early in the morning on May Day and wash their faces in the dew to keep their skin silky and youthful." Cora sighed. "Guess I missed it this year, so if my skin wrinkles and I look old and ugly, I'll blame the Japs." The three laughed, it was a sound seldom heard in the tunnel.

After the laughing stopped Cora became serious, "Speaking of back home." She stopped, then breaking the silence added, "I was used to coal-mining accidents and seeing the injured, and the dead brought up out of the mines covered with coal dust and blood. I was even prepared to hear the wailing of their families." She paused and took a couple of puffs of her cigarette, picked up the hairbrush resting in her lap and began brushing her hair.

"Oh that sounds awful," Betsy said. "Did anyone in your family die in the mining accidents?"

Cora stopped brushing, "Yes, my oldest brother, my grandfather, two uncles and —" She got up off her bunk turning away from Betsy and Claire to conceal her moist eyes. She pulled a deck of cards from her pocket, "Anyone for a game of rummy?" Cora asked forcing a smile.

"Sure," Betsy said, "Anything to get our minds off this place."

"Yea that's a swell idea." Claire moved so they were sitting in a circle. "I'd led a pretty sheltered life before Pearl Harbor was hit. About the worse thing I had seen at Central Maine Medical School in Lewiston were a couple cases of diphtheria, car wreck victims and sledding casualties. After school I joined the Army.

"None of us were prepared for this atrocity. There is no way we would have believed it could happen or even imagined the cases we see each day." Cora said as she shuffled the deck of cards.

"What will you tell your family about this place?" Betsy asked looking at Cora.

"I don't know. I'm sure they wouldn't understand, or need to know." She paused. "I think I will just try to forget this part of my life."

"What about Flint?" Claire asked.

"I don't know that I'll ever see him again, so I can't predict that." She finished dealing, "Let's play."

* * *

Brice continued improving but to his disappointment he was not cleared for a new assignment. Cora enlisted his talents of talking to patients, especially new arrivals. He was a natural at lifting the patients' spirits. When she walked past the bed of a depressed young soldier she heard Brice say, "Okay Lieutenant, are you ready for me to beat you at rummy again? Or will I have to pull rank on you?"

Brice voluntarily read to patients, told stories, played games, helped feed the men and offered a hand at rolling bandages for the nurses. He was greatly appreciated, but Cora knew he felt like a caged bird that needed to be released.

"I've never felt so helpless in my life," Brice said to Cora while helping her change a patient's bandage. "I shouldn't be here! I should be up in a bomber helping us win this war! If there are any B-17s left!"

"You are helping!" Cora snapped. "And you could put others in danger if you were unable to control the plane with that arm!"

"Yes but—"

"We need you here now and we certainly don't have time for self pity. Would you please get a glass of water for the guy on the top bunk." She turned and left Brice standing with his mouth open.

Cora marched out of the ward and to the north

entrance where she listened to thunder as rain pounded the rock. She took several deep breaths of fresh air and her mood improved. She returned to the ward and found Brice playing cards with another patient. He looked up and flashed his famous Oklahoma smile, "Feeling better?"

She returned his smile, "Yes, sorry I lost my temper."

"I don't recall you loosing your temper." Brice studied his hand and looking at the patient said, "Your play."

Cora went about her job realizing how lucky she was to have Brice as a friend.

* * *

On 2 May at zero seven hundred hours the shelling began and lasted five hours with the continual noise and vibration putting everyone's nerves on edge. Thirteen waves of enemy aircraft bombed the island before the day ended and entrances to the tunnel were hit. There were no injuries, but everyone feared surrender was near.

"Okay, we're all here and I want you to listen." Captain Jennings stood erect in front of her nurses. You will remain dressed in your khaki uniforms at all times and carry your gas masks. Be brave and remember why we are here. We have a job to do and we will continue to conduct ourselves as Americans and members of the Army Nurse Corps. May God bless us all." The Captain turned and exited the lateral.

No one moved or spoke for several minutes. As they finally began to leave the meeting Claire whispered to Cora, "What's going to happen to us?"

"We're going to surrender, only this time we're not being evacuated."

Betsy caught up with Cora and Claire. "Looks like we're going to meet the Japs. Remember what we must do if we are in physical danger."

They nodded and indiscreetly checked their hidden drug.

On 5 May the Army Nurses were ordered to meet with the head nurse again. With a grim expression the woman said, "Go to the lateral and remain there when you are not on duty. You are to wear the Red Cross Armbands you have been issued. Do not remove them for any reason." Captain Jennings looked out at her nurses, "This may be our last time together, do you have any questions?" She paused but silence filled the air. Before leaving she again said, "Good Luck and may God bless us all."

While the nurses waited in their lateral, Cora removed her locket and wrapped it in gauze and adhesive tape. Next she cut pieces of her hair and wrapped the strands around the package. Then brushing her hair, she twisted it around the locket and the lethal dose of morphine before forming a neat tight bun.

"I know we have orders to get rid of our money before we're captured, but I just can't! I've never disobeyed an order, but I can't destroy money," Cora said.

"Neither can I," Betsy said and Claire nodded in agreement. "We've worked hard for this money and if we get a chance to escape it could mean the difference between life and death." She pulled out one of the innersoles of her combat boots and placed her dollar bills inside and carefully replaced the innersoles. Claire and Cora did the same.

An officer and the head nurse entered the nurse's lateral. The officer spoke to the ladies. "The Japanese have

116

landed down the beach northeast of the tunnel at a location called Monkey Point. And I understand there is another landing of Japanese barges loaded with artillery are also close." They left the nurses alone.

Officers and other men who had been in the tunnel for months came to say good-bye to the women. The men were wearing steel helmets and armed with gas masks and guns, equipment they had not previously needed in Malinta Tunnel.

The tunnel radio reported that General Wainwright would surrender Corregidor on 6 May at twelve hundred hours. A bugler played "Taps" as the American Flag was lowered. A white flag, a bed sheet, was raised while United States Officers burned the red, white and blue flag. The shelling continued for another fifteen minutes. When the fighting finally ended many walking wounded found their way to the tunnel for treatment.

*This will be the last. I don't know what will happen to us, but at least there won't be any more casualties,* Cora thought to herself as she anxiously waited.

Nurses not on duty at the hospital stayed in their lateral. The group remained solemn speaking only in whispers. All fifty-four nurses and fifteen civilian women who worked on Corregidor waited in fear.

"What will happen to us now," one of the younger ones asked.

"My guess is they will send us home," answered someone several bunks away.

Cora had her own ideas and being sent home was not one of them, but she chose not to share. She knew what they did to women who were taken prisoner.

Betsy caught Cora's attention. "We'd better keep our

117

thoughts to ourselves, she whispered."

Cora nodded in agreement.

When the Japanese arrived at the tunnel, their superior officers gave their English-speaking officers permission to enter the hospital. The Japanese doctors, most of who were trained in the United States, discussed the condition of the patients with the American doctors. The Japanese officers were shocked to see women working with the men in a war zone. At first they did not know what to do with the nurses, but it didn't take long to figure a way to use them to their advantage. They ordered several nurses to report outside the tunnel. They were ushered past Japanese standing guard with rifles and bayonets. The women walked out showing no signs of fear. A Japanese officer with perfect English spoke to the nurses. "I lived in Boston for six years while I studied medicine. We are not going to harm you." He ordered the guards to lower their weapons. "We are taking your picture to send to your General MacArthur to show him how well we are taking care of you." He bowed and left them with a short officer that stared at them through thick eyeglasses while a wide grin exposed his oversized upper teeth.

After the pictures were taken the women were returned to the nurse's lateral and Captain Jennings arrived with a Japanese escort. "The Japanese military or anyone under their authority will not molest the nurses," the head nurse explained as she read the conditions of surrender to her nurses. "The only conversation you are to have with our captors is to discuss your patients, and only with their medical personnel."

She relaxed her stance. "Most of the Japanese doctors studied in the United States, so watch what you say in their presence, they will understand you!"

The next few days were tense, but the nurses became accustomed to being rousted out of bed several times each night for inspections. "If this keeps up, I don't know how we are to get enough sleep to do our jobs!" Claire complained. "Not to mention our beauty rest."

"Several of us need to complain to Captain Jennings and the Officers in the hospital," Betsy suggested.

The next morning a few of the nurses complained and that was the end of the nighttime inspections.

"We are running out of food," Claire mumbled staring into her bowl of cooked cracked wheat with dead weevils floating on top.

Betsy looked at Cora as she busily scooped out the weevils. "Did you hear about the inspections in the hospital?"

"No," Cora and Claire answered.

"The Japanese physicians inspected the wounded and forced those that could walk to go outside where they were shoved into prisoner-of-war pens with no protection from the scorching sun. I understand there were about four hundred." She paused then added, "Brice was one of them."

"Oh, that's awful! What about the patients too sick to move?" Cora lowered the spoonful of the disgusting gruel.

"I don't know," Betsy answered.

"The Japanese doctors are working with our doctors and seem to be getting along fine, Spencer said when we got to talk briefly yesterday," Betsy said changing the subject from Brice. "Spencer was a student at Penn with one of the Japanese officers. They have been catching up on classmates and reminiscing.

"Some of the guards are friendly," Cora said. "One

real young soldier showed several of us a picture of his girlfriend or wife. Then he showed us a picture of a countryside and we guessed that was where he lived."

"Most of them, like us, aren't here by choice. They have relatives back home worrying about them too," Claire stated and pushed her half-empty bowl aside.

"Yea, but their families know they are winning the war!" Betsy added ending the conversation.

On 25 June the tunnel hospital was moved to the renovated hospital topside. Bombs had blown off the roof, but the fresh air was welcomed along with the fresh pleasant scent of the blooming gardenia trees.

"Even under these conditions I think everyone's attitude is improving since we moved out here, don't you?" Cora asked Betsy while they were boiling bandages.

"Well if not their attitude at least their breathing. The patients appear to be more comfortable too since we found the mosquito netting for them. And of course the extra food is improving their attitude and strength."

The following week Claire came rushing into where Cora was checking the drug supply cabinet. "Cora! All of our doctors, medics, and orderlies are being taken out to that freighter!" She pointed out the window to a large boat with the name LIMA MARU printed on the side in large letters.

Cora watched as doctors, medics and orderlies carried patients on stretchers to the docked ship. "Where are they taking them?"

"No one knows. The Japs aren't talking."

"What are we to do without patients?"

"Maybe they intend to take us too." Claire said, but her expression said otherwise.

That night the nurses learned that the boat was going to Manila.

The next morning the LIMA MARU had been moved farther out in the bay. A Japanese officer met with the nurses. "Gather your things and you will be taken by small boats to the ship."

Excitement laced with fear spread among the nurses, they were all talking at once. "It's only a three hour trip to Manila! We'll be with our patients! We'll get real food!"

Rose added, "Yes fresh mangos and bananas too."

Cora, Betsy and Claire huddled close together in the small boat. "Oh no!" Claire said. "Look at how we are to expected to get aboard!"

Cora and Betsy had seen the long ropes they would need to climb, but were too tired to panic.

"I can't do it," Claire sighed as the three stared at the heavy rope. "This is the end, I'll be eaten by sharks."

"No Claire, after all you've been through, climbing a rope is nothing," Cora insisted fighting back her own fears.

"This is not the end! We are going to survive and don't you forget it!" Betsy snapped.

"She's right. If you desert your patients you'll never forgive yourself. Believe me, we know," Cora said rather matter-of-factly.

"Claire just put your mind to it. You can do it!" Betsy's tone turned to encouragement. "Remember, Spencer is out there on that big bathtub!"

"No, I can't do it!"

"Claire," Cora said gently placing her hand on her friend's arm. "Did you ever climb trees when you were a kid?"

"Yes," Claire mumbled.

121

"Okay, think back to your childhood. Picture yourself at home and remember your confidence and lack of fear. Be that kid again and race the others to the top. You're a winner. I know you can do it!"

As the boat banged against the freighter the ropes were tossed over the side. When it was their turn they each grabbed the knots of three ropes in a row. "Ready?" Cora shouted.

"Yes," Betsy shouted. They looked at Claire and she gave an insecure nod.

"Let's do it, we can't disappoint Spencer and Brice." Cora willed her former tomboy training to take over and shimmied up the rope stopping only long enough to make sure her buddies were following.

Cora and Betsy reached the deck as did Lydia and Shorty. They watched over the rail hoping the men would grab hold of Claire and pull her aboard before she gave up. In unison they released a sigh of relief as Claire tumbled onto the deck. She did not move until Cora and Betsy lifted her to her feet, then she fainted.

"You did it Claire! You did it!" Cora and Betsy shouted as she regained consciousness.

"Now we will sit here and rest," Cora said pointing to a spot next to Rose and Lydia. "We'll need our strength when we reach our patients and a real hospital." Cora dropped her bags and propped herself against a stack of wooden crates. Betsy and Claire followed her lead.

"There may not be any protection from the bright sun, but look," Betsy said pointing to a guard serving the nurses tea and rice cakes. The women aboard appreciated the nourishment they received knowing their weak dehydrating bodies needed replenishing.

As the freighter approached the Port of Manila the women raced to the side of the ship and leaned over the rail for a view of the beautiful tropical paradise ingrained in their minds.

"Oh no!  Look what they have done!"  Claire said. "Manila is destroyed!"  The sight was devastating.

"It's nothing but ruins," Claire whimpered.

"I wonder if anything is left standing?" Cora's voice trembled.  She stared at the half-sunken ships and pieces of steel from oil tanks protruding out of the clear blue water like dolphins frozen in the middle of dives.

After several attempts to dodge debris in the port the ship managed to dock.  The ambulatory men were quickly ushered ashore by guards waving rifles fitted with bayonets. Once off of the ship the prisoners were forced to stand in lines in the hot sun.

"Look," Betsy pointed to the patients too weak to walk being loaded onto trucks.  "We are nurses with patients again.  I can't wait to see the medical facility set up in the school the Japs told us about!"

"It is in Paranque.  I can't wait to get there either!" Claire added with a newfound enthusiasm.

The women stood in the hot sun watching the trucks filled with their patients leave in the direction of Paranque followed by a parade of medical personnel and prisoners following close behind on foot.

"I wish I could see Brice," Betsy said standing on her tiptoes.  "He's so tall I should be able to find him.  I don't see Spencer either."  The three shaded their eyes and searched the hundreds of men for a glimpse of Brice and Spencer, but did not locate them.

Once the patients were on their way the nurses were

taken ashore and herded on to three separate trucks. Again the trio stuck close together as the trucks began to move. "Wait," Betsy yelled, "We're going in the wrong direction." The others quickly surveyed the area and realized she was right. They all began screaming at the Japanese guards and pointing in the opposite direction, but the guards only laughed at the women while the trucks continued moving farther and farther from their patients. Finally the women could no longer see the men through the dust.

During the course of the ride the nurses pretended to be fixing their hair, or pushing it off of their moist foreheads. They had the narcotic to use if necessary and no one displayed fear; they acted as model prisoners proud to be serving their country.

**Malinta Tunnel**

**One of the guns on Corregidor**

**Destruction on Corregidor**

**Corregidor Memorial**

**Pesky monkey**

**The author and Dr. Venerando Maximo in front of the Main Building on the Santo Tomas Campus.**

# Chapter Eight

## 2 July 1942

Three flatbed trucks with temporary wooden sides bumped their way along the dilapidated streets through the ruins of Manila for an hour before reaching their destination. They drove past a tall wall and through large iron gates onto the campus formerly known as Santo Tomas University. Lush tropical trees stood in front of the high concrete fence topped with barbed wire enclosing the pristine campus.

The women looked out from the trucks at the people milling around. "They look so tanned," Claire whispered.

"And healthy!" added Betsy.

"This looks like a resort. Look," Cora pointed to a woman lounging under a palm tree reading a book, then to a man swinging a golf club.

Shouts announcing the arrival of new prisoners erupted and the prisoners confined inside the fence rushed the truck. Japanese guards attempted to control the crowd with little success. The civilian prisoners were yelling questions at the nurses, hoping to get information about relatives and friends. Some of the prisoners held signs with the name of a missing relative printed on it. The entire prisoner population wanted news and the nurses were saddened by their helplessness.

The trucks carrying the United States Army and Filipino nurses and a few Filipino auxiliary women drove down Espans Boulevard toward the entrance of a large ornate building in the middle of the campus.

"We must look starved to them," Betsy said as the women accepted fruit being tossed to them.

"Well, we are starved!" Cora said stretching to catch a banana.

The ill and starving women hid their fears and forced smiles as they waved their thin weak hands to their fellow comrades.

"Do you realize this is the first fresh fruit we have had in six months," Betsy said as juice from a mango ran down her chin.

"Yes. That is kind of them to share with us isn't it?" Claire said. Everyone agreed as they stuffed their mouths with fruit.

"In some respects this place reminds me of the Army-Navy Club," Cora said to those standing around her. "Just look at the detailed architecture on the buildings."

"No talk! No talk." The nurses' attention turned from the internees to the guards ordering them to get off of the trucks.

Looking straight ahead the nurses stood on the back of the trucks refusing to move.

Speaking through an interpreter the head nurse said, "We are nurses. We will not get off of the trucks until we are taken to the hospital where we can treat patients. " However the Japanese guards armed with rifles and bayonets quickly persuaded them to disembark.

After they were unloaded in front of the large three-story Main Building, the armed guards rushed them inside. The tired and hungry nurses helped those too weak to walk as they were marched down a long marble-floored hall that surrounded a well-manicured courtyard. Two sets of polished mahogany stairs with brass railing led to the upper floors where the courtyard could be viewed through marble arches. Claire, Betsy and Cora stayed close together. The guards continued to enforce the no communication between internees and the newly arrived nurses.

They were led into a stark room. "Do I smell food or is it my imagination?" Cora whispered, "Are they going to feed us?"

"I smell it too," Betsy answered.

"So do I, but it's probably not for us," Claire whispered dampening their hopes.

The room had been transformed into a dining room where the women were served a dish consisting of carabao meat, rice and pineapple.

"Umm," Cora uttered after a sip of rich steaming hot chocolate. "This is much tastier than chocolate bars dissolved in cold water."

"No wonder. This is made with real milk!" Betsy exclaimed. "I've been dreaming of fresh milk and chocolate."

"I think we are being served more in this one meal than we've had in the last three months," Cora said.

"Yes, and it's going to be hard not to eat too much and become ill," Betsy said.

"And this fresh pineapple will help fight beriberi too," Claire said then added, "I hope it's not too late."

They knew they were suffering from malnutrition with the possibility of developing beriberi. The disease came in two dreadful forms, dry and wet. Both types were painful and the wet beriberi ended in an agonizing death. The threat of beriberi concerned all of them causing them to quickly consume all of the pineapple they could.

Before leaving, the room was transformed into an interrogation area. They were informed that they were in a civilian prisoner of war camp. "You are our prisoners. You are in Santo Tomas Internment Camp," an interpreter said. The women were searched while guards made fun of their belongings, especially panties and bras. One smug guard marched around the room holding his sword high in the air with a size D cup bra hanging on the tip of it. The laughter was loud and humiliating. Many of the undergarments were kept as souvenirs.

Each woman was questioned through a less than adequate interpreter. *These questions are silly,* Cora thought. *Why is my favorite color important to them? Our name is the only information they've asked for that is of any importance.*

After all of the women had been questioned and searched they were herded back on the trucks. They stood holding on to the wooden rails with no idea as to where they were being taken.

"Where are they taking us now? Was that our last meal before the execution?" Cora whispered to Betsy so Claire could not hear. Betsy did not respond.

Much to their surprise they were driven across the campus, outside the wall then across the boulevard to a building hidden behind another high fence laced with sawali, making it impossible to see through. Japanese guards ushered the women into a large house and upstairs to two large rooms. There were enough beds made with curved bamboo frames for all of them. The structures resembled the chaise lounges they had spent hours relaxing in before the war.

"When I toured Old Manila I read a brochure about the place across the street," Claire said. "Before the war it was Santo Tomas University with six thousand students and three-hundred faculty. It was a Dominican academy founded in the sixteen hundreds by Spanish Dominican priests. I think it's named after a Saint." She paused and twisted her lips while she thought. "I think I remember that it has something like a sixty-acre campus."

"Do you know anything about this place?" Cora asked, looking around the large bare walled room they were placed in.

"No, just that the sign said, Santa Catalina Convent."

"It must be a women's dormitory or a home for nuns," Betsy said.

"Or a home for wayward girls!" Claire added. "Didn't you see the fence?"

They nodded. Then with a glint in her eye Betsy addressed the situation. "Well, we're certainly not young girls and I don't think we classify as wayward either."

"I guess there is nothing for us to do but rest until we're given more instructions." Claire said. "Doesn't that sound great! No sirens announcing incoming enemy aircraft, just quiet rest."

"We were told not to go downstairs except for our meals, so we don't have much choice but to sleep or at least rest. Maybe after we rest they plan to take us to the hospital," Betsy said.

"I'm going to take advantage of this quiet time, our survival may depend on rest, nutrition and a healthy attitude," Cora said. "We're tired and have a full stomach so I think a nap is appropriate."

"I know I can sleep," Claire yawned and flopped down on a bed.

"Cora is right, the only way to survive is to rest and eat right. We also need to stay active and maintain a healthy outlook," Betsy said and continued. "Let's start by claiming these two beds next to Claire's."

"I've been tired for so long I hope my body remembers how to rest," Cora said. After they staked out their beds, she sat for a while holding her bags with all of her personal possessions before stowing them under the bed.

"I can't get all of those beautiful healthy, round-eyed children across the street out of my mind. Did you see them watching us as the truck drove through the campus?" Cora asked.

"Yes, several looked to be Courtney's age. I felt like we were in a parade as they waved to us," Claire answered. "Do you realize that we haven't seen many children since we left Manila?"

"Just a few village children and don't forget General MacArthur's son on Corregidor, that's about it," Betsy said.

"I think I recognized a couple of the women I saw, did you?" Claire asked.

"I thought I saw Smitty and Dottie, but I'm not sure. They waved and smiled, but I was too frightened to return the smile," Betsy said. "They looked so nice and we . . . well we don't."

"Yea, they looked like models, but I always thought

the Navy nurses were more attractive than the Army nurses anyway," Cora said. "I am ashamed for anyone to see me in this condition."

"The place across the street reminded me of a country club back home," Betsy said. "Those women sitting under umbrellas reading and the men practicing their golf swing. They all looked so healthy and happy!" Claire slid down on the makeshift bed and added, "For the first time in seven months I feel safe, I only wish I knew where they took Spencer and Brice and if they are safe."

"I wish I knew too." Betsy was lying on her back with her head resting on her hands and staring at the cracks in the ceiling. "But how can you feel safe here? We're POWs, at the mercy of the Japanese Imperial Army!" She turned toward Claire and raised up on one elbow, "Frankly, I think we are in the most danger we've been in since this war started."

"But they put us in the care of Filipino Nuns. Do you think they will harm us with all of those nuns downstairs?" Claire asked.

"I think she's right Betsy, let's put our fears aside for now and get some rest. If we're going to survive, the first thing we have to do is regain our strength."

A slow silence drifted across the two rooms as the women's sleep deprived bodies gave in to tranquil slumber.

The next morning internees from Santo Tomas brought the women's meals to the convent; however, the nurses were not permitted to go downstairs to eat until the internees disappeared from the premises. Then one of the nuns summoned the women to a nutritious meal, of fish, rice, eggs and fruit.

"I wish we were allowed to speak to someone besides

that one nun and the minister that conducted that boring Sunday service," Cora said after one of their meals several days later.

"Well we're permitted to talk with the Japanese guards now," Betsy said sarcastically. "Of course they probably don't have a clue to what we are saying. Their English is pathetic!"

"And your Japanese is not?" Cora asked as the three sat down on the floor between their beds to write letters.

At the end of two weeks the nurses were rested and ready to go to work. "I'm bored," Claire said while painting her toenails. "With such few beauty aids we can't keep primping."

"Yea, I'm surprised we still have a few cosmetics, but then we've never had the time to use the creams, lipsticks and things we brought from Manila." Cora said.

"Why are we fixing ourselves up when there are no men to see how nice we look?" Betsy asked.

"Practice," Rose answered from across the room. "I want to remember how to fix myself up when we get to be with men again. I saw plenty of Filipino men across the street!"

"I'm just happy to have my figure back. Well almost back, I still need to gain a few more pounds," Lydia said joining in on the conversation. "I can't wait to dance again."

The days passed slowly as the women ran out of things to occupy their time.

"I'm going crazy with nothing to do!" Betsy shouted. "I need patients to care for, news, music – something – anything!"

One of the older nurses spoke up, "I suggest we

arrange the two rooms into an Army barracks like we were accustomed to before we came to the Philippines. Then get some military discipline and order back into our lives."

"Yes, I agree. We need some order to our lives!" Another older nurse added.

"And this place could use a good cleaning. I'll check with the nuns about getting us cleaning supplies," Betsy said.

Before long the women were scrubbing floors, windowsills and beds. They began singing and talking more as they worked together. After the beds were lined up in the two rooms, the women placed their few belongings underneath and enjoyed a space more familiar to them. They began to feel like individuals again.

"We've turned this place into a finishing school," someone said when the work was completed. From that day on it was referred to as "The Finishing School."

"Now all we need are patients," Cora announced while playing bridge with three women.

"Hey, that's a great idea Cora," Shorty said.

The following morning, after much planning, the nurses set aside an area for their few comrades who were still having bouts of dysentery, malaria, dengue fever and hookworm. They made up a schedule and took turns caring for the ill. Being back on a schedule and working as a team performing various tasks was a boost to the nurses' spirits.

Lydia got several balls of yarn from the nuns and told Cora that they promised to furnish all the yarn and knitting needles the women needed.

"That's great," Cora said. "Claire is already knitting a pair of socks."

Betsy agreed to work the laundry detail, which was done on the first floor under the supervision of a nun. The nuns supplied ironing boards and irons, and several women took on the responsibility of the ironing.

A wealthy local lady began arriving at the convent every week in her limousine filled with boxes of clothes, sweets, fruits, cosmetics and various necessities and luxuries for the women. She was a friend of Captain Jennings before the war broke out and due to her dual citizenship, she was British and her late husband was German, she was permitted visits without a guard present. She always left with a list of the nurses' needs and a promise to return the following week.

"I just realized that even though we have been working side by side for the same cause, we really don't know each other," Cora remarked to Shorty one afternoon. "In surgery or on the ward we can practically read each other's minds, but we know very little about each other's background or personal lives."

"You're right. We don't, but I think that is being corrected," Shorty answered.

The Finishing School provided time for the women to form bonds of friendship while sharing cosmetics, cigarettes, books and dreams.

"Have you thought about how much in common we all have?" Cora asked the book group sitting in a circle on the floor discussing John Steinbeck's, *The Grapes of Wrath*.

She received a few curious looks and a couple of blank stares. "Think about it, all of us that are nurses survived nursing school and served as Army nurses in the States for at least two years and then Manila. Some of us served on Bataan, we all served on Corregidor and we've all survived. Now here we are serving together as prisoners of war."

"You're right Cora, we should learn all we can about each other and share what we have too. I'll begin by contributing the books I've been carrying around with me and if others would like to donate theirs I will operate a library for us," A tall nurse from Alabama volunteered.

"That's a great idea and we can add the books we've been getting in our care packages from Captain Jennings' friend too, and I'll be glad to help you," Claire said.

"Great then, we agree?"

All heads nodded. "Good, we now have The Finishing School Library!"

They took advantage of their free time whether it was to share recipes, play cards or just sit around talking. Some offered to share their talents. Claire and two other nurses volunteered to give knitting lessons and another nurse offered French lessons. Lydia and Rose offered classes in Tagalog.

"Do you think we will ever have contact with the rest of the camp?" Claire asked one evening as she sat on the floor knitting. Cora was giving herself a manicure and Betsy was concentrating on a game of solitaire.

"I don't know, but I did hear a couple of the nuns whispering and one said we were being held here until they could brief us. She said they don't want us telling the other prisoners what took place on Bataan and Corregidor," Cora said.

"Is that all you heard?" Betsy asked.

"Yes."

"But I don't think they plan to keep us here long,"

Cora stopped filing her nails.

"Oh really, what gives you that idea?" Betsy asked.

"That real short guard with the annoying cough told me that across the street at the main campus there is a hospital and clinics. We are going to care for the prisoners," Cora answered. "So I'm thinking we should enjoy the rest and food before we are moved again." She stood, placed her hands on her lower back and stretched before adding, "He also said there are about nine hundred children of all nationalities here at STIC, that's what they call The Santo Tomas Internment Camp."

"While I was in the laundry one day the short fat nun told me there is an Executive Committee made up of internees that make the rules and enforce them. They report directly to the Japanese Commandant. There are also committees for safety, entertainment and education made up of internees. It is run like a city," Betsy said.

"Listen," Cora whispered. "It is so quiet," she moved to a window with Claire and Betsy close behind. "And look." They stared out at a half moon and thousands of stars. "I still can't get used to the silence; it's sad that the strafing and bombing had become so normal isn't it?"

Claire lowered her brow, "Yes, and that's scary."

"I still waken and listen for the chatter of the monkeys and the hooting of the owls," Betsy added.

"Yes, sometimes it's hard to remember what life was like before the war and yet it has been only seven months," Claire said.

"Remember our first evening in Manila?" Cora asked. Claire and Betsy nodded. "It was much like this evening. The sunset was prettier than a picture postcard and the fragrance of honeysuckle drifted with the gentle breeze coming off Manila Bay."

"I remember our second evening better," Claire remarked. "Remember we had just met Spencer, Brice and Flint?"

"We were so excited when they wanted to show us the city and take us to dinner at the Army-Navy Club," Betsy reminded them. Cora drifted into a trance remembering the good times in Manila.

"Cora, Cora!" Claire said. "You've been standing there a long time, we need a fourth for bridge, want to play?"

"No, not tonight, I'm reminiscing," she said and tried to remember her time with Flint. *Why couldn't I see he was glad to see me?* Cora decided to continue her thoughts while she showered and washed her hair. Flint had been a gentleman and did not appear upset by the cool reception she gave him. Unlike her, he was patient, loving and kind.

That night Cora sat on her bed and thought of home. *There was always enough to eat, I never left the table hungry. My clothes were not always new or stylish, but they were clean. Dad worked hard in the mines and Mother sacrificed so that her children did not have to go without. I never really appreciated what they did to raise me.*

Cora got up and pulled her small bag from under her bed, and removed a folded linen handkerchief her grandmother had given her. A gasp escaped her lips as a picture slid out from the folds and fell to the floor. It was the last picture taken of her and Vincent Rapuano. *It is our* engagement *picture.* She picked it up and stared at it. *I feel like I'm looking at strangers. I have no feelings. I can't even cry for the strangers.*

## Chapter Nine

*24 August, 1942*
*Santo Tomas Internment Camp*

Six weeks after their arrival a Japanese Officer stood at attention at the bottom of the convent steps. The women prisoners descended the stairs with their personal belongings in tow. An English-speaking Japanese Officer taught them how to execute a proper bow and explained they would be expected to bow upon meeting their superior Japanese captors.

"You will not speak of anything that happened on Bataan or Corregidor. Is that understood?" He asked when they had mastered the bow.

"Yes," they answered in unison and bowed twice as instructed.

The women were escorted from the Santa Catalina dormitory to their new home across the street, the Santo Tomas Internment Camp. They were issued a metal cup, a spoon and a bucket before being met by one of the Executive Committee members. The British prisoner informed them that the committee had negotiated on their behalf to obtain permission to work in the medical facilities on the campus.

"The Japanese will be giving you assignments after we have met with your commanding officer," he announced.

The army nurses stood tall showing no outward display of emotion, but Cora sensed the excitement. She did not look at Betsy or Claire for fear they would start jumping up and down and screaming with joy.

The nurses were assigned to living quarters separated from the civilian women. Their quarters were on the second floor of the Main Building where four classrooms had been converted into a dormitory. The limited area provided each nurse with a six by three-foot space.

"Okay ladies, this is our new home so let's make the best of it!" Captain Jennings said. "We have only a foot between each bed, so we will sleep head to foot to help eliminate the spread of colds and other diseases." The aging head nurse glanced around one of the rooms. "Stow your personal things under your bed. I'm leaving now to work out your assignments," she said with her lips slightly curved.

From the windows the nurses watched prisoners milling around in the main courtyard below, but across the yard stood a symbol of lost freedom. From the tall guard tower, three armed guards stood watch over the grounds.

Later that night the women received another reminder of their confinement. At nine o'clock a goodnight song played over the public address system, the lights went out and the doors to their quarters were locked. They learned that roll call was every night and every morning.

The next morning Claire suggested she, Cora and Betsy explore the camp together. "I'm not sure one day will be enough time for me to learn my way around," she said after they had agreed to join her on the excursion.

The new prisoners spent the day orienting themselves with the campus and meeting acquaintances from the Sternberg hospital. With each greeting they learned more about their new home.

"Look at the ornate statues and Greek symbols," Cora exclaimed as she pointed to the Main Building. The embellished figures were breathtaking.

"I used to like Spanish styled stucco buildings, but I'm not so sure any more," Betsy sneered.

"Well it sure beats the jungle floor and the cave!" Cora snapped.

"Well, I certainly can appreciate the architecture, just look at the duplicate wings extending from the front entrance!" Claire said. "I think I remember that from the brochure. Also, it seems like it said that this building is about one and a half city blocks long."

"I can believe that. It sure looks that long. And look there is a third story above our floor, plus that two story tower above the front entrance." Cora pointed to the tower. "If we lose our watches we can always check the time on that giant clock in the tower."

"I didn't see any of this when they brought us here for interrogation, did you?" Claire said.

The three women nodded and shaded their eyes against the bright morning sun as they observed the large white cross above the tower. "It's beautiful," Betsy said as they stood in awe.

By the end of the day they could get to their food stations and most of the internees were eager to explain how the systems worked.

"It's too much to digest in one day," Claire said as the threesome sat on the lawn after dinner and listened to records played over the public address system.

Just as Cora and Betsy began to relax, the two Navy nurses Betsy had spotted the first day joined them. Smitty and Dottie offered to help show the nurses around and help them adjust to prison life.

"When were you brought here?" Claire asked.

"We were brought here when the Japanese took Manila," Smitty answered. "Almost everyone that's here came then. The civilians from other countries that are here didn't have time to get out of the city and of course the Japanese saw them as threats of espionage."

"It's really not so bad here, nothing like we heard you were experiencing!" Dottie said as the three stared at her with questioning expressions.

"How do you know that?" Cora asked. "We were given orders not to speak about it."

"News gets in and out of here, sometimes later than we wish but it does get in and out," Smitty answered. "You'll be surprised at our underground systems."

"But you didn't hear that from us," Dottie added.

Cora, Betsy and Claire nodded their heads showing they understood.

"How many nurses are here?" Cora asked changing the subject.

"Eleven Navy nurses and several local civilian nurses," Dottie answered. "We have a 'Campus Health' program that we broadcast over the public address system. Smitty and I are responsible for it and hope you will help with it."

"How often is it broadcast?" Cora asked.

"Every Monday at eleven hundred hours. We cover health issues dealing with the conditions here, such as malnutrition, malaria, tuberculosis and sanitation."

"There are some very educated internees here. The occupations represented by the prisoners in this camp are equivalent to a normal city. We have doctors, lawyers, teachers, ministers, cooks, florists, mechanics, bakers and it goes on and on," Smitty said. "In fact the internee you hear announcing the tunes being played was a local radio announcer in Manila."

"I thought he sounded familiar," Betsy said.

Smitty continued, "He was allowed to bring records with him and later hundreds more were donated."

"How many internees are here?" Betsy asked.

"The last count I saw was in the camp newsletter a week ago and it was thirty-three hundred," Dottie said as she turned to Smitty. "Does that sound right?"

"Yes, and there are almost as many nationalities represented as there are occupations," Smitty added.

"A newsletter?" Cora repeated.

"Like we said, you will be amazed at the organized activities here," Dottie said, "But it's time to go inside, we'll have to finish our conversation later. By the way, the clinics are over there in the education building and the gymnasium." She pointed to buildings located on opposite sides of the main building.

"Goodnight," Smitty said as they reached the second floor of their new home.

"Goodnight and thanks for the orientation," Cora said with Betsy and Claire echoing her words.

"Under different circumstances I would be thrilled to call this magnificent historical structure home," Claire said.

"Even with these long narrow halls and the open stairwells that magnify sounds and hold in stale odors? Uck!" Betsy said. "Not me." She paused, "But it's better than what we've had for the last six months."

Captain Jennings posted the duty roster the following morning and the healthy nurses dressed in their khaki skirts, white shirts and white oxfords were eager to work. Before reporting to work however, the women carried their meager eating utensils to the chow line where they learned about vendors coming into camp to sell and trade. Everything available in the stores were brought or ordered for later delivery. Fruits, vegetables and meats were the most popular, with reading material and clothes being a close second.

The threesome looked at each other and nodded. Cora knew they were thinking of the money they had smuggled into camp. Not knowing what they would be permitted to keep, half of the money remained in their combat boots and the rest had been hidden in their nursing oxfords.

Working under the scrutiny of guards the newest interned nurses began their first assignment. It was disappointing to find they would not be working with patients, instead they were ordered to set up a hospital facility in the Santa Catalina School building.

"Well Betsy," Cora said, "We're becoming experts at setting up hospitals, do you think there is a future in it back in the States?"

Cora ignored the disgusting look Betsy tossed her and continued toward her designated working area. They were split into small groups and as instructed by the Japanese they set up two wards on the second floor, one for men and one for women.

"Next we are to organize a clinic on the first floor," Capt. Jennings informed her nurses. "I know we're tired but we have to show these Japs that we are strong and we don't give up."

"Did we really say we missed working?" Betsy said wiping perspiration from her brow before opening another box of supplies.

"I think what we said was we missed caring for patients, which I might add we have not yet seen!" Claire answered.

"I've learned that the patients with communicable diseases are housed in the Isolation Hospital located in back of the Main Building by the camp garden," Claire told Betsy and Cora. The children under age sixteen are housed away from other patients too, they are in a separate pediatric ward."

The nurses worked for several days without patients. Determined to show up the Japanese, the Americans and Filipinos did not show outward signs of discouragement or disappointment.

Betsy was working next to Cora. "Can you believe those instructions on how and when to bow to the Japanese guards and officers?"

"No. I was afraid if we didn't learn they would have kept us in the convent."

"I think it's silly to stop and bow twice each time I meet a guard and bend my tired back, especially after spending hours working while the guards do nothing," Claire said when she joined in the conversation.

"It's to show our respect," Betsy said in a mimicking

sort of way. "Next they will have us taking tiny little steps like the Japanese women."

"Well they are not turning me into a Geisha Girl," Cora said with conviction.

After carrying out their first order, Cora, Betsy and Claire stood in line waiting with the other nurses to receive their rotating work schedules. The sun was disappearing behind the buildings as Captain Jennings arrived.

"The day shift is like it was at Sternberg Hospital," Captain Jennings said. "Because of heat and humidity it is divided into two four hour day shifts. The night shift is eight to twelve hours. If you prefer to work the same shift continuously, put a request in to the Executive Committee. They run the camp for the Japanese, so if you need something don't go to the Japanese, go to the committee or see me."

Cora, Betsy and Claire met after receiving their assignments. "I will be working on the floor in the main hospital, starting with the night shift," Cora informed her companions. "An eight-hour shift. "Where will you be?"

"The clinic in the Main Building, first dayshift," Betsy said. "It's not the emergency room in Chicago's Cook County Hospital, but at least it's work."

"Listen to this, I'm being sent to work in a civilian hospital outside the compound," Claire shook with fright. "I'll be working the first dayshift doing general floor duty." She looked up from her written orders, "What do you think I'll find when I get outside? Will I be treating Japs or Filipinos? How will they treat me? Will they trust me? Can I trust them?"

Both Cora and Betsy shrugged their shoulders. "Just do what you were trained to do, and you will do fine,"

Cora answered. "That's all any of us can do."

"It's been a long time since I worked on the floor, I've been in military post surgical wards for a long time. What if I can't remember what to do?"

"It's like riding a bicycle, or climbing a rope – you don't forget," Betsy chided.

"Claire, you're a good nurse, you'll do fine." Cora put her arm around Claire's thin narrow shoulders.

Cora was pleased with her shift. *I will be busy through the night and that will help me get through the lonely hours. During the day there are enough activities to keep my mind busy.*

"Let's get our utensils and head for the chow line," Claire said scrunching her nose. "I'm sure it will be more of the same mystery goop."

"I can't believe you're complaining!" Cora said and they managed to laugh at their predicament. "The proper term is moogow served over a scoop of lugaw. Moogow and lugaw — sounds rather exotic don't you think?"

"No! It is still a few grains of rice floating in water poured over cornmeal mush!" Betsy said. "And to me that's goop!"

"I like to say moogow and lugaw. It sounds like a couple of comic strip characters," Claire said.

The following morning Betsy and Claire got up before the zero six hundred hours wake up call which was music playing over a public address system. When they arrived back in their small space after taking showers, Cora was sitting on her bed smoking a cigarette. She had finished working the night shift, and since she started an hour early her relief was always an hour early. This arrangement worked well for them.

"I'm glad Dottie shared her secret of getting a shower ahead of the others," Claire said.

"So am I! Three hundred women scurrying around to use the three showers is bad enough, but only five toilets and lavatories!" Betsy said. "It could take all day for us to get a shower."

"Yeah, the jungle bathing facility was the Ritz compared to this!" Cora said.

"Have you forgotten the critters and flying insects?" Betsy asked. Cora ignored the question and continued enjoying her cigarette.

"I just hope we are up every morning before the music starts," Claire said.

After they finished their tea and rice Betsy walked with Claire to the front entrance of the Main Building. Cora joined Betsy to see Claire and Shorty off on their first day in the civilian hospital. A truck similar to the one that had brought the nurses to STIC arrived and armed guards took Claire, Shorty and two U. S. Navy nurses out through the large iron gates and turned toward Manila. Cora and Betsy waved before going inside the sweltering, noisy building and up to the dormitory.

"She is so frightened," Betsy said. "I wonder what she will find when she gets there?"

"I don't know, but I'm anxious to find out," Cora answered.

Ten minutes later Betsy announced, "I'm going to the clinic now. You had better get some sleep before it gets any hotter in here."

Lying in bed Cora thought about Betsy's words. *Sleep? As tired as I am I know I won't be able to get into a deep sleep. These guards coming in for unannounced inspections, the children running up and down the halls screaming, the older women arguing and the noise drifting up from the chattering down on the lawn. It is worse than the trains being filled with coal and switching tracks at the coal mines. I learned to sleep through that, so I suppose I'll learn to adjust to this too. If only I could substitute the coal dust odors for the body odors here.*

That evening Claire explained her assignment in the local hospital. "I work with a guard watching over me, but he leaves for long periods of time, so I feel a little freedom." She paused and lit a cigarette. "Everyone was nice, but cautious, but then so was I," she said with a nervous giggle.

"What about the patients, were they Japanese?" Cora asked.

"Most of them were elderly Filipinos, there were a few Jap soldiers."

"Do you have a good supply of drugs?" Betsy asked.

"I think so. I didn't see much of the hospital except the floor I'm working on. I do know that the drugs on that floor are locked and I'm not permitted to go into that area."

Betsy and Cora shared the experiences of their first day and then the three joined a group of nurses on the lawn to listen to the evening music.

Little by little they learned the camp rules and routines. Though not a lot of talking was allowed they learned their way around the compound. After the first two weeks of working and adjusting, the three were granted the permanent shifts they requested. Betsy and Claire worked the first day shift, and Cora the night shift.

"I think we should have some of the men build us a shanty. What do you think?"

"I think it's a great idea! Many of the internees have them and even if they are only two sided, it's better than sitting on our beds or in the hot sun."

"What's a great idea?" Claire asked catching up to them.

"A shanty. We think we should have one built for us. We're together most afternoons and it would be nice to get away from our sleeping quarters."

"That sounds like a great idea!" Claire shrieked. "Those odors in the dorm are unbearable. I won't even mention the noises."

"Let's go right now and claim a spot," Cora suggested, and the trio was on their way.

"After we find a spot we will have to get a permit from the executive committee," Betsy said.

The women walked past several of the small structures standing around the inside of the fence away from the permanent buildings. In some areas they were three rows deep, separated by walks, referred to as streets, avenues and boulevards complete with handmade signs.

"These shacks resemble the hobo shacks down by the railroad tracks in Chicago," Betsy said.

Cora laughed, "I bet your Chicago hobos never had little flower or vegetable gardens around them like some of these do."

"No, I just meant the architectural design," Betsy said. "But I think theirs were made from wooden crates and cardboard."

"Maybe ours won't look like a hobo shanty. What material should we use?" Claire asked.

"I don't know. Most of these are made from wood or nipa palm leaves, but I like the ones made from strips of used metal," Betsy said.

"I think the metal would be best if it doesn't cost too much," Cora said. "I met a carpenter yesterday, I'll ask him about getting it built and if we need to buy the materials ourselves."

"I like this spot," Claire said. "It's not far from the Main Building and we could stay here longer than if we are at the other end of the rows."

"Look! There's a mango tree here too," Betsy noted as she inspected the blooms.

Cora and Betsy agreed. "Yes, this will do and I think the name, My Hometown Avenue, has a nice ring to it too," Cora said as they inspected the sign.

"It sounds better than Boardwalk or some of the other streets," Betsy said.

"The other choices don't sound as cozy as My Hometown Avenue does," Cora said. "So, does this spot suit us?"

Betsy and Claire nodded their approval. "Well, let's go stake our claim," Cora said, and they went from the site directly to the office of the Executive Committee.

"This will be fun," Claire said when they left with their permit and walked to their property. "We will have a place to sit protected from the sun, and if we can locate one of those little stoves we can cook food bought from the camp canteen and the vendors."

"Here it is, our home away from home!" Cora said, and the three sat on the grass at #3 My Hometown Avenue. "Our little piece of privacy."

They sat on the future site of their shanty discussing recipes and foods they were going to cook until time for curfew. It was nearly time to leave when dark clouds appeared overhead, and they ran reaching the Main Building as the first rain drops hit the ground.

"You were right Claire, it will be nice having our shanty close to our bedroom," Betsy said when they were inside and sitting on their beds.

"Are they still treating you okay at the civilian hospital?" Cora asked Claire.

"Yes. Actually I look forward to going everyday, especially the ride when it isn't raining."

"Do you think they trust you now?" Betsy asked.

"I'm not sure. At first I didn't think they did, but now some of them seem to. It's like most hospitals, some of the staff are friendly and some aren't."

"Speaking of friendly, have either of you heard about the secret loan operation here at STIC?" Cora asked.

"No, how does it work?" Betsy asked.

"Well, I heard there is a lending service arranged by men on the Executive Committee." She stopped and lit a cigarette. "If I understand it, some of the businessmen will make loans to nurses knowing that we will receive our back-pay when the war is over. Some of the men are Americans with connections to Swiss and Chinese banks through their companies."

"I guess we are good risks, that is if we live to get back home," Betsy said.

"My back-pay never entered my mind. I've not even figured how much I'm owed," Claire said with a puzzled expression.

"Well I know and I feel like I've earned every penny of it!" Betsy said.

"I know exactly what I have coming too and I plan to make it home to collect!" Cora said.

The metal shanty was completed and paid for by the monies they had smuggled into camp. The following week after the three elated nurses finished their final inspection they sat on the green grassy carpet under the roof and visited.

"Have you heard of a group called Good Samaritans?" Claire asked during their free time.

"No, but I hope they are reflections of their name," Cora said.

"They are sympathizers or family members of the internees who are allowed into camp to bring packages for the prisoners, like clothes, bedding, food and necessities plus newspapers, books and games. These are supplies the Japanese do not have to acquire for us, especially the food," Claire said.

"When do they get into STIC?"

"The guards let them come in with the vendors. They fill the area inside the main gate as far as the shoe and cot repair building," Claire answered. "I understand that is how we can get messages in and out of the prison."

Cora drew her brow down and gazed at Claire, "Who would we send messages to?"

"I don't know. If we find out where Spencer and Brice are we could send them money and maybe food."

"Okay, let's get close to the gate tomorrow so we'll have a chance of seeing more people and see if we recognize anyone we knew before the war. Let's also keep asking where the POWs from Corregidor were taken. Someone has to know!" Cora said.

"Maybe we can find someone to mail letters for us too," Betsy added.

The following day when the gates were opened, a

156

wide-eyed Cora, Claire and Betsy were among the prisoners waiting.

The three watched the faces in the crowd but saw no one they knew.

"This is exciting but I'm not sure what we are seeing," Betsy said. "Look at how the internees and the Good Samaritans are gesturing. It looks weird to me."

"Me too," Claire said, "And there are guards everywhere."

"I may be wrong," Cora said, but I think all the strange movements are a type of code"

"I think you're right," Claire said. "It is nonverbal contact taking place through a code of strange body movements."

"I thought they were having seizures but they're just communicating and the guards can't understand it." Betsy laughed, "And neither can we."

"They must have worked out a code through the messages they pass back and forth," Cora said. "Enough of this, let's go, we have shopping to do!"

"This is like going to an open-air market," Betsy said as they checked out the vendors merchandise to furnish their empty shanty.

"Look! Here are two lawn chairs and the man over there has another one," Cora shouted as she pointed to the third chair. "I'll buy these two Claire, you get the other one."

"Okay."

When Claire returned she said, "I bought this little table too."

"That's just what we need. We can't carry any more, we need to get back to the shanty." Cora glanced around the crowd, "Have you seen Betsy?"

At that moment, Betsy appeared with her arms full. "Look! I found four plates, four bowls, two pots, one skillet and three bananas. I didn't find a stove but I couldn't have carried it if I did. The vendor said he would bring one the next time he comes." She stared at the table and chairs. "Wow! Those are great. Are you ready to head home?"

*Home.* Cora thought back to the company house her parents rented from the coal mining company. It wasn't large or fancy and she couldn't wait until she would be old enough to leave and seek out adventure and a better life. *Well I 'm having the adventure, but certainly not a better life. If I were still there I wouldn't be hungry. I would be safe, loved and free.*

Back at the shanty the three set out to make the structure a home for daytime use. It was not freedom but it was a good substitute.

"This reminds me of fixing up the old chicken coop on the hillside in back of my house," Cora said. "My brothers helped me turn it into a charming little playhouse. My grandmother made curtains and I moved my dolls and a bed my dad made for them into it." She paused while they bowed to two Japanese guards. "My grandmother used leftover yarn to crochet a rug and my cousins gave me a small table and chairs." She smiled, "I hosted tea parties and played nurse with my dolls."

"My playhouse was temporary," Claire added. It was a tent made out of old quilts my mom helped me drape across big boxes and two saw horses under a weeping willow tree in our back yard. I thought I was something when I crawled in there with my dolls and a trunk that held their clothes. Mom liked to sew and she used scraps of material to make lovely outfits for my dolls. Some days Mom would bring my lunch to me and when it was really hot she would come out and we would have a tea party with peanut butter and jelly sandwiches washed down with ice cold lemonade."

Well, as you know, I had brothers," Betsy said matter-of-factly. "So I played in a tree house and no dolls were allowed. Girls weren't allowed either, but Mom made them change the rules so I could go in too." She lit a cigarette and smiled, "I think the boys were jealous because I could shimmy up the rope faster than they could. I wasn't afraid of anything and they didn't like that. Dad called me his little tomboy. I refused to allow my younger brothers to out-do me." Betsy took a drag on the cigarette and as the smoke drifted upward she looked at the Chester-field she was holding. "Come to think of it that is were I learned to smoke these things."

"Probably more than that," Claire chided.

"Well I did have my first taste of alcohol there too." She paused. "And my second and my third."

"We get the picture," Claire said.

After arranging their purchases, Cora stepped back and took inventory. "They fit great in here," she said admiring the lawn chairs and table.

"If we entertain guests' we will have to sit outside," Betsy announced.

Claire left the shanty and returned half an hour later with an orange crate, three sets of flatware, a small knife, a tin security box, a box of crackers, a jar of peanut butter and three chocolate bars. "Check these out," she said drop-ping her wares on the table.

"It looks like dinner to me," Betsy commented while examining each item.

"We can store our food in this tin box," Claire said handing it to Cora for approval.

"It's great, you've thought of everything," Betsy said.

With their new purchases arranged in the shanty, the three sat on the chairs watching the sunset. After a meal of crackers, bananas and peanut butter they savored the sweet chocolate bars.

"Maybe tomorrow we will get our stove and some drinking glasses," Claire said.

"I think we are going to make three men very good wives, don't you?" Cora asked. Shaking their heads her friends frowned.

"Yes, and maybe "Good Housekeeping" will show up to interview us complete with snap shots too!" Betsy answered.

Ignoring her, Claire said, "It's my turn to do our laundry and I think I'll take care of it tomorrow afternoon. You two check out the vendors again and I'll pay for my share." She brushed crumbs from her lap. "Maybe you can find some flower seeds. I love working with plants and they will give this place more of a homey atmosphere."

"That's a good idea, we need you to stay with our clothes. Even with the area being patrolled by camp police I still hear of laundry being stolen while it is on the ground drying."

"Well take a book to read while you wait in line. It gets crowded around that cement laundry trough. Then you'll have to wait while the clothes dry too." Cora said and added, "I hope it doesn't rain!"

"Well the camp garden sure doesn't need any more

rain," Betsy said. "The garden laborers have worked hard and too much rain could ruin the whole seven acres of vegetables."

"Yes, the first rains were great and they were able to stop carrying water to the plants, but they still work hard hoeing and hand weeding. It's hard on their backs, but I'm thankful for the vegetables in our broth."

The camp garden was responsible for about a thousand pounds of vegetables for the camp kitchens, which were operated by the internees. It offset the thirty-five cents operating expenses the Executive Committee had to feed each internee per day.

Later that day Cora asked, "What's wrong Claire? You've seemed preoccupied all afternoon."

"I'm not quiet, I'm just concentrating on my knitting."

"Betsy's right Claire, you've been quiet and you've been irritable too. Are you feeling well?" Cora asked.

Claire dropped the knitting needles into her lap, her eyes filled with tears. In a light whisper she said, "I've just got to tell someone, but they said I'm not supposed to tell anyone."

"Tell what?" Cora asked.

"Who?" Betsy added.

"When I got back into camp today I was given a message saying the Executive Committee wants to see me."

"Who gave it to you?" Cora asked.

"I don't know his name. I was walking away from the truck and he slipped a cigarette into my pocket. I didn't know what it was at first and when I pulled it out there was a piece of paper wrapped around it."

"Why can't you tell anyone?" Betsy asked.

Claire shrugged her shoulders, "The message said not to."

"It could be a trick or it could be dangerous," Cora said.

"I know, but I have to meet with them in ten minutes."

## Chapter Ten

Claire returned an hour later appearing more distraught than before the meeting. She met Cora and Betsy on the lawn where they could talk and walk. "They asked about my acceptance and treatment by the hospital staff and then questions about the hospital security. They appeared interested in my well being and wanted to know if I liked going there each day." Claire stopped and her friends followed her lead. She twisted her mouth as though thinking about the questions. "Then they asked a weird question. They wanted to know if the staff trusted me."

The three bowed to a Japanese Officer. His condescending smile was disgusting as his squinting eyes followed the shape of the women's bodies as if undressing them.

"That was it?" Cora asked as though they had not been interrupted.

"Yes. It really was nothing. I shouldn't have gotten so upset."

The worried expression that Betsy and Cora displayed was met by Claire's questioning eyes. "Do you think it means something?"

"No. They probably just wanted to know if we're being treated okay," Cora calmly answered.

* * *

The last day of September arrived and Claire had heard nothing more from the Executive Committee. She shrugged off the inquiry telling Cora she thought it must have been a courtesy because of working out of the camp. With the end of the month came a halt to the flow of packages into the compound. An earlier inspection had revealed messages getting through to the prisoners.

When the package lines were allowed again a week later, Cora said to Betsy and Claire, "The Japanese must have realized they had to feed those that had been receiving packages of food."

"I doubt that we'll get a package, but it sure would be nice," Cora said.

"I wonder if our families know they can send packages?" Claire said to no one in particular.

"Well, one of us should be at the line just in case." Cora paused then added, "I'll volunteer." They went their separate ways with Cora making her way to the package shed to the right of the main gate by the guard's quarters.

"2nd Lt. Cora Adams" was announced as the packages were being distributed. She rushed up to the Japanese officer and bowed, shaking so badly she could barely hold her arms out to accept the parcel addressed to her in bold printed letters. She bowed again as she had witnessed the other internees doing, then rushed toward the shanty.

Privacy was rare in STIC, and as Cora dropped into a lawn chair she remembered that Betsy and Claire were involved in sport activities allowing her to enjoy her treasured mail alone.

Tears trickled down Cora's cheeks while she read the label through blurred vision. It was addressed to her in care of Santo Tomas Internment Camp in Flint's handwriting! He sent it directly to the prison instead of her State Side address. *My mail got off the rock before the Japs got there! Flint found out where we were taken. He knows I am here!*

With the package on her lap, Cora slowly removed the brown paper and found canned meat, two cans of Carnation Milk and a box of Whitman's chocolates. Cora's heartbeat sped up as she continued examining the contents. Next she removed a bottle of Kreml shampoo, a cake of Cashmere Bouquet, Mum deodorant, Ipana toothpowder and six bright hair ribbons. *He is so thoughtful, he must have heard how difficult it is to buy personal items!*

The next item had a note attached. *"For Cora, Betsy & Claire."* She unwrapped the gift. To her delight it contained Nescafe coffee, four packs of Lucky Strikes, two packs of Chesterfields, three bottles of Vimms vitamins and a deck of cards.

Cora held the colorful ribbons as tears rolled down her cheeks. *I guess he doesn't know that I have to wear my hair in a bun to hide the morphine.* Regaining her composure she took down her bun and braided her hair with one of the ribbons and twisted it into a bun concealing her secret.

Words were cut out of his letter, but Cora knew the Japs censored the prisoner's mail. As she read the words, Flint's voice filled her head and she understood his message. She stayed in the shanty savoring her new gifts until her friends returned.

"Would you care for a piece of candy?" Cora asked Claire as she entered their abode.

"Where on this earth did you get that?" She asked.

Cora slowly opened the lid on the box of Whitman's Chocolates; "An admirer sent it to me."

"You heard from Flint! Didn't you? How is he? Is he okay? Did he send anything else?"

Cora could barely contain her excitement, "Yes, just look at all of this." Cora pulled the package out from under her chair.

"Oh my, with this added to our Red Cross package we're not going to starve, at least not right away." Claire looked sheepish, "That is if you care to share with Betsy and I."

Cora smiled and nodded before she saw Betsy shuffling down the walkway to their shanty. "Here comes Betsy, quick, set out our cocoa and I'll get the Carnation Milk. We'll see how long it takes her to spot them."

"What is that?" Betsy asked immediately as she stepped into the shelter. "Am I having hallucinations?"

"No, it's just what it looks like," Claire answered. "Cora got a package from Flint today! Isn't it wonderful?"

"Look at all the things he sent," Cora began showing Betsy the bounty. "He is still sailing on hospital ships, but I don't know any more than that."

"Does he know where Spencer and Brice were taken?"

"He didn't say and his letter was censored."

Overflowing with excitement Cora made an entry in her journal that evening:

*24 October 1942*

*I have survived twelve weeks on the main campus of STIC and it seems like a lifetime. The main campus is run much like a city or a military base. There are committees for sanitation, policing, entertainment, food preparation and other components of government necessary for a city to function. I'm sure that if I weren't so tired and scared I would find it all very fascinating.*

*We have been having typhoon force winds and rains. We all feel like sewer rats. Last month we had to surrender our flashlights. I'm not sure why we can't have them and we miss them especially working the night shift.*

*Betsy, Claire and I are the owners of a house. It is a two-sided shanty that cost 117 pesos, which is fifty-eight dollars and fifty cents in American currency. The three of us have served together as friends and comrades for over a year now and we will soon be celebrating our second Thanksgiving together. We have become closer than many families. We've been through more than most families!*

*It's hard to picture the trees turning brilliant colors on the mountains back home but I hope to see them next fall. It takes most of my strength just to survive while I wait for the troops to arrive and free us from this nightmare.*

Cora tucked the journal back in her bag and under the bed, or as she had learned to call it, her bejuco. The humidity made sleeping more difficult than usual and the children's playful screams and laughter were carried through the building like cheers through a megaphone at a ballgame. Most days Cora's head ached and today was one of those days.

The following day the Executive Committee ordered every able-bodied adult to work two hours a day. There were numerous jobs to be preformed by internees with and without special skills. Volunteer police made sure everyone worked.

"Let's get ready for our scoop of lugaw and moogow," Cora said. The words no longer sounded funny to the trio. After being served the same meal twice a day every day, the nauseating words often induced the gag reflex.

"I hope I win the lottery today and get a slice of an unidentifiable vegetable," Betsy said.

"I wouldn't get my hopes up too high if I were you." Claire said.

"My parents taught me not to complain but always be thankful for any food we had, but it is getting more difficult every day!" Cora said.

"I understand that not everyone gets a noon meal," Claire said.

"That's right, I heard that only internees over eighty years old, teens, children and those with a doctor's written order can receive the lunch. Of course those working in the camp kitchen or medical facilities are also permitted to eat.

"After we finish eating let's go to the open-air theater and listen to the concert the Freedom Chorus is giving," Claire suggested.

"Okay, that should take our minds off dinner." Betsy said.

Cora nodded in agreement and said, "The entertainment committee has been working hard and have scheduled entertainment for next month too." She paused. "But maybe we won't be here then."

Several of the internees were professional actors, comedians, singers, dancers and musicians, and a talented playwright always had a show in the planning stages.

That evening several singing groups joined the Freedom Chorus and performed at the "Theater Under The Stars." While the crowd was involved in the tunes, a man tapped Claire on the shoulder motioning for her to move over so he could sit beside her. He didn't stay seated long after he slipped a note into her hand. When he had disappeared into the crowd Cora gave Claire a questioning glare. Claire hunched her shoulders and remained silent.

"Did Betsy or anyone else see him give me the note?" Claire asked in a hushed tone.

"I'm sure Betsy didn't, she had her eyes closed during the whole song and I don't think anyone else noticed either."

The programs always included "Boogie Woogie Bugle Boy," sung by three women and even though they were not the Andrew Sisters the group loved their harmony and cheered loudly when they finished.

"I wonder what the top ten tunes are?"

"It doesn't matter, we never hear any new songs and without a real paper we'll never know. At least we have the weekly paper STIC publishes," Claire said.

"Yeah, it's not the *Chicago Tribune* but it's news," Betsy agreed.

"I think we're lucky to have a real cartoonist here too. I look forward to his take on the shenanigans going on around here. I fail to see any humor until I see his cartoons," Cora added. "For instance the way we form a circle and walk round and round through the small trickle of water the Japs call a shower, while we're smoking!"

"Yeah, no one back in the States would believe that!"

They laughed and Betsy added, "It is kind of funny."

"He does give us all something to smile about for a few seconds. Maybe someday he will have them published in a book and we'll look back and realize we didn't have it so bad after all," Betsy said sarcastically. "And let's not forget to add that after the camp paper is read and passed around it serves as a necessity in the bathroom. Toilet paper is not something I gave much thought to until it was rationed to eight sheets a day!"

When Betsy stopped ranting the three were near their dormitory and she was told about the note Claire received. They walked to a less populated area and Claire read the note while her friends stood watch.

"Well?" Cora asked when she heard Claire tear the paper into bits.

"I'm to meet a man at the shoe repair building tomorrow afternoon."

"Do you know who?" Betsy asked.

"No."

"That's just great! Do you want us to be there when you arrive or go with you and wait outside?" Betsy asked.

"No. I shouldn't have told you. The note said to tell no one."

The following afternoon Cora and Betsy waited in the shanty for Claire. "I can't believe we've been worrying about this war for nearly a year and now we have these notes to Claire to be concerned about too," Cora said. "I'm beginning to get worry lines!"

"I'm glad we didn't destroy our money. With the war lasting so long it is helping us survive. Without money we couldn't take advantage of the extended canteen hours," Cora commented, while they watched for Claire to return from her mysterious meeting.

"I wish Claire would get back from the shoe shop, I'm getting worried. Who knows what she is being set up for!" Betsy said. "I know about the gangs in Chicago and I wouldn't be surprised to find fragments of them here too."

"I'm sure she's okay and she'll be back soon," Cora responded. "Look, there she comes now!"

They jumped from their chairs and rushed to meet her before she reached the shelter. Simultaneously they bombarded her with questions.

Claire held her hands up and said, "One at a time."

"What happened?" Cora asked.

"No one can hear this." Claire looked around to see if anyone was close enough to hear. "Let's go into the shanty." When they were inside and she was sure no one was close Claire continued, "Tom, one of the men on the security committee, approached me."

"What did he do to you? Did he . . ." Betsy's eyes flared.

"No. No nothing like that. He wants me to deliver messages to someone at the hospital that will then deliver them to the guerrillas."

"That's dangerous!" Betsy said raising her voice. "It's also crazy!"

"Be quiet!" Claire said.

"You can't do that! How could he even ask you to put yourself in more danger?" Cora whispered.

"Someone has to and I do get along well with the people at the hospital. He knows I speak a little Spanish

171

and that I've been taking the Tagalog class. It might as well be me as someone else and it would be helping our boys."

"When will this begin? That is if you do it," Cora asked.

"As soon as I find someone I can trust."

"Oh that's just great. You could get killed if you ask the wrong person!" Betsy said.

Claire's eyes became misty, "It's a chance I'm willing to take."

\* \* \*

"Happy Thanksgiving!" Cora called out as she stepped into the shanty to join Betsy and Claire. "We're having a turkey feast. Tables are set up on the lawn in front of the Main Building."

Many internees planed the November 26th holiday for the sake of the children, keeping a near normal routine for them was important. It was also a mental exercise and distraction for the organizers.

"I can't wait!" Betsy said. "I heard there will be sweets and my sweet-tooth is killing me!"

Food prices were increasing rapidly with sugar being rationed to three tablespoons a day. The Sanitation Committee had declared war on the rats to save food for the internees who dreamed of food every night.

"I heard we're having a traditional American football game after the feast too!" Betsy informed her companions. "The East End of camp and the West End of camp chose their best players and a coach for each team."

"A real football game?" Claire asked. "It's not cold.

How can you have a football game in this humidity?"

Betsy ignored the second question. "Yes, a real football game and being true to the American way, it is a bowl game. It is **The Talinum Bowl.**"

"Talinum Bowl?" Cora repeated.

"That spinach-looking vegetable the internees grow in the garden?" Claire asked, with an expression of disgust on her face.

Betsy nodded and laughed, "That's it, talinum." They laughed with her.

The holiday began as the entire camp enjoyed the early afternoon feast of roasted turkey. The amount of meat per person was meager, but everyone got a taste of the traditional thanksgiving bird.

"This brings back memories," Cora said savoring the small bites of turkey and thinking of her family and friends in the United States. A Filipino woman and her two-year-old twins were seated beside her. Listening to the little boy and girl giggle brought smiles to Cora while watching them fill their shrinking stomachs.

Cora's thoughts wandered. *I never thought that I would miss my family like I do. I know there is a time difference, but I can see them all sitting around a table filled with turkey, dressing, mash potatoes, gravy, sweet potatoes, lima beans, coleslaw, hot rolls and at least a dozen pies – Grandma's pumpkin pies and mother's pecan pies.* For an instant she imagined she smelled her mother's homemade yeast rolls, then realizing her mouth was watering, she swallowed and blinked away the blissful past.

Cora's table companion introduced herself, "I am Zeneida Sullivan, but everyone calls me Zennie and these are my children, Patrick and Peggy, they will be three years

173

old on December 7th. Their father was an American from Oklahoma."

Before Cora could respond Zennie added, "He was one of the pilots killed at Clark Field."

"I'm sorry."

"Thank you," Zennie said then asked, "What were your family thanksgiving meals like before you joined the Army?"

Cora felt the corners of her mouth turn upward as she formulated her words. "Well early, about four o'clock Thanksgiving morning, my mother would stuff the turkey, put it in the oven and then prepare a special breakfast of homemade cinnamon buns. About nine o'clock my dad, brothers and uncles would gather at our house to go rabbit hunting. The older children took charge of the younger children, keeping them occupied while the women cooked and baked. It was a house full, but we had so much fun we didn't mind.

Peggy and Patrick's eyes widened as they listened to the American woman talk about Thanksgiving Day in the United States.

Cora smiled at the children and continued, "At noon the men would come home, clean their game then sit in the living room reliving the morning's adventure. Then at two o'clock we all gathered at the table, but before we could sit we had to tell one thing we were thankful for that day. Next, my granddad would offer the blessing and when he said amen you would have thought a flock of magpies had landed in our dining room. Everyone talked at once and laughter filled the house, it was wonderful."

Zennie thanked her for sharing the tradition and as they talked Cora knew she had a new friend. She liked

Zennie's positive attitude; they shared other stories while enjoying their meal with the children.

"I help with the first grade in the school over there," Zennie pointed to a block building. "You must come and visit me there. It is on the first floor."

"I would love to come," Cora said. Then looking down at the twins she asked, "Are you in school?"

Their round faces framed by straight ebony hair bobbed up and down. "We are in that building," Patrick answered and they both pointed to the structure.

Not to be outdone by her brother, Peggy said, "Our teacher is Miss Madeline and she's nice."

"Miss Madeline is real pretty too," Patrick added.

Cora removed a clean folded handkerchief from her pocket and placed it on the table. She talked with the children as she folded it in a triangle then rolled the sides to the middle, next she pulled the underneath corner down and up over the two hanky babies forming a cover for them. This delighted the children, and Patrick's dark eyes danced as he pulled it apart and begged Cora to make it again while Peggy scowled at her brother. Each time Cora made twin hanky babies the twins giggled.

Claire and Betsy were sitting several seats down from Cora, but after the meal they walked back to their shanty together. Relaxing in their vendor purchased chairs they relayed the conversations that took place during the feast.

"Some of the internees are making toys and other gifts for Santa Claus to give the children for Christmas," Claire announced.

"I know the Sullivan twins I just met are looking forward to Santa coming. I hope they won't be disappointed," Cora said.

"We could make some toys," Claire said. I have yarn, I can knit dolls like my grandmother used to do for me."

"My granddad taught me to whittle, I can do train whistles," Cora added.

"I know how to make rag dolls," Betsy said.

"Good. We need to get started, there are four hundred and thirty-five children under twelve, including my two new little friends," Cora informed them.

The following week, as promised, Cora paid a visit to Zennie's first grade class. She helped with the art and music classes. The music class sang a song for Cora, bringing tears to her eyes.

"Thanks for coming Cora, I look forward to seeing you again," Zennie said as they left the building together.

"They are so innocent, how do you explain this to them," Cora asked. Zennie shrugged her shoulders.

"I wish I could," Zennie said.

When they reached the lawn Patrick and Peggy ran to their mother, both talking at the same time. After scolding them she insisted they remember their manners.

"Good afternoon, Miss Adams," both children said.

Cora stooped down and gave each a hug, "Good afternoon to you Patrick and to you Peggy." Their black hair glistened in the tropical sunlight.

"Our birthday is almost here," Patrick said through a wide grin.

"It is! When is it?" Cora asked.

"It's December uh," Patrick paused and drew his brow then said, "You tell her Peggy."

"Our birthday is December 7th," she proudly announced.

"Well, I'll have to remember that won't I?" Cora said.

176

The twins smiled and nodded before Zennie led them away.

*I haven't felt this good in months*, Cora thought. *There is something about the innocence of children that is refreshing, even in this horrible place.* Before going to the shanty she went to the second floor in hopes of taking a nap before standing in line for the evening meal. There she found Betsy, Claire and four other nurses busily searching their cots for bedbugs. Most cots were made of reeds, but luckily Cora's had wooden slats.

Claire was exasperated, "I can't find them but tonight they will bite me again. I know they are here!" She poured more hot water on her cot, but did not find the tiny bugs. Cora convinced them to go the shanty with her and work on the Christmas items. Betsy readily agreed and Claire finally gave up on the bedbug search and joined them.

"The Sullivan twins' birthday is next week and I'd like to give them something. Any ideas?" Cora asked while they sat in the shade of the shanty crafting Christmas gifts.

"Something sweet!" Betsy suggested. "I really miss cookies and candy. I also miss sugar in my tea. Last night I dreamed I was chasing Oreos. They were rolling down a hill like bicycle tires and I couldn't catch them!"

"Sweets! That's a good idea," Claire agreed. "I know how Courtney loves sweets and I think every child does, plus it gives them energy too."

"Okay, sweets it is. I'll try to locate some candy for them," Cora said. "I don't know how much I'll have to pay?"

"I'll check with some of the women at the hospital in

town tomorrow," Claire said. "They may have a black market source."

"Great. With everyone hungry all the time I'm not sure we'll find any."

"We'll find some! There are residents hoarding sweets just waiting for someone like us willing to pay more than it's worth," Betsy said.

Before going to their sleeping quarters they took a walk over to the grassy area near the theater. They sat and listened to the evening music playing over the public address system until it was nearly time for lights out.

Cora smoked a cigarette and mentally replayed the day's activities while waiting in her room for time to report for her shift. She found thoughts drifting from her world to Claire's dilemma. Having had time to think about it, she realized Claire's shy childlike demeanor would not draw suspicion, but she was too trusting and that could be a problem.

Weakened by hunger, Cora was not sure she could make it through the twelve-hour shift without fainting. All around her people with sunken cheeks and hollow emotionless eyes stared into space.

Arriving at the shanty the day of the twins' birthday Claire proudly held out an egg, "We're going to celebrate. See what I got today,"

"What did that cost?" Betsy asked.

"Sixty cents and I bartered for coffee too."

"I bartered for a pineapple," Cora added holding the fresh fruit up for them to see.

"Well, I was going to surprise you later, but look what I got!" Betsy reached into her pocket and pulled out three chocolate bars. "One for Patrick, one for Peggy and one for us!"

Claire let out a loud squeal.

"Shhh," Cora warned.

"I got three too," Claire said.

"That's great, they will be so happy," Cora said.

"So will we!" Betsy added.

"I'll cook the rice we have and add the pineapple. If we boil the egg it can be sliced on top of our tropical gourmet casserole," Cora said.

"Cora, you stay here and protect our bounty, Claire and I will take our buckets through the chow line. If we're lucky there may be a few strands of some unidentifiable meat in our stew to add to the casserole."

"And if not we will just add the weevils for protein," Claire said.

The trio enjoyed a rare nutritious meal and later met with Zennie and her children on the lawn under a palm tree. Two chocolate bars for each of the twins were wrapped in paper Claire salvaged from a patient at the hospital. The three nurses presented Patrick and Peggy with the gifts for their third birthday. After hugs were shared, Zennie took the children in to put them to bed.

Cora, Betsy and Claire sang as they returned to their humble daytime home. Then worked on the Christmas gifts with little conversation until it was time to get to the Main Building for roll call and lights out.

"I'm so tired and my back aches," Betsy said as they started toward their sleeping quarters.

"I don't know where you find the energy to play softball, that's probably why your back hurts," Claire said.

"Oh no, look what's heading this way," Cora said. "Nine guards walking single file."

"I don't think I can bow once, let alone eighteen times!" Betsy groaned.

"Remember our orders. We are American nurses representing our country," Claire whispered. "So we will bow with pride, and be thankful that they don't know what we are thinking!"

"Just smile and grit your teeth," Cora said.

"No, let's separate before we reach them," Betsy said mischievously, "And force them to bow twice to each of us too."

"That was almost fun," Claire said after they passed the guards.

The following morning when Cora's shift ended she joined Betsy on the steps of the Main Building. They waited again with Claire for the truck to take her to the hospital in Manila. She informed them she had tossed and turned all night. "When I did not feel bugs crawling on me I dreamed they were all over me."

"I experienced the same thing," Betsy said as they shivered. As the truck drove out of the compound, Betsy turned to Cora, "Claire told me there is an orderly she works with that worked at Sternberg and she thinks he might be sympathetic to Americans, but she's not sure."

"Is she going to approach him about the messages?"

"She isn't sure. She's heard him talking to another orderly about Bilibid Prison. She's going to ask him if the prisoners from Corregidor were taken there. If he says no, and since we have heard rumors that they were, and his mannerism is such that she feels he is sympathetic, she will ask him if he knows where they were taken."

Cora smacked her lips, "And if not?"

"She will change the subject. Claire will be fine; she

won't take any unnecessary chances. No one will expect timid Claire to be smuggling messages."

"I sure hope she knows what she's doing. I still can't get the picture out of my mind of what happened to those three internees that escaped."

"They should have known they'd be caught," Betsy said.

"Yes, but making the whole camp watch them stand before a firing squad? That was cruel! Especially to insist the children be present."

"But you have to admit it was a good lesson for anyone considering an escape," Betsy said and left for work. Cora went upstairs to her cot hoping for a few hours of sleep in the hot humid room filled with body odors and noise.

\* \* \*

That afternoon the three were together again and before the interrogation began Claire said, "I did see the orderly again that I told Betsy about, his name is Rafael. He was shocked that I remembered him from Sternberg and especially pleased that I remembered his name. He was friendly and said he recognized me too."

"Is that all?" Cora asked. "Just a reunion?"

"No. I told him that I remembered he was a friend of Dr. Kirby's. He said yes, good doctor but lousy poker player." Claire chuckled. "Then Rafael smiled and asked me where Dr. Spencer Kirby is now."

"I told him I didn't know, but he was brought here from Corregidor on the same ship the nurses were on."

"And?" Betsy leaned closer to Claire.

181

"A Japanese soldier came into the room and we pretended to be discussing the number of linens Rafael had taken from the shelves. I began yelling at Rafael. He then returned two of the sheets and apologized in Tagalog and I accepted in Tagalog.

"Do you think the Jap bought your act?" Cora asked.

"Yes, I saw him smile as he turned to leave, but he may be a problem later, he keeps flirting with me." Claire made a disgusting face and shivered. "He's all teeth and no eyes!"

"Then you didn't get a chance to ask Rafael about Bilibid?" Betsy asked.

"No. I think I should try to build up a friendship and trust first." Claire paused. "Maybe I'm being too cautious, but I'm scared."

"That's it then?" Betsy asked.

"No, not quite. When I was leaving the hospital Rafael handed me this mango, I think he likes me." She tossed Cora the mango and said, "Will you do the honors of serving it for our snack before we eat the food from our relief kits?"

"Sure," Cora said catching the fruit. She picked up a knife and starting cutting, but halfway through the fruit she stopped. "Something is wrong here!"

"What?" Claire jumped up from her lawn chair turning it over in the process of rushing to Cora's side. Betsy arrived in two giant steps.

"I'm not sure, but I wouldn't get too friendly with Rafael just yet," Cora answered.

"Oh no, it's a grenade!" Betsy yelled as the trio stepped backwards, never taking their gaze from the mango.

## Chapter Eleven

"I don't think so," Cora said stepping closer to the fruit. "The texture is tough." Cora stood at arm's length from the mango and extracted the knife wedged in the fruit. Gently pulling the fruit apart along the incision, she peered inside then reinserted the tip of the knife. The other two cautiously moved closer. Cora wiggled the knife and gently removed a wad of tightly rolled paper.

"What is that?" Claire asked standing on tiptoes while staring over Cora's shoulder.

"It's a piece of paper; here you take it, it was meant for you." Cora thrust the paper with the knife attached toward her.

Claire took the note, unrolled it and read it aloud. *Belong to group that helps prisoners in STIC. If there are three pillows on the windowsill of room C-3 tomorrow meet me at the drug cabinet at 9:00.*

"That's great!" Cora said clapping her hands.

"Yes, I don't have to worry about him reporting me. I just have to worry about getting caught."

"You don't think he would set you up in order to catch the smugglers here in camp, do you?" Betsy asked.

Claire did not answer for several seconds. "No. At

least I hope not."

"Can we eat what's left?" Betsy asked sniffing and punching the destroyed mango.

"There is no fruit. It was removed through a hole cut in it and after the note was placed inside and the hole was plugged." Cora picked up a piece of wood and began whittling.

"That's pretty clever!" Betsy said. "Even though I was looking forward to a slice of fresh fruit." She paused. "But this is exciting. If he finds out where Spencer is then we'll be able to find out if Brice is with him and we can communicate through notes." Lost in her thoughts, Betsy continued making rag dolls, and then said, "They are probably as worried about us as we are about them, don't you think?"

Both Cora and Claire nodded, then Cora prepared a snack from the relief kits.

Cora spent her shift in a ward of malaria patients while pushing aside thoughts of the decreasing food supply and Claire's predicament.

When Cora returned to the dorm, she slept until noon, then after tea and rice went to the classroom building to see Zennie and her students.

The children, like the adults, were suffering from malnutrition and diseases. Somehow working with them brought joy into the day and the time passed quickly as she shared her love with them.

* * *

In December truckloads of parcels for the prisoners arrived from the South African Red Cross. The emaciated male internees willingly unloaded the trucks while their captors watched.

"This came just in time," Betsy said as she, Cora and Claire sat in their shanty unwrapping the packages from their allies.

"In time for what?" Cora asked looking up from her parcel.

"Yeah, in time for what, Betsy," Claire added.

"To keep me from going stark raving mad! I'm starving to death and if I don't get something sweet soon, my whole system is going to shut down!"

They laughed while excitedly examining the contents of the packages.

"I never gave much thought to the Red Cross until these packages started arriving, and now I have a new appreciation for the work they do," Betsy said.

"You're just saying that because they sent chocolate cake!" Claire said.

"The cans of bacon and tomatoes look great to me!" Cora said then added, "And they sent real tea and sugar."

Betsy's head jerked up, "Sugar?"

"Yes, a meat spread and crackers too," Claire announced while proudly holding up each item.

"Oh, they sent marmalade and a pudding!" Betsy screamed.

"Maybe we could sell her some of our sweets," Claire suggested to Cora.

"Have you forgotten, we're about out of money, but she would probably get a loan to buy sugar and chocolate," Cora said and they shared a rare time of laughter.

"I think Cora should be in charge of protecting and stretching our food supply," Claire said, and Betsy nodded in agreement while clinging to the marmalade and pudding.

"It's only a couple of weeks until Christmas and I've heard we will have another feast with special sweet treats," Betsy said.

"And remember, we have no assurance that there will be other relief kits," Claire said. "But tonight we won't go to bed hungry, thanks to the South African Red Cross," Betsy said and inhaled the chocolate aroma of the cake.

* * *

A few days before Christmas, Capt. Jennings called all of her Army nurses that had served on Corregidor to a meeting. "Merry Christmas ladies, from three of our engineers that the Japs have kept on Corregidor to work in the tunnel." Their leader then divided the gift the men had sent equally among her nurses.

Cora, Betsy and Claire accepted their portion of the gift and returned to their shanty.

"I know our soldiers are great guys, but I still can't believe they would smuggle this money to us," Claire said holding on to her share.

"Look, this money was stashed by American Soldiers before they were captured. The army engineers found it and have no use for it," Cora said.

"Captain Jennings said they didn't want it to fall into the hands of the Japanese and they don't know if the Japanese will allow them to live after they complete the work in the tunnel," Betsy reminded them.

"That's all true, but still it was nice of the three of them to think of us, especially right before Christmas,"

Claire said.

"They were taking a big chance getting this money off the rock," Cora said, then quickly added, "They are true American heroes and I hope some day we will get to thank them in person." A lump developed in Cora's throat as a voice in her head said, you *know what the Japanese plan to do with the engineers when they finish the job.*

With misty eyes the three Army nurses thought back to their days in the tunnel. "You know, we touched a lot of lives in that hospital," Claire reflected. "And a lot of lives touched us."

"Yes, there and at the Jungle Hospital. Most of them were frightened boys and to them we were not just nurses. We were substitute mothers, sisters, friends and family back home," Cora said.

Claire lowered her head, "We were all they had from home."

The three nodded in silence, and several minutes later Betsy spoke. "All of us know there is more to healing than treating a wound or illness. You don't learn everything from a textbook."

"That's for sure and with our experiences we could write a textbook," Cora added.

\* \* \*

The Entertainment Committee worked hard during the months leading up to Christmas. The camp buzzed with excitement that the Japanese did not understand, but the guards were caught up in the festivities and smiled as they walked around the grounds.

A midnight service was not permitted so the day started with worship services. The children ran about the compound enjoying a day off from school while anxiously anticipating the appearance of Santa Claus.

"Look," Cora said pointing to two Japanese photographers milling about the crowds. "They are taking our pictures for propaganda! Even though they don't understand what they are seeing, they are getting pictures of happy prisoners."

"Everyone is too busy enjoying the day to give them much thought," Betsy said.

The internees organized the activities for the celebration and the Commandant made a special concession. Visitors were allowed into the camp.

Hundreds of visitors bearing gifts of food, clothing, toys and much more arrived. Families and friends were permitted to spend the day together, laughing and crying as they celebrated. They shared food, eaten picnic style from a blanket on the ground, while reminiscing about holidays past. Some visitors brought seeds for the garden and many brought books for the library.

When Claire returned from work she sat at a table, a door placed on two sawhorses, and accepted donations to the Anchor Library.

"The Commandant is permitting mail delivery today!" One of the Navy nurses shouted to Cora and Betsy. They waited in the line and received their letters as well as Claire's. Cora wept as she read one from her brother telling her of their mother's heart attack.

When she saw an envelope with Doc's return address she ripped into it, though the Japanese had opened it. She could hear him speak the words written on the paper as she imagined smelling his Half and Half tobacco rising above his curved pipe stem. In the last paragraph he described her mother's condition. She had suffered a slight heart attack and was recovering. He also assured Cora that her sisters and brother were providing excellent care for her mother and that he checked in on her every time he was in the mining camp.

Flint's letter was saved until last. He was still stationed on a hospital ship but he could not reveal his location or destination. *"I hope you, Betsy and Claire are well. I am looking forward to our meeting again after we . . .* (words cut out) *war." Most of the days go by fast, but we could use you and your two friends' expertise here. Don't give up – Think of our future. . .* (Words cut out)

*I wish I could write what I want you all to know, but as you know our mail is censored.*

When Cora, Betsy and Claire finished reading their mail and digesting the information, they shared their letters.

Claire's aunt and uncle sent newspaper clippings announcing the weddings of her friends and of those leaving to join the war effort. Their words of encouragement and how they longed for her return brought tears to her eyes. There was a P.S. saying they hoped she was enjoying the care packages they had been sending.

"I'm not getting any of their packages! They probably have chocolate chip cookies in them too! Oh just thinking of some Jap eating my chocolate chip cookies makes me want to scream!" Claire's face flushed while her big brown eyes appeared to get bigger.

"Maybe you should get word to your aunt to cut up those little chocolate laxative squares and use them in place of the chocolate chips. That would teach the Japs to stop stealing our packages from home!" Betsy said.

As angry as Claire was she managed to laugh at the suggestion.

Betsy learned her grandfather had died, but the rest of her family was thinking of her, reading the newspaper and listening to Edward R. Morrow on the radio everyday. Her youngest brother had joined the Marines, but her family didn't say where he was fighting or where her other brothers were either. She understood why.

"Mom says women all over Chicago and the country are saving their bacon fat for the government. She says they are donating scraps of metal too."

"Listen to what Doc says, 'People all over the Country are planting small gardens in their back yards, calling them Victory Gardens. They provide food for their families and friends, allowing food that they would buy to be sent to our military.' Isn't that great?" Cora looked up from the letter. "Too bad we're not getting any of the produce, but the soldiers need it more than we do."

"I just knew we had support from the States and that they would come through when we needed them!" Betsy said lighting the cigarette butt she had found on the ground near the ball field. "Yes, it seems like the Americans back home are helping in every way they can. Mom wrote that in April sugar was rationed. They are making sacrifices too. I know it's not easy for her, she has a weakness for sweets like I do," Betsy admitted.

After reading their mail several times, they began putting the finishing touches on the gifts they had made. With the task completed, they walked over to the nurses designated area for the feast.

The three arrived in time to help decorate the table placed behind the Main Building. There were handmade crocheted ornaments and others made of wood, dried plants and wire. Many decorations were made from old Christmas cards donated by friends who had remained in Manila.

"There is no way this hot, humid temperature or the guards standing over us is going to dampen my spirits today," Betsy said and began humming *Silent Night.*

"I don't think it will dampen any spirits in camp today," Claire added.

"Aren't we fortunate to have a turkey and all the trimmings delivered to us from our wealthy friend again?" Cora stated. Later a slice of fruitcake and the singing of Christmas carols ended the afternoon feast.

Religious services conducted by missionaries and priests continued throughout the day giving everyone a chance to worship and reflect on their religious beliefs. Cora, Betsy and Claire attended the service and were joined by Zennie and her twins. *This is my family now*, Cora thought. while she listened to one of the missionaries read Luke 2:8-20.

Cora left the service and walked to the hospital to visit her patients. Reaching the ward she stopped at the first bed, a middle-aged woman suffering from malaria.

"See, Mrs. Hill," Cora said. "I told you I would come today to wish you a Merry Christmas."

"I knew you would come," the elderly English lady said, and turned her head toward the woman in the adjoining bed. "Didn't I tell you she would come?"

"It wouldn't be Christmas if I couldn't be with my friends and wish them a Merry Christmas," Cora explained.

"What's it like out there?  Is everyone having a good time?"

"You bet they are!  After dinner the nurses sang carols and a group is forming to come caroling through the hospitals later."  The smiles were a welcome sight.

"Is there a Christmas tree?"  Another patient asked.

"Yes, it's behind the Main Building."

"Have the gifts been given to the children yet?"  A patient several beds away asked.

"No, but I understand we have almost two thousand gifts for the children under age twelve," Cora answered. "And they are exuberant."  After wishing the patients a Merry Christmas she moved on to visit other patients.

In the late afternoon on Christmas Day when the visitors said their sad good-byes, Cora emerged from the hospital and gathered with the prisoners by the Christmas tree. When Santa made his appearance the Japanese guards watched as the explosion of excitement erupted from the children as well as older residents welcoming the man in the red pants and shirt sporting a cotton beard.  Before he reached the crowd the prisoners burst into singing, "Here Comes Santa Claus."  The bewildered expressions on the guards' faces went unnoticed by most of the prisoners.

Santa Claus and his eager helpers, some wearing red hats, handed out the two thousand gifts the internees had made and wrapped and the gifts donated by family, friends and sympathizers in Manila.

"Mama, Mama," Patrick and Peggy cried out.  "Look what Santa brought us."  Four little hands shot up filled with their gifts.

"Look," Peggy said.  "I got a puzzle and a book."

"Mama, I got a yo-yo and a ball!" Shrieked Patrick. Zennie looked at their gifts as she fought back tears of joy and sadness. "I'm going to share my yo-yo with Peggy and she said I can read her book."

"Um-um, those are nice gifts and it's very nice of both of you to share, now run along and play," Zennie said.

"Patrick! Peggy! Wait!" Cora shouted to be heard over the crowd. "Betsy, Claire and I want you to come to our shanty in about half an hour." She looked at Zennie and winked, then turned back to the children. "And bring your mother too."

Patrick rolled his big round eyes as he grinned and Peggy lowered her head trying to hide her smile. "Okay," they said and ran toward a group of their friends.

"Claire!" A man called out.

Many internees exchanged token gifts, and to Claire's surprise a man she knew only by sight said, "Merry Christmas," as he gave her a small package tied with twine.

"You must have me confused with someone else," she said.

Cora, several steps ahead of Claire, turned in time to see the transaction take place.

"Merry Christmas, Claire, from the Executive Committee," he said in a near whisper. "You'll know what to do."

At that moment a guard moved up beside them. "Oh thank you," she said, and hugged the man as though they were close friends. She continued thanking him until the guard was out of hearing range.

"Good luck," the man said, tipping his head and disappearing into the crowd. Claire turned from him and rejoined her companions.

## Chapter Twelve

Cora, Betsy and Claire arrived at the shanty and began preparations for their holiday visitors. Betsy set out cups while Cora heated canned milk diluted with water. Claire stashed the gifts and then added the broken chocolate bars to the hot mixture.

When the drink was finished Claire stepped out behind the shanty with the gift from the Executive Committee in her hands. A few minutes later she returned to find Cora stirring the hot chocolate and Betsy spreading marmalade on crackers. The two women stopped and questioned Claire with their eyes.

"It contained a sealed envelope and instructions for me to get it to a band of guerrillas working near Manila," Claire said. "It is important that I get it into the right hands at any cost, and it must go out of camp tomorrow."

"How do you know who to give it to?" Cora asked.

"Yea," Betsy said. "What if you give it to the wrong person?"

"I will be approached by one of the priests carrying a bouquet of flowers. He will not be one from here. He will ask me about a certain patient, only he will have the wrong name and illness," She whispered.

"That could happen by accident and then you would give it to the wrong contact!" Betsy said.

"No. I have to respond with, 'You look tired, Father,' as I look at him. And if it is my contact he will say, 'And you also.' "

"It still sounds risky to me," Cora added in a hushed tone.

"Well, I don't think it is but just in case something does go wrong, I have prepared a letter to be sent to Courtney. I keep it in the bottom of my musette; please promise me you will try to get it to her."

"Of course we will, but nothing is going to happen to you! You are smart enough to be careful and trust your instincts," Cora said placing her arm around Claire.

"Put on your happy faces ladies, our guests are arriving," Betsy announced.

Cora set out the last of the refreshments as the Sullivan family arrived. After a round of hugs the guests sat on the three chairs and the hostesses sat on the ground while everyone enjoyed the special treats.

The women smiled as Patrick spied the gifts under the table and whispered to his sister, who in turn told him to mind his manners.

"They are good kids," Cora said to Zennie. "You are very lucky to have them."

"Yes I am, the Japanese could have separated us. They are all the family I have."

"You have no one else?"

"No, I grew up in an orphanage after my parents drowned in a fishing boat accident when I was five years old. Then when I finished my schooling, I went to work at Clark Air Field where I met Sully, my husband," Zennie paused. "Sully was eight when his parents were killed in an accident, and he was raised by his grandmother until she died. He was sixteen then and he lied about his age to join the Army."

The twins finished their hot chocolate and crackers and squirmed while the adults visited. "This seems like a good time to give you your presents," Cora said. "Or we could wait."

Patrick looked at Peggy then said, "Miss Adams, I think this is a real good time." He nudged his sister.

"Yes, I think it's a good time too," Peggy said attempting to conceal her excitement.

"Claire, will you see if any of those packages over there are for Patrick and Peggy?"

Claire moved over to the table and pulled the gifts out and examined each one slowly.

"This one is for," she paused while the children squirmed, "Patrick, and this one is for Peggy!" The well-behaved children stayed in their seats and waited for Claire to give them their gifts.

The children's big round eyes sparkled as they tore off the colorful paper. Patrick jumped off his chair and ran to his mother with Peggy two steps behind.

"Look, Mama, it's a whistle," he blew into the mouthpiece. "It sounds just like a train whistle!"

"Mama, I got a doll. Isn't she beautiful?" Peggy said, holding the doll out for her mother to admire. "I'm going to name her Lulu."

"Yes, my goodness, they are both very special gifts." She glared at the children and waited.

"Oh yeah," Patrick lowered his head, "Thank you."

"Thank you," Peggy echoed, never taking her eyes off

of her new doll.

"You are welcome," Cora, Claire and Betsy said together and accepted hugs from each child.

"There are still gifts under the table," Betsy said and Claire pulled them out.

"This one is for," again Claire paused and silence filled the shanty, "Zennie!" Claire handed the small parcel to their Filipino friend.

"You didn't have to do this," Zennie said, with tears puddling in her eyes.

"We wanted to Zennie, open it," Cora said.

"This ribbon is beautiful," Zennie said.

Cora smiled knowing Flint would be thrilled knowing the red ribbon made a sad woman smile on Christmas.

"Merry Christmas Zennie," the nurses said in unison.

Patrick and Peggy were staring at one last gift under the table. "There's another one," Patrick said pointing to it.

"Where?" Claire asked.

Both children yelled and pointed to the gift, "Under there!"

"Oh, I see it now," Claire said teasingly. She retrieved the small package and read the label. "It is for," again she paused and looked at each one. "It is for Patrick *and* Peggy!"

She handed it to the children and they each tried to get it unwrapped.

"Oh boy," Patrick said taking one of the chocolate bars and giving the other one to his sister.

"What do you say?" Zennie said.

"Thank you," they said together.

"We must go now, you two need a nap if you are

going to the concert later tonight." Zennie thanked Cora, Claire and Betsy again for the gifts and the party.

Alone in the shanty after a busy day, Betsy, Cora and Claire enjoyed a cigarette from the package Flint had sent. The day's events and Christmases past were discussed, renewing a sparkle in their hearts.

"Let's open our gifts now," Claire suggested.

"That's a good idea," Cora said and reached under her lawn chair and pulled out two packages that had been hidden under two towels. Betsy removed a small package from each pocket of her skirt, and Claire retrieved two packages hidden in the corner of the shanty under a shirt.

Cora opened her gift from Claire first, "Oh, they are great Claire."

"The potholder is so you won't keep burning yourself on that dangerous little stove and the bobby pins are to keep your hair up so it doesn't catch on fire." The three laughed and Claire gave Betsy a deck of cards.

Betsy gave Cora a light blue scarf to tie around her hair and a yellow print scarf to Claire. Cora gave Claire a skein of bright yellow yarn and a set of bamboo knitting needles made by an intern.

Cora presented Betsy with a novel she had bought from a vendor. It was, *For Whom the Bell Tolls*, by Ernest Hemingway. "I heard you say you hadn't read it and I think you'll like it. I read it when we were on our way to Manila, but left my copy behind."

The three enjoyed a small piece of dry fruitcake and a cup of tea before going to hear the choruses. When they were seated on the lawn a man squeezed in between Cora and Claire and sat down.

"Can you make your gift work," he asked quietly.

"Yes, I'm sure I can," Claire answered keeping her eyes focused straight ahead."

"Good." He moved to another area of the crowd.

All of the camp's choruses joined together in a special concert followed by more than two thousand internees joining them in singing Christmas carols. It was an exceptional time.

"Couldn't you just feel the unity among everyone?" Betsy asked.

"Yes, I think all of us forgot our hardships for a while by remembering what today is all about," Cora said.

The hustle and bustle of the day died down as curfew neared and the internees returned to their dormitories for roll call and lights out.

\* \* \*

On December 26th Cora and Betsy anxiously awaited the arrival of the truck transporting the nurses back to camp from Manila.

"I see her, she's on the truck," Cora said squeezing Betsy's hand, but showing no outward sign of excitement. Silently they waited.

They walked up to the second floor living quarters with Claire, and while she changed from her uniform to a regular dress she gave bits of information when she thought no one was listening.

"Get some sleep, Cora, it's over, no problems," Claire said. "It was like playing a game and winning.

"Did Raphael know about it?" Cora asked.

"He didn't work on my floor today, so I didn't see him."

"You act like you enjoyed it," Betsy whispered disgustingly.

Claire smiled, "I did." Her eyes twinkled, "I'll tell you both all about it this afternoon."

As promised, Claire eagerly elaborated on the sequence of events later that day. "I was nervous, but I kept busy until I saw an elderly priest come into the ward carrying flowers. He walked over to the patient and asked about her; of course he used the wrong name and the wrong diagnosis. He watched diligently as I changed her bandage, then I told him he looked tired today."

"Then what happened? Was it the right priest?" Betsy questioned.

"He responded correctly. We made eye contact and exchanged a smile. He then suggested he could bless me if I had the time, and I agreed as I had been instructed. When he finished he took my hands in his and told me to kneel in front of him. As I did I removed the note from my skirt pocket and when he placed his hands over mine I transferred the note into his hands."

"That's it?" Betsy asked.

"Yes."

"Well it sounds like it went well this time, but I hope you don't have to do it again," Cora said.

Claire smiled.

\* \* \*

New Year's Day 1943 arrived with little fanfare, a football game was played and late that night off in a distance the sounds of firecrackers, whistles and horns reminded the internees of their fate. The idea of beginning

200

another year at the hands of their captors brought about mass depression.

Five days later Betsy reported news to Claire and Cora, "I heard one of the prisoners who unloaded the Canadian Red Cross Ship yesterday say it was supposed to have arrived here before Christmas. He said the sailors told him it had been setting at the Manila Dock since 26 December."

"Well I'm sure we'll appreciate it as much now as we would have then," Claire said.

"That's not all he said. The men also saw stacks of medical supplies from the American Red Cross setting on the docks in the hot sun," Betsy said. "When the Executive Committee heard this they contacted the Commandant and of course he denied any knowledge of such supplies arriving."

"That shouldn't surprise us," Cora said.

After another five days the comfort kits from the Canadian Red Cross that had been shipped to arrive for Christmas were given to the prisoners. Crackers, cheese, jam and sardines were Cora's favorite and Betsy loved the raisins, prunes and tea. Claire was thrilled with sardines and soup. All three enjoyed the corned beef and the nurses traded with each other and with other prisoners to get what they liked best and to get more nutritious food.

The month of January gave way to the month of February and preparations were underway for Betsy's birthday on the twelfth. She would celebrate her twenty-fifth birthday in captivity. Though she did not mention the event to anyone, Cora was determined to bake a cake and invite several nurses to share in the festivities.

The day arrived and Cora slept for three hours after

her shift ended before going to the shanty to begin preparing the food. With the milk, chocolate and sugar from their Red Cross kits and the flour and baking powder she had bartered for days earlier, she made a birthday cake. When the cake was cooled one of the nurses placed a candle on it.

"Happy Birthday!" they shouted when Betsy returned from an errand Cora had sent her on. Betsy shook with joy. Her friends had remembered her, and tears fell into the cake as she blew out the candle. "Thanks," was all she could say.

Claire's gift to her was a hat made from twine to wear in the sun and Cora had her made a set of knitting needles to replace the ones she had broken in her attempt to learn the craft. Other gifts received were a book, a pair of knitted socks and homemade candy.

Later that day Cora and Claire walked over to the ball field to watch the girl's softball team. After the game the team sang happy birthday to Coach Betsy. Zennie and the twins were waiting for the birthday girl when she left the ball diamond.

"Here Miss Brown," Peggy said. "We made this picture for you," she handed her a colored picture of trees, sunshine, birds and a big black fuzzy dog.

"It's a picture of your dog, Fluffy, you told us you had when you were a little girl. I colored the trees and the dog and Peggy colored the grass, sunshine and the birds," Patrick said with a big grin stretching across his face.

"It's lovely. I've never had anything so beautiful, and it looks just like Fluffy too!" Accepting the picture, Betsy asked the twins, "How did you two know that it was my birthday?"

They giggled. "A birdie told us," Patrick answered

and cupped his little thin hands over his mouth attempting to muffle his laughter.

"That was so sweet of you two to do that," Cora added seeing that Betsy was fighting back tears.

"How would you like to have a piece of my birthday cake?" Betsy asked.

After a burst of shrill screams, they proceeded to the shanty where the twins ate the remainder of the small cake.

*I wish we could give them a big glass of milk*, Cora thought. *They are getting so thin.*

The day ended with Betsy, Cora and Claire lying under the stars listening to the recorded music drifting across the lawn.

A large population of mosquitoes ushered in dengue fever in epidemic portions. Whooping cough also became a problem for the overcrowded hospitals where little medicine was available. Fortunately, most of the nurses remained healthy enough to put in extra hours caring for the sick.

Betsy developed a constant headache, then began suffering severe joint pain. She managed to hide her discomfort until Cora noticed the rash covering her body.

Claire and Cora had discussed Betsy's headaches but now with the rash they were sure.

"It's breakbone fever," Cora said in a whisper and Claire nodded.

"We need to get her to the hospital regardless of her arguing."

"I think she will go," Cora said. "I also think she knows that it is breakbone fever."

The two found Betsy resting on the ground in the shanty, and with no resistance from her they supported her weight until they reached the admitting area of the hospital. It was at this point that Claire and Cora realized how advanced the infectious disease had become.

Breakbone fever lasted about ten days, followed by a year of immunity. With the support of her upbeat shanty-mates Betsy escaped the mental depression many victims experience. Each day of her confinement in the hospital Cora and Claire took food to her and massaged her back and joints. Their upbeat conversations were part of the treatment plan.

With help and encouragement, Betsy recovered her mobility and strength completely in two weeks and was released from the camp hospital. Her friends also made sure she ate when she returned to the dormitory. They insisted on plenty of rest and watched over her like a couple of mother hens.

One sunny afternoon before Betsy was well enough to report to work Claire went to the shanty to sit with her. "You look a little down today," she said. "But this should raise your spirits." Reaching into her pocket and pulling out a garlic plant, she continued, "Look, we can plant it with the flowers and use it to cover up the nasty taste of the stuff we eat."

"Great! When we cook weeds we can add the garlic and pretend it is spaghetti or some exotic Italian dish," Betsy answered.

Cora joined the two, "Well Betsy, I see you are acting like your old self, but maybe this will change that sarcastic tone of yours." Cora placed a small rag tied with twine on the table and gingerly untied it for Betsy to see.

"Sugar! Where on earth did you find it?"

Cora ignored the question. "I also have real tea, three

cans of milk and three packs of American cigarettes."

Claire looked at Cora and grinned, "He actually went for it?"

"Yes," Cora answered, "I told you he would."

"Will someone tell me what you two have been up to? Who went for what?" Betsy asked.

The two looked at each other. "Go ahead, Cora, you tell her."

"Okay. I traded my rhinestone necklace to one of the guards."

"You what!" Betsy said raising her voice.

"I know it's against regulations, but I knew I would never have an opportunity to wear it in here."

"Do you know what they would have done to you if you had been caught?" Betsy shook her head. "How did you know he wouldn't report you?" She paused. "Your rhinestone necklace?"

"Yea, I know," Cora said and without missing a beat continued, "And when we do get out of here we'll have enough back-pay to buy all of the rhinestone necklaces we want."

"How did you do it?" Claire asked.

Cora smiled, "I put it on and the rest didn't take long. I noticed one of the guards staring at it. I slipped my hand under it and held it up. He came closer, never taking his eyes off the jewelry. Then I said, you like?"

"That was it?"

"Yes he offered to trade," Cora said.

"But didn't you say the necklace was a special gift to you?" Betsy asked.

"Yes it was."

"Care to tell us about it?" Betsy asked.

Cora hunched her shoulders. "It's a long story."

"We have time," Claire said.

"Yes, I suppose we do." Cora stared off into the distance and lit one of their new cigarettes. After a couple of puffs she tilted her head back slowly exhaling a stream of smoke into the humid atmosphere.

## Chapter Thirteen

"It was a cold November day," Cora began. "I was walking home from school, I was a senior. As I started down the hill, the dreaded loud piercing whistle began echoing through our coal mining camp. I dropped my books and ran toward the mine. A dark cloud of soot and smoke was erupting from the entrance.

"It was like slow motion in a movie. I remember trying to think if my brother was working that shift. I knew my fiancé, Vince, was scheduled to work, but he had told me he was thinking of taking the day off to deer hunt." Cora paused and inhaled the stimulating nicotine.

"I reached the wash-house, that's where the injured men would be brought. Inside men were moving benches to make a temporary infirmary; the closest medical facility was sixty miles away. I stepped out into the hysterical crowd. The air was filled with sulphurous fumes. I took a handkerchief from my pocket and held it over my nose. My eyes were stinging. I couldn't find my brother, Dad or Vince.

"Doc and I began setting up the infirmary, though there rarely are survivors. To my surprise, my brother was carrying the first stretcher. Later I found he had come out of the mine minutes before the explosion. My dad showed up next, but no sign of Vince.

"Doc assessed the injuries and instructed me how to help him. Sometimes I would remove a headlamp. One time a man's scull came off with it. I remember that is when I had to go out back of the wash-house and throw up; then I was okay until I saw Vince being carried in on a stretcher." Cora paused, crushing her cigarette under her foot.

"I remember screaming, 'No,' over and over. I could see people's mouths moving, but couldn't hear anything." She paused. "It was much like the day Manila was bombed. Next I remember being angry with Vince and screaming, 'You promised me this wouldn't happen.' He coughed and I removed his headlamp exposing his dark curls. I assured him he was going to be fine. He coughed again, his chest heaved and he died.

"You see, after my graduation we were going to be married and move north to Wheeling." Cora stood. "The sad part is I don't feel anything anymore. I try, but there is nothing. It seems like it happened to someone else."

Betsy and Claire gave her support through hugs. "The rhinestone necklace was a gift from Vince?" Betsy asked.

"Yes. I know he would want me to trade it for food to survive. He would be pleased to know he gave me something I could trade. I still have memories of him, and the Japs can't take that away."

"Do you have a picture of him with you?" Claire asked.

Cora nodded, "Yes, it's in the dorm."

"We'd like to see it when you are ready to show us,"

Betsy said.

After several minutes of quiet thoughts, the discussion reverted back to bartering. "I have a ring my parents gave me when I graduated from Nursing School, we can trade it when we need more food," Betsy added.

"And I still have the silver cigarette case," Claire added.

"That's swell! Our prized possessions may just keep us alive," Cora said. "Now I think we should invite Zennie and the twins for crackers and milk tomorrow if that is okay with you. I feel sure that Zennie has been giving the children her food portions, she is getting very weak. We need to help her all we can."

"I feel bad for Patrick and Peggy, they are much too small for their age," Claire said and the other two nodded in agreement.

* * *

On 14 May 1943, eight hundred of the strongest and youngest men at San Tomas Internment Camp boarded buses for Los Banos, fifty miles southeast of Manila, to establish a new internment camp at the Agricultural College of the University of the Philippines. The Navy nurses volunteered for the assignment of setting up the hospital under the direction of a civilian physician they were serving under at STIC. It was a solemn time as the internees watched their friends and loved ones being forced to leave.

"Good-bye, Good-bye," Cora, Betsy and Claire shouted from the steps of the Main Building. The grounds were filled with those left behind. As the first truck moved out toward the large opened front gate, the loud speaker produced a burst of static followed by "While the Caissons Keep Rolling Along." The last truck rumbling toward the open gate carried the Navy nurses, and "Anchors Aweigh" blared across the lawn as the remaining internees watched through tear-filled eyes until the trucks turned onto *Calle Espans*. The gates were closed.

The music stopped and a man standing on the steps raised his head and in a deep boisterous voice began singing. His voice bellowed out across the lawn and those remaining in camp joined him in singing "Onward Christian Soldiers." The song ended with a cloud of sadness hovering over the camp. The only hope was a promise from the enemy that all of the internees at STIC would be going to Los Banos when the camp was completed.

Claire glanced at her watch, "It's almost time for my ride to the hospital."

"I'll wait here with you. I don't feel much like sleeping today," Cora said.

"Do you think Dottie and Smitty will find the conditions at Los Banos to be what they are anticipating?" Claire asked.

Betsy and Cora stared into her questioning eyes. Finally, Cora answered, "No Claire, these are the Japs we're dealing with and as much as I'd like to think they'll find a better facility there, I fear they won't."

Betsy added, "And don't get your hopes up about us joining them either."

"I won't," Claire said. "I've been concerned about them since I heard about the transfer, but hoped I would be wrong"

"Yeah, but remember they are tough. They can take anything the Japs dish out," Betsy said. "In a way I wish we were going too. I could use a change of scenery."

"I'll take my chances and stay here, thank you. At least we know what we're dealing with here," Cora said.

"Me too," Claire agreed.

"By the way, Claire, I have a book from the library I want to read this afternoon, if you'd like I'll go with you to do our laundry," Cora said attempting to take their minds off the Navy nurses.

"Great, I'd love the company while I wait and knit. Here comes my personal carriage, right on time," Claire said as the truck pulled up to the Main Building. "I hope they will replace the Navy nurses that went with me," she said. "How does my hair look?"

"Fine, I can't see a hidden thing," Betsy whispered as she hugged Claire. "Be careful."

Cora was relieved that Claire's meetings with Rafael and the priest had gone undetected. Both of her contacts were competent, but she still worried about Claire being caught. Three messages had successfully been delivered into camp and two out of camp. Claire had shared information with her two friends about several large guerrilla outfits operating near Manila.

* * *

That afternoon as Cora and Claire stood watch over their laundry an elderly man interrupted. "Miss West, here is the yarn you wanted."

Cora never looked up from the book she was reading. *The less I see the better off I'll be.*

"Thanks," Claire said while placing it in her worn knitting bag. She picked up her needles and continued knitting golf balls out of twine.

"Can you get cotton tonight for me to stuff these balls?" Claire asked.

"Sure, that's one thing we still have plenty of, I just have to remember to get it."

"I want to deliver these to the guys that brought their golf clubs with them. They seem to be nice, decent men," Claire said.

"Oh? Is that all?"

"Yes, of course it is," Claire said defending herself. "Besides, they are married; I've met their wives at the library."

Cora smiled, "Good."

"Tomorrow I will start knitting each of us a bra and a pair of panties with the yarn I just received, and if there isn't enough I'll alternate rows with the softer twine I have been saving."

"That will be great. I've noticed our clothes are not going to last through many more washings, and I doubt the Japanese will supply new uniforms for us either." Cora lowered her voice, "You didn't ask for any yarn did you?"

Claire dropped her knitting needles into her lap and looked up at the sky. "No," she said then paused. "No, I don't think it will rain tonight." Claire gently shook her head and Cora understood the answer.

Cora picked up the dry laundry. "Let's put these away and then go to the shanty. Betsy should be back from softball practice by then. I'm glad she feels like coaching those teenagers again."

"Me too. The girls missed her and she hasn't been as grouchy since she went back to coaching."

When they were all in the shanty where Cora and Betsy could stand guard, Claire checked the message she uncovered in the ball of yarn.

"Listen to this!" she whispered. "This is going to Bilibid Prison. *Prepare medicines/supplies for doctor being transferred here to smuggle in.*

"What does it mean," Betsy said after Claire told them what it said.

"It sounds like we are finally getting a doctor to replace Dr. Green. We could use at least three more doctors," Cora said. "Since he went to Los Banos there has been a steady increase in the population and sickness."

"We need nurses or medics to replace the Navy nurses that left too," Betsy added.

"But we'll take anything we can get," Claire stated.

"Maybe the doctor will have information about the men from Corregidor," Cora said before taking a drink from her canteen.

"I hope so. Rafael would like to help, but so far he hasn't been able to. He says he is being watched constantly when he isn't in the hospital," Claire said.

"I know the Japanese could change their minds and we won't get a doctor, but if we do get one it could be tomorrow or it could be next year if we are still at war."

"Yes," Betsy and Cora agreed.

A few days later Betsy said, "More prisoners were brought in today, I wish our new doctor would get here. More were brought in than were transferred out. There were two hundred children all under the age of five, seventy women and the rest were elderly men."

"Wow! We had better get more doctors and nurses soon," Cora said.

"What about food? How will the Japs feed them?" Betsy asked. "They can't feed us now!"

* * *

On 25 May 1943 Cora celebrated her twenty-fifth birthday under the control of the Japanese Imperial Army. Chuckling to herself, Cora pictured her family and friends giving up on her finding a husband and getting married. In West Virginia if you were not engaged or married by the time you were sixteen you were doomed to be an old maid. Cora could still hear her grandmother's words on her sixteenth birthday. *A spinster is what you are going to be Cora Leigh. You just mark my words. You spend entirely too much time reading them books of yours. You can't expect to get a husband from no books.*

A small celebration took place, but there were no staples for a birthday cake; however, her friends remembered her and sang "Happy Birthday." Patrick and Peggy presented her with pictures they had drawn and she hung them on a post in the shanty.

Later, Cora and her friends spent the evening sitting on the lawn playing cards and listening to music. Close attention had to be paid to the selections and the order in which they were played. Many of the songs portrayed news from the battlefields in a code only the internees understood. Often, the title reflected victories and loses, causing bursts of clapping or shouts of anger, while the guards stood by confused and puzzled.

If "There'll be Bluebirds Over The White Cliffs of Dover" played followed by "Stormy Weather," everyone knew England was involved in difficult battles. There were songs for all of the countries at war and it took some imagination to break the code. The Japanese assumed the outbursts were a show of enthusiasm for the music. The guards always joined in the excitement when "Waltzing Matilta" played, unaware of the news from Australia it proceeded.

The following night while Cora moved from patient to patient her thoughts were again on going home. Two men in her care died that night, but with the death toll increasing monthly it had become normal. Medicines were needed, but nutritious food and better sanitation were needed more than the medicine. The camp population had increased by one thousand during the last four months while food and medical supplies continued to dwindle.

"Good afternoon, Zennie," Cora sang out to the frail woman the following afternoon.

"Hello Cora, my but you are in a good mood today," Zennie answered. She was difficult to hear. Her voice had grown weak. Cora continued encouraging her to eat, but she knew Zennie was giving most of her rations to her children.

"I brought you some crackers," she said and handed them to her.

"Thank you, the children will be so happy."

"I know they will, but you have to keep your strength up too. Please eat some of the crackers," Cora pleaded.

Zennie tucked the food into her dress pocket. "You know, Cora, we have more young children in camp now and we need volunteers to teach classes. We would like to expand our afternoon class. You are good with the children, will you consider teaching?"

"I'll think about helping but I'm working longer shifts

now."

Cora and Zennie walked across the lawn to meet the twins.

* * *

The end of July arrived and there had been no news from Los Banos.  Spirits in the camp were down.  Cora and Betsy greeted Claire in the dormitory after her shift in Manila.

"Claire?  What's wrong?  You are pale as death and you're shaking," Betsy asked.

"I'm fine."  She ripped off her khaki uniform.  "Meet me at the shanty in ten minutes," she said changing into her dress.

Fifteen minutes later Claire handed Betsy a letter hidden in a book.  "The orderly, Rafael brought it to me just before my shift ended.  I placed it in my shoe before I left the hospital.  I tried to stay calm as I boarded the truck. There are rumors that we are going to be searched before we leave camp and when we get back.  I was so nervous my insides were trembling.  In fact they still are."  Claire lowered her tired body into her lawn chair.  "The thought of being searched before I could get this to you made me ill," she said to Betsy.

"To me?" Betsy asked.

"Yes, it's from Brice."

Betsy grabbed the paper from Claire's hand and read the short letter several times before reading it aloud.

*My Dearest,*

*I am well. I was transferred from Bilibid Prison to McDonald and before they recorded our names, I volunteered daily for a water detail. We walked several miles from camp to get water from a stream. One day I waited until the guards were looking the other way and I slowly backed-up into a thicket and kept walking. A group of guerrillas saw me leave the work detail and a day later approached me. I joined them and have been working against the enemy since then.*

*I am taking a chance with this letter, but with no names and a reliable courier I am confident it will reach you. I know where you are and how the conditions are there. We'll be together soon, don't give up.*

*Say hello to my friends. I long for the good old days. Arm is doing fine.*

*Where our friend S.K. is imprisoned they sleep indoors on concrete floors and spend the days in an open courtyard. All 1,162 use a common bathroom. He hopes to get a transfer where he can be more useful.*

*I do spend a lot of time thinking about you and the ranch back home. I plan to get both you and the ranch back when this filthy war ends.*

*All my Love,*
*Your Cowboy*

"Rafael also agreed to help me get messages out to the guerrillas," Claire said. "We are going to tie one shoelace horizontally and the other one vertically when we have messages. The pillows we were using get moved and we think the Japanese guard may be doing it. Rafael thinks the shoestrings will work, at least for awhile."

"Where will the messages be?" Cora asked.

"In the janitor's supply closet. There is an old can of furniture polish and the little that is left in it is dried up. The can is on a bottom shelf out of sight."

"Oh Claire, it sounds awfully dangerous," Cora said.

"This whole life of ours is dangerous."

After reading the letter several times, Betsy held her cigarette to the corner of the paper and watched Brice's words go up in smoke. When the last flame when out she said in a matter-of-fact tone, "We diagnosed a case of infantile paralysis today in an eight-year-old Filipino boy."

Cora lifted her head, "Are they sure that's what it is?"

"Yes, I'm afraid so."

"Can you imagine what an outbreak here would be like? It would be disastrous, with the lack of nutrition plus the poor sanitation conditions," Claire said. "And the rains aren't helping either."

Cora's thoughts were immediately on Patrick and Peggy. *They are so young and have seen too much sorrow in their short lives, and now the possibility of polio.*

## Chapter Fourteen

"Well, we've read about typhoons and heard about them and now we are getting to experience one," Claire said to Cora and Betsy during their evening meal of watery, meatless vegetable stew. They sat on their cots in the dormitory because of the heavy rains.

"Personally, I prefer reading about them, I never wanted to be in one," Cora said.

"The monsoons this fall have been bad enough, and staying inside is driving me nuts!" Betsy added. "Do you realize it's been raining for three days now? Everything is soggy, including me!"

"If this keeps up we'll all drown anyway," Claire added.

"Well I heard something today that will take our minds off the rain," Cora said.

"I hope it's not more cases of polio," Betsy said.

"No. Food rations are being cut again and we will be getting a ration card for our clothing."

"That's a joke, we don't get much clothing now," Betsy said.

"And how much more can they reduce the amount of food we get?" Claire said.

"I don't know about the food, but we will get a dress, pants and a pair of socks with our card," Cora answered. "And we certainly need them!"

"How long is the card good?" Betsy asked then added, "I'm beginning to think we may live out our lives here." No one commented for several minutes as they imagined their future.

"Come on now, we can't give up. They say we will be getting another one in six months," Cora answered.

"I'll have to continue knitting our socks and under-garments," Claire sighed.

"The socks you've knitted out of the heavy twine rubs blisters on my feet, especially in this rain," Betsy said. "I prefer to go without socks, unless they are made with the thin twine."

"I have a little of the thin left, but not much."

Cora walked over to the window and looked out, "I wonder when the electric and gas will be back on?" she asked no one in particular. "This weather is certainly destructive."

"I'm wondering if the Japanese will restore the utili-ties," Betsy said. "Boy, what I wouldn't give for a piece of chewing gum." Her companions ignored her last state-ment.

Claire's assignment at the civilian hospital was can-celled due to the heavy rains and she was ordered to work twelve-hour shifts in the children's hospital. To reach the hospitals during the typhoon, the nurses held on to thick ropes made of hemp that the men had stretched over a twenty-five-foot long and twenty-five foot wide depression filled with water. The men held the rope tight and the women wearing shorts, which was against regulations, trudged through water up to their hips. They held their khaki uniforms over their heads with one hand and the rope with the other until they were on the other side of the large water hole.

"We can be thankful that the outbreak of infantile paralysis has decreased, even if the cases are increasing our work load," Betsy said when she and Claire returned to the dormitory after their shift. Cora gave up on sleep and sat up, "Were there new cases again today?"

"No," Betsy answered.

"Well, at least the scare of an epidemic is over," Cora said. "I'm concerned for all of the children, especially the Sullivan twins and the little ones in the class I'm helping with."

"It's still raining, so what shall we do today? Play cards?" Claire asked.

"I'm going to write to Flint and hope I can get one of the priests or a missionary to take it out of camp for me.

"I'm not sure I can stand in the chow line today. The measly amount of food we get after waiting in the rain and wind is inhumane!" Betsy complained. "And it's not worth it."

"I hope we secured our furniture in the shanty with enough ropes to keep it there," Claire said. "I'm anxious to see if the structure is still standing."

"Our little bit of food is in the tin box, so it may be okay," Cora reminded them.

"I didn't know it was possible to rain this much and this long," Betsy said. "We should have built an ark!"

"Well, get used to it, it could last for several more days. Look on the bright side, maybe it will plump up our dry skin," Claire said.

"Actually, I feel like I'm getting several free showers everyday. Of course I'm up to my ankles in mud," Cora said pulling her musette from under the bed.

"I'm going to write to Courtney," Claire said and took a photograph of the child from her bag under her cot.

"You really miss your little sister, don't you?" Cora asked.

"Yes, since Mom died all the family she has is Aunt Irene, Uncle Jake and me."

Cora also took advantage of the free time and began a letter to Flint.

*18 August 1943*
*My Dearest Flint,*

*We just received great news – we've heard from Cowboy and he is safe. Our other friend we think is in Bilibid Prison. I've not heard anything good about the place only the opposite. I have not shared my information with C, but she probably has heard it too.*

*The children here have been good for me. I laugh with them and love the way they care for each other. Their outpouring of love works magic on B, C and me.*

*I must close before the guards stroll by and order an inspection.*

*Love,*
*C*

*P.S. I think of you often and wish we could talk. There is so much I want to know about you.*

* * *

"This Thanksgiving will not be celebrated like the one last year," Claire said when someone mentioned the upcoming holiday. "But at least the rains have stopped."

"That's for sure. There won't be the traditional turkey meal for the camp but the children are drawing turkeys and doing a play about the pilgrims. We have to keep the tradition alive for them, and it gives us something to look forward to," Cora said.

"But mostly something to reminisce about, and quite frankly some of my memories are fading," Betsy said. "I'm having trouble remembering what pumpkin pie tastes like, I know it smells good but I can't remember that either."

"That's because we are suffering from psychological torture," Cora said. Her friends nodded in agreement.

* * *

The solemn Thanksgiving celebration ended while Cora made an entry in her journal.

*Thanksgiving Day 1943*

*There was no celebration except a skit put on by the children. Spirits are low and we wonder if we will ever get out of here. The grounds are not kept as clean as they were our first year here, but then there are more people and many are old. Everyone's energy level is lower because of the food rationing.*

*The nurses continue to work and keep busy. We also pool our money, what little we have, to buy fruits and vegetables. Last night we had baked peanut loaves for protein since we rarely see any meat in our meals. We had peanut sauce made from boiling peanuts and we poured that over our moldy rice. We always go to bed hungry. It is a constant feeling that is difficult to explain, but those of us experiencing it hope that someday it will be over and we will never have this feeling again. I worry about the children and the forty-five babies we delivered last year. What is their future? When will it be too late for them to physically develop normally? I want to cry when I look at the children's and the teenager's teeth. They are going to lose most of their permanent teeth, and some of the younger children are beginning to show signs of bone deformities. If we are not liberated soon, it will be too late for them, maybe for all of us.*

*The psychological problems continue to grow and the hospital has expanded the psychiatric ward to handle the internees that cannot cope. I am thankful for my job and the sisterhood of the nurses to share this horrible burden.*

*We did not have our "talinum bowl" football game. The men have lost interest in the sport and are probably too weak to play.*

* * *

After a small celebration for the twins' fourth birthday, Cora, Claire and Betsy enjoyed a quiet time together.

"Can you believe that today is the anniversary of the bombing of Pearl Harbor? We have been at war a full two years!" Claire said as she dealt the cards for a game of rummy.

"And we and a lot of other people thought it would be over in a week or two," Cora said as she shuffled the cards and began dealing. "A month at the most. Boy would I love to have an American cigarette!"

"Me too, and hear some current news from the outside," Claire said as she picked up the hand and arranged the cards,

"Yes, all the news we seem to hear has to do with food rations and the lack of sugar!" Betsy said. "I continue to dream of Oreos, only now each time I attempt to pick one up it rolls away and I start chasing it and it stops until I reach for it and then it rolls away and is joined by life-savers. All rolling down a Carmel coated hill."

No one laughed. "We are all having similar dreams," Cora said. "I dream of an orchard where oranges, apples and bananas all grow on the same tree, then there is another one with pineapples, grapes and pears, then another, but the fruit is too high for me to reach. I'm too tired to jump. I just sit and look at it."

"Milk," Claire said.

Her friends looked up from the cards they were holding.

"I can't remember what milk tastes like but I know I liked it," Claire said.

The women swapped recipes as a way of compensating for their cravings as the card game continued.

"You know the library has a cookbook section. I enjoy reading different ways to cook meats, but there are also books on Jell-O recipes and casseroles," Claire informed them.

"Are there any on just desserts?" Betsy asked.

"Yes, that's the largest category.

"What do you miss most when you think of food?" Cora asked.

"Homemade ice cream with fudge sauce," was Betsy's quick response. "And next would be hot dogs smothered in onions and so much chili sauce that it would be dripping off of my elbows with every bite."

"Blueberry pancakes with butter melting on top and swimming in Maine maple syrup," Claire said, licking her cracked sore lips. "Of course, the blueberries would be Maine low-bush blueberries!"

"I never thought I would say this but I crave fried bologna and baked beans. I hated it because we had it so often when I was growing up, but I can almost taste it now!" Cora said.

Passing around cookbooks and copying recipes, drooling over pictures and dreaming of home-cooked meals became a way of life at STIC. The nurses used their military discipline and their jobs of helping others to give them strength and keep going. They continued talking and planning their lives after the war ended. Keeping their hopes up and having plans gave everyone something to hold on to while waiting to be liberated.

A couple of weeks before Christmas, Betsy asked Cora and Claire if they had heard about the comfort kits from America.

"No, where are they? When do we get them?" Cora asked.

"Some of our men found them. The Japanese had hidden the kits," Betsy said.

"Are you sure?" Claire questioned. "It could be some kind of a cruel joke."

"No, it's for real and they will be handing them out this afternoon," Betsy insisted.

When the internees produced the kits, the guards were

furious and cut open some of the cans and removed all of the labels from the others. They opened boxes of raisins and poured them on the ground for the ants while insisting that they were searching for messages."

"Did they give the Committee what was left of the kits when they finished?" Cora asked.

"Yes. They will be giving them out soon."

Within the hour the news came over the loudspeaker and the prisoners reported to the food stations and received their package from the United States of America.

"Real coffee!" Cora shouted when she returned to the shanty. "The Japs kept our cigarettes, but we can have a cup of good old U.S.A. coffee!"

"Did you hear what some of the internees are selling their kits for?" Claire did not wait for an answer. "Six thousand pesos! That's three thousand American dollars! Can you believe that anyone here would give up this food for money?"

"No, they don't have the knowledge of how their bodies work, especially the digestive tract, and we do. Still, it's hard not to overeat," Betsy said holding a can of Spam and a package of cookies. Her hands trembled.

"If we continue to eat what the Japanese give us and slowly eat this nutritional food along with it, we will be less likely to suffer from malnutrition," Cora suggested. "Already our hair is getting thin and our gums are bleeding."

"Yes, that's what we'll have to do," Claire said. "We must eat small amounts because our shrunken stomachs will not be able to handle a large amount all at once anyway." She paused and sadness filled her eyes. "Rationing food from our kits may be our only chance of survival."

"We have no idea when we will receive another kit or even if we will. This has to last as long as possible," Cora said holding onto some of the food. "Do we agree?"

Claire and Betsy nodded in agreement.

"The packages are less frequent now and if the Japs are winning we may never get any more," Claire added.

The entertainment Committee again made plans to celebrate another Christmas behind the wall at Santo Tomas Internment Camp. Cora, Claire and Betsy made gifts for the children. "How many of these rag dolls do you think we can make?" Betsy asked her friends.

"I don't know," Cora answered and continued to sew on an arm. "Our supplies are limited."

"I hope to have ten knitted dolls done by Christmas Eve," Claire said.

\* \* \*

Christmas arrived with less enthusiasm than a year earlier, but the children were excited and their excitement carried over to the adults.

The nurses set up a separate table in order to celebrate together as a group again and they received special gifts and food from Captain Jennings's wealthy friend in Manila.

Cora and Zennie made arrangements to meet after the meal and Cora gave the twins the balls she had made by crocheting small casings out of twine and packing them tightly with cotton balls.

"Thank you," Patrick said, and his sister echoed his words.

*They are a year older and taller than they were last Christmas, but neither of them has gained weight. I worry about their bone development,* Cora thought.

"I have two chocolate bars for you too," she said and handed each of them her last two until the next care package.

"Zennie, this is for you," Cora presented her with a linen handkerchief. Cora had crocheted lace around the edges and when Zennie saw it she cried.

The children's big round eyes searched their mother's expression.

"It's okay children, it's just that Miss Cora has made me so happy." Zennie reached out and hugged the twins. "Why don't you give Miss Cora her gifts now?"

"Zennie!" Cora said, "You shouldn't have."

"The children need to learn to give as well as receive."

They each gave Cora a bookmark they had made from cardboard and colored with crayons. Zennie gave Cora a book of poems.

"Thank you so much," Cora said. "I won't lose my place when I am reading now." She placed the book markers in the book. "This is a great gift." She hugged the children. "And Zennie, I will treasure this book all of my life. Thank you."

As soon as the gift exchange ended Patrick and Peggy left to show their gifts to their friends.

The combined camp choruses sang and had a sing-along for the audience. As a special treat, a cast of one hundred and fifty put on the play, "Cinderella," which the adults as well as the children enjoyed.

For a day the miseries of daily life were shoved aside;

however, all were saddened by the Commandant's refusal to allow the two thousand visitors standing at the gate to enter the camp. Defeated and heart broken they turned and walked away taking the gifts of food, clothing and other necessities and luxuries with them, though many tossed the gifts over the stone wall in hopes of their relatives or friends finding them.

Cora was disappointed that there was no mail this Christmas, but she wrote a letter to her mother hoping the missionary could get it out of camp. He was only permitted to leave twice a month now instead of two days a week.

*Dear Mother,*

*I hope you are getting better and not giving Doc a hard time about taking your medicine and resting. I am doing fine; my friends and I work together. Today is Christmas and I hope you are enjoying a beautiful tree and a great dinner. I'm picturing a white Christmas there and all of the family gathered together, what a wonderful sight.*

*We have a lot of children here. Give my best to everyone.*

*I love you,*

*Your daughter*

She then wrote to Flint hoping he would receive it – if he were still alive.

*25 December 1943*
*My Dearest Flint,*

*This is our second Christmas here at STIC, we never thought we would be here this long. If it were not for the comfort kits we receive I would think our country and allies had forgotten us. We are united and our spirits are still high but I don't know how long that will last. We are hopeful that the worsening conditions here are a sign of allied successes. No visitors were allowed to come in for Christmas and we did not receive mail.*

*We hear a lot of rumors here and some news. I've heard that our hospital ships are being bombed even though there are large crosses painted on the decks. Don't think it is because the Japs can't see the crosses through those thick glasses they wear. I know they can see. Sometimes I think the guards have eyes in the back of their heads too. There has been no word from our friends lately.*

*We had a nice meal with turkey. The children enjoyed the day with gifts and singing. Most of the adults exchanged token gifts. Tomorrow it is back to our regular routine under the Japanese guards.*

*Will we ever be free again?*

*Lovingly yours,*
*C*

Cora placed the letter in her poetry book and walked over to the dormitory. Christmas 1943 was over.

* * *

Walking from the hospital late one morning, Cora noticed one of the camp doctors and another man coming toward her. "It can't be!" She whispered and tried to shade the sun from her eyes. The glare did not keep her from recognizing the familiar silhouette. She blinked her eyes several times thinking the mirage would disappear.

## *Chapter Fifteen*


Cora stopped, her hands moved to cover her mouth; the two men continued walking towards her. Suddenly her feet moved and she ran into Dr. Spencer Kirby's embrace. The man he had been walking with continued on. "Cora? Cora? Is it really you?"

"Yes," she said stepping back to look at him. "Are you okay?"

"Of course, I'm here, aren't I?"

Cora gave him another hug and when she stepped back he asked, "Are Claire and Betsy here too?"

"Yes, we've been together since Corregidor."

"Oh, I can't believe I'm with you three again! I hoped to find you all here, but I'm learning it is best not to get my hopes too high."

"Yes, I know." Suddenly her emotions took over and tears of joy flowed down her cheeks. "When did you get here?"

"Yesterday," Spencer answered. "Are the three of you okay, I mean are you able to work?"

"We are all fine, we keep busy and try to survive while we wait for our boys to come and rescue us."

"How is Claire?"

"She is fine too, but she has been worried about you. We're all doing well considering, but I do believe we look better than you." Cora grinned.

"You're the only one we hadn't heard from."

"You've heard from Brice?"

"Shhh," she cautioned. "Let's walk."

"Yes, he is safe, or at least he was a few months ago. Betsy will tell you all about him." They stopped and sat under a coconut palm. "We can talk here."

"What about Flint, when did you last hear from him?" Spencer asked.

"Several months ago," Cora's thin drawn face lost its smile. "We've heard that many hospital ships have been blown up, but I try not to think about it."

"You get news about the war in here?" Spencer glanced at their guarded surroundings.

"Yes, I'll explain that later too," she said smiling. "I'm so glad you are here. We didn't think we would get the doctors that had been requested," Cora said.

"I'm the only one sent from Bilibid," Spencer said. "I can't believe I got out alive." He lowered his head.

"Betsy, Claire and I were hoping they would send you."

"Where and when can I meet with all of you, or is that possible?" He asked as they stood to leave.

"This afternoon, if you can make it. We are losing some of our privileges, but unlike Bilibid this is a prison for civilians, so we are treated better than the soldiers in the military prisons."

As they walked, Cora explained their shanty to him, and before the shift ended arrangements were made for the four to meet there in mid-afternoon. "We no longer get a noon meal, but we try to have some sort of a treat each day."

*I don't know if I can sleep,* Cora thought when she crawled into bed. *I can't wait to see the surprised look on their faces when they see Spencer, especially Claire's, but Spencer is so thin.* With joy and sadness in her heart she drifted off to sleep.

Cora got up and in the process of sorting real life from her dreams, and then she remembered the afternoon plans. Walking through the trickle of water the Japanese called a shower, she rehearsed the afternoon plans. *With Claire working in the library for two hours and Betsy coaching softball, I'll be able to have everything prepared by the time they all arrive.* She dressed and walked to the shanty to make preparations for the long-awaited reunion.

Cora found a little flour not infested by worms and made a pie crust. Matches were scarce in the camp, but she was able to light the little cook stove with her cigarette lighter that still contained lighter fluid. Baking was not an easy task on the stove, but she had mastered the technique.

After the crust baked, Cora filled it with a lemon like filling made from calamancis. They were smaller than lemons and looked like limes; they would be a great substitute for lemons. Yesterday she had traded Betsy's ring for two duck eggs and sugar. The duck population, as well as other animals, was diminishing as food became less available.

While the pie cooled, Cora placed the crackers, cheese and jam they had saved from their comfort kits onto a chipped plate. Next, she heated water to make "Micky Finn," a soybean coffee substitute.

As planned, the guest of honor arrived before Claire

234

and Betsy. Spencer looked fresh and thrilled at the thought of their reunion.

His sunken eyes widened when he saw the pie. "Is that a real lemon pie?" He asked sniffing the air.

"Almost," she said, looking up in time to see Claire and Betsy sauntering across the lawn toward Hometown Avenue.

"Quick hide!" Cora said, before he could bolt toward them.

"Where?" He looked at the cramped area between two walls.

"Behind the wall, quick or they will see you." Spencer did as instructed and Cora thought she could hear his heart beating through the thin structure.

"Wow! What's the occasion," Betsy asked.

"Yea, it looks like you are expecting guests, is Zennie bringing the twins over?" Claire asked.

"No, sit down I have a surprise for you," Cora could barely speak. "Quick sit!"

Betsy and Claire looked at each other then back to Cora.

"Sit!" Cora insisted and pointed to the lawn chairs.

"Shall we humor her?" Betsy asked Claire.

" Yeah, why not, that pie does smell good and that's the only way we will get her to share it."

"Okay!" Cora shouted and before her mouth closed Spencer stepped around the wall. Betsy and Claire shot out of their chairs like balls out of a cannon, nearly knocking Spencer to the ground.

"Spencer!" They shouted. "When did you get here?"

Cora was speechless as she watched the three hugging, then they grabbed her and danced in a circle.

*Oh, how I wish Flint and Brice were here too. No that is being selfish, but I do miss them.*

They ate, laughed, cried and attempted to catch up on all that had transpired since their separation.

"Betsy, tell me what you heard from Brice," Spencer whispered and she gladly recited his letter.

"But it couldn't have happened without Claire's work," Betsy said.

"What do you mean?" He looked from Betsy to Claire and back to Betsy.

"Oh, I think she had better tell you."

Claire blushed. "It's really nothing," she said before informing him she passed messages in and out of camp.

"The priests smuggle letters out for some of us, but they can only take a few when they make their hospital visits outside of camp," Claire said. "Then some of the missionaries are permitted to go out of camp and they take mail for the prisoners, especially for the nurses.

"Claire passes requests to a guerrilla contact, like the one for the doctor being transferred from Bilibid to smuggle in extra supplies. Did you get that message?" Betsy asked.

"Yes." He turned to Claire. "You risked your life to get that message to Bilibid?"

"I'm just doing what I can to help us win this war, it's nothing that any of us wouldn't do if asked." Claire shrugged her shoulders as if shrugging off the danger.

"Well," he looked back to Betsy and Cora, "I was able to bring more than was packed for me, but the men there need supplies too." Spencer swirled the cup of imitation coffee and took a sip. "This isn't too bad."

"Bilibid must have been as bad as we heard if you

like this stuff," Betsy said before taking another drink of the hot liquid.

"Yes, Spencer, tell us about the conditions there and how you were chosen to be sent here," Cora said, and as she did Spencer's expression changed. A wave of horror and fear cut through the silence.

Through clenched teeth he said, "Maybe at another time, lets celebrate now." He glanced at the pie, then at Cora. "When do we get to taste that pie, Cora?"

"Oh, I forgot about it." She jumped up, cut the pie and served them.

"This is the first piece of pie I have had since the first month on Corregidor," Spencer said as he savored each bite.

After the pie was eaten, the conversation continued until Claire suggested they give their new guest a tour of the grounds.

"That's a great idea," Betsy said and Claire took Spencer's hand urging him to get up.

* * *

As midnight ushered in New Years Day 1944, a dark cloud of silence fell over the camp. The absence of bells ringing, whistles and horns blowing in Manila did not go unnoticed. No one in the camp felt like celebrating the holiday; however the Entertainment Committee did arrange for a football game although little enthusiasm existed among the weak teams and spectators. After the game, Claire and Spencer strolled over to the grassy area where Cora and Betsy were lying on their backs, heads resting on their hands and staring up at the sky. Ten minutes later they all headed for the shanty.

"Auld Lang Syne" echoed across the camp several times during the day and evening from the loud speakers, with most internees, including Spencer, Claire, Cora and Betsy showing little outward appearance of a holiday. Each day, week, month and year ran together like lava down the side of a volcano. Past days became hardened in the internees minds like volcanic rock.

\* \* \*

Six days later the Japanese military took charge of Santo Tomas Internment Camp and other prisoner of war camps around Manila and STIC turned into a *military* prisoner of war camp. Package lines were stopped and the nurses' friend from Manila could no longer supply them with necessities. The Japanese closed most of the hospitals outside of the camp, especially those housing older prisoners whom they transferred to STIC into overcrowded wards. The nurses were forced to work longer shifts.

"I've been assigned to the psychiatric hospital," Claire told Betsy and Cora.

"That's going to be quite different from your job in town," Cora commented.

"Well, at least I will be working the night shift, that shouldn't be as bad as working days."

"But I hate to see an end to the smuggling of information," Claire said. "My secret missions have ended and now I wonder if they were worth the risk. We're still here, so maybe I didn't help after all." Claire's shoulders drooped as she sighed.

"We don't know that! I'm sure you helped, we just

don't know how," Cora answered placing her arm around Claire.

"The missionary doctors are no longer permitted to come and go," Spencer told his three closest friends.

"Where are they going to work?" Betsy asked.

"They were given the choice of working outside of STIC or being confined here in the prison camp," he paused. "They all have chosen to stay here where they feel they can best serve."

"Do you realize what this means?" Cora asked.

Betsy sighed, "Yes, our private Post Office just closed."

"But we'll have them helping here all the time now," Cora said.

* * *

"Zennie came to the clinic today," Betsy told Cora. "She said you had insisted we examine her. She was admitted to the main hospital. They tried to make her comfortable by placing pillows under her knees and elbows, but it didn't give her any relief."

"I know, she waited too long," Cora paused. "It's too late isn't it?"

"Yes," Betsy shook her head. "Zennie's hands, arms, legs and feet are so swollen she can't move them. I told her you would be stopping by to see her."

"We all knew she had advanced beriberi. If only she would have eaten all of her rations, it wouldn't be so severe. The malnutrition here is now starvation!" Cora bit her lip attempting to stave off nausea. "She's been giving most of her food to Patrick and Peggy, she is a good mother. I tried to make her understand that she needed to stay healthy for them . . ." her voice trailed off.

"The poor little tykes, what will they do without her?" Betsy asked not really expecting an answer.

"I don't know," Cora said shaking her head.

"I wish we had been able to give her an injection of thiamin when we first saw the symptoms, but if any was ever shipped to us the Japs kept it for themselves!" Betsy said.

"I didn't realize how bad she was until it was too late. Some friend I turned out to be."

"Cora, there was nothing more you could do. We shared our food from our kits and you told her how important it was for her to eat, that's all you could do."

"Well, with the wet form of beriberi the only thing that could help now would be a blood transfusion from a healthy person, and that's impossible," Cora said. "How long does she have?"

"I'm not sure, maybe a week. Her friend that helps with the twins has agreed to watch them for her."

"I'll go see her now and then talk to Patrick and Peggy before I report to work." Cora stood and forced her tired body to walk to the hospital.

Cora visited Zennie that hot February day and promised to explain to the twins where she was and to sneak them in to see her the next day.

"Miss Cora!" the twins shouted seeing her outside the school.

"Did you two learn anything today?" Cora asked and they both talked at the same time, showing her the pictures they had drawn.

"Where's Mama?" Peggy asked looking in all direc

tions.

"She couldn't come today, that's why I'm here."

"She's sick ain't she?" Patrick asked, and both children looked at Cora with big sad eyes.

"Let's go over there and sit under that tree," Cora pointed to a palm tree. When they were seated and staring at her Cora continued.

"Yes, your mama is sick, very sick, and she saw Miss Betsy at the clinic today."

"Where is she now?" Patrick asked as he reached out for his sister's hand.

"She's in the hospital that I work in and I went to visit her before I came to meet you." Cora paused to make sure her voice was confident. "She asked Mrs. Sanchez to take care of you, and Betsy, Claire and I will be helping Mrs. Sanchez. Your mama wanted me to ask you to be good for her and to be brave." Cora looked at them waiting for a response.

Patrick and Peggy lowered their gaze, "Yes ma'am we will," they mumbled.

"She needs to rest today, but tomorrow right after you get out of school I am going to take you to visit her, okay?"

Their little heads popped up, "Yes!" they said looking at each other with wide grins spreading across their thin little faces.

"I'll walk with you to see Mrs. Sanchez then I'll see you tomorrow. You might want to bring the pictures you drew to your mama."

The children were pleased that they would get to see Zennie, and Cora deposited them in the care of the elderly Filipino woman, who was not in much better shape than Zennie.

241

The next day, Cora visited Zennie before going to meet the children. She combed her friend's long black hair and made two braids tied with the red ribbons Flint had sent.

Cora smuggled the little ones in to see their mama and stood watch at the door while Zennie spoke to them in a low whispering voice.

"After fifteen minutes, Cora stepped into the ward. It's time for them to leave," she said to Zennie. "Give your mama a kiss now."

As they did Zennie said, "Remember I love you very much and you must do as I have asked. Promise?"

Patrick and Peggy nodded and waved to their mama. Cora shuddered remembering her promise to Vince as he was dying. The twins placed their hands in Cora's, pulling her from her memories. They looked back over their shoulders until they were out in the long dingy hall.

When Cora returned from depositing the twins in Mrs. Sanchez's care, Zennie said, "Cora I have something to ask you and there isn't much time for you to think about your answer."

Cora sat on the edge of the cot, "Of course Zennie, what is it?"

"Under my pillow is an envelope, will you get it please." Cora removed a tan legal-sized envelope.

Zennie took it and held it close to her heart. Cora I want you to promise me you will take Patrick and Peggy with you when the Americans come." Cora started to answer, but Zennie stopped her. "Wait. I want you to take care of them, I know you will see that they have a good home and education. Your Flint sounds like he has a big heart like my Sully. It would all be legal. Mr. Benson, one of the internees, is an attorney and he has given me papers." Zennie's weak voice cracked. "They are adoption papers, and I have signed them and I hope you will too."

Cora gently hugged Zennie. They cried. When they gained control of their emotions, Zennie continued as tears rolled down her dry scabby cheeks. "You know I'm dying, please give me peace by promising me you will care for my children."

## Chapter Sixteen

At first Cora thought she had misunderstood, but looking into the woman's pleading eyes she knew she did understand.  Speechless, Cora took Zennie's hands in hers while collecting her thoughts.  "I will take the children with me and care for them.  I promise." Cora swallowed forcing the lump in her throat to disappear. "I will treat them as my own. I'd be honored Zennie, I'll sign the papers."

A witness watched as Cora signed the adoption papers. "Do the twins know about this?" Cora asked.

"Yes, but I'm not sure they really understand.  But I know they love you."

"I know they do and I love them too.  I will keep you and Sully alive in their hearts by telling them all that I know about their parents." Cora said.  Both women quietly sobbed and before Zennie drifted off to sleep she looked into Cora's eyes and whispered, "*Bahala na.*"

Cora new the familiar phrase well, it meant, *what will be will be.*  When she was confident that Zennie was asleep, Cora went to her quarters to prepare for her shift.

The next morning when her shift ended, Cora stopped in Zennie's ward to check on her. "I'm sorry, Cora," the attending nurse said. "She slipped into a coma last night.

Her vital signs are very weak, she can't last much longer."

"I'll stay with her."

*Why? There is no justice here! This is all because the Japs are not giving us food and Zennie is such a good mother that she would rather starve than see her children hungry!*

An hour later Zennie died, with her friend holding her hand. Cora stepped out of the ward and sobbed. *The twins, I have to see the twins. No, they are asleep. I'll take them through the breakfast chow line and after they eat I'll take them to the shanty and tell them. I will explain that I promised their mother that I would take care of them. I'll get another one of the mothers to care for them at night and I'll watch after them during the day. Yes, that will work.* Cora wiped her eyes and walked to the dormitory.

"Mrs. Sanchez, Zennie died last night," Cora whispered to the older woman the children call "Grandma Sanchez." As Cora expected there was no reaction. Many of the internees, especially the elderly and ill, no longer expressed feelings. "She asked me to care for Patrick and Peggy and I plan to, but I need someone to watch them during the night. If you will do that for me, I will tuck them in before going to work and be here to take them through the morning chow line." Cora studied the woman's expressions and added, "Will you watch them for me?"

"Yes, I can do that. They are good children, Zennie was a good woman."

Off in a corner the twins were playing with other children while Cora spoke with Mrs. Sanchez. When they saw her approaching they ran to greet her. Cora stooped down, held out her arms and received their hugs. *They are so small for their age, they should be gaining weight.*

While they were still cradled in her arms Cora said, "I came to have breakfast with you."

"Yeah!" they shouted jumping up and down. Patrick ran over to the old woman, "Grandma Sanchez, Miss Cora is going to breakfast with us." Without waiting for a response he skipped back to his sister and Cora. Hand-in-hand they walked to the chow line.

Cora had eaten at the hospital but managed to get another meal ticket so she could give the twins, her new family, extra food.

After receiving a banana for breakfast, Cora took the children to the shanty and gave each one half of her banana and a few raisins left over from her comfort kit. She did not like raisins, but hoped they did.

"Can we go see Mama again today?" Peggy asked.

Cora turned away then lowered herself onto the lawn chair.

"Can we Miss Cora?" Patrick asked as he and Peggy sat on the ground next to her.

"Children, I want you to be brave because I have some bad news." Cora pulled them close to her. "Last night your mama went to live with Jesus. She wanted to stay here with you, but she was too sick and Jesus will take care of her."

"You mean like Daddy?" Peggy responded.

"Yes. Peggy, like your daddy." Cora felt their little bodies shake and she tightened her grip on them.

"We won't ever see her again?" Patrick asked.

"No, not until we are all in heaven, then we will all be together."

The three cried.

"Yesterday, your mama asked me to take care of you and I promised her I would because I love you very much and I loved your mama too. Grandma Sanchez will be with you at night while I work at the hospital and I'll take care of you during the day and tuck you in at night. You will still go to school and after school you may come here and visit with Miss Claire and Miss Betsy too. Okay?"

"Yes, Miss Cora."

"They love you and I'm sure they would like for you to call them Aunt Claire and Aunt Betsy. How does that sound?"

They each whimpered, "Fine."

"Your mama wants you to go on to school and do the things you do everyday like you did when she was here and I will try to learn how to care for you, but I will need your help." Cora pushed them back and looked into their little tear stained faces.

"Will you be our mama now?" Peggy asked looking into Cora's eyes.

"I can never take the place of your mama, Peggy, but yes, I guess I am your new mama."

"What are we supposed to call you?" Patrick asked as Peggy looked on clutching Lulu.

Cora stammered searching for an answer. "What do you want to call me?"

The twins looked at each other and said nothing.

"Why don't you think about it and let me know when you decide, until then you can still call me Miss Cora. Okay?"

Patrick looked at his sister as they thought about their decision. Peggy hunched her shoulders and Patrick nodded his head as they said, "Okay."

"Now it's time to go to school." She inspected each child then gave each one a kiss and a hug. "I love you," she said. "You come back here after school, I'll be waiting for you." She watched them walk toward the education building and several yards away Peggy reached over and took Patrick's hand in hers.

Later in the morning the guards allowed a few vendors into camp and Cora retrieved the last of the money received from the soldiers on Corregidor. The prices continued to increase and she was appalled that it now cost one dollar and eighty cents for a loaf of bread. She bought it and two eggs for her new family. *I wonder how Flint would feel about marrying me and the children?* Keeping that thought she tried to sleep on the floor of the shanty protected from the hot sun.

Cora dreamed of being dressed in a long formal gown and long silk gloves sitting at a banquet table filled with meats, vegetables and desserts. Before she could make a decision on what to take first, she jerked her eyes open. Patrick and Peggy were squatting beside her and staring into her face. Worried expression on their faces changed as she sat up. *Oh dear, they must have thought I was dead.* She quickly hugged them and asked how school was and what they had learned.

Cora sent the children to play with their friends after Claire and Betsy arrived. After hearing about their friend Zennie's death and Cora's new responsibilities, Claire agreed to stay at the shanty and guard the bread and eggs while Cora and Betsy took the children through the evening chow line.

"I'll go later or just have a slice of bread and jam.

I'm really too tired to eat," she said.

When they returned with their watery vegetable broth, Cora scrambled the eggs using her Pacquins cold cream as fat. She divided the eggs between Patrick and Peggy.

Her first attempt at establishing a bedtime routine included reading the children a story from a library book Claire had brought them. Next, Cora made a half of a peanut butter and jam sandwich for everyone. Cora felt guilty that there was no milk to wash it down, but seeing the smiles on the children's faces as they ate made the guilt disappear. When they finished she wiped their faces and walked to the Main Building; a child on each side clinging to her hands.

In their room, they fell into their normal routine of getting ready for bed and Cora observed, helping only when needed. Zennie's bed had been given to another internee, but Mrs. Sanchez's cot was next to Peggy's.

Cora kissed her new son and daughter goodnight before walking over to Mrs. Sanchez. As Cora approached the woman stood and handed her a small bundle. "These are Zennie's things. There are pictures and things the children will appreciate later."

"Thank you, thank you for everything. Cora kissed the woman on the cheek."

Claire and Betsy were waiting outside the Main Building when Cora came out. As the three were walking back to their shanty, they stopped. "Look at that!" Betsy yelled.

"I don't believe it!" Claire added.

"Well, we knew the Japanese Army was making a ten foot security line inside the fence, we just hadn't stop to think that they would take out the shanties in their path."

"I'm glad we had ours built on Hometown Avenue, I don't know what we'd do without our little sanctuary," Claire said. "But I feel sorry for everyone that is losing theirs."

Later that evening, Cora learned more about Zennie as she sifted through her personal belongings. They were the same age. Her parents and the dates of their deaths were recorded in her bible, as was her marriage to Grady Sullivan, his death and the births of their children. Cora entered the date of Zennie's death. She found several pictures tucked inside the pages, one of Zennie as a young girl, one with her standing by Grady and one of her and Grady with a date written on the back, *"Our wedding 6-15-36."* The next photograph was of the twins when they were six months old and the last one was a family picture taken in November of 1941. *I must make a mental note to ask Brice if he knows any Sullvians in Oklahoma – if I ever see him again.*

The Sunday after Zennie's death, Spencer came to the shanty to visit Claire, Betsy, Cora and her new family.

"Patrick, Peggy, I would like for you to meet your new uncle," Cora said. "This is Uncle Spencer."

"Wow! We have an uncle?" Patrick asked.

Cora smiled, "Yes you do."

He said hello to each of the children and asked them if they would like to join him in a game of catch later in the afternoon.

"Yes!" Patrick squealed. "We both have a ball."

"Santa Claus gave them to us," Peggy added, then looking at Cora asked, "Will it be okay to play with them Mama Cora?"

Cora knew her face was beaming with pride at being

called Mama Cora. "Yes of course it will, and Aunt Betsy, Aunt Claire and I will be the cheering section."

The twins were never removed from their routine, but Cora could not interpret their reactions to their mother's death. They played and laughed, but when she would find them alone they were often quiet and somber. Cora knew they missed their mother and she tried to fill their time with activities and still allow time for grieving. They had become inseparable and Cora was thankful they had each other for support.

By the time March arrived, Cora's main concern was finding enough food for Patrick and Peggy. Thanks to Zennie's sacrifices they had received more than most of the children. With the package lines shut down, the camp was not receiving food or messages from the outside. They were shut off from the outside world except for a radio that had been smuggled into camp.

One afternoon while Claire was at the laundry station, Cora and Betsy sat in the shanty watching the twins play with friends. "I'm really worried about the twins getting enough to eat since the Japanese Army took over our food supply," Cora said.

"Don't worry, Cora, you know you can count on Claire and I for help. We'll get food for them," Betsy said.

"I know you will, but they only allow such few vendors in now and without the sympathetic Filipinos we have no one to help us. I can't even request clothing for them." Cora sighed. "We are almost completely cut off from the outside world."

"The vendors that do come in don't sell much because of the high prices," Betsy added.

"There is no coffee any place in camp except the

Japanese-operated Canteen and it is forty pesos a cup!" Cora said.

"Have you heard that none of the patients will be transferred to other hospitals regardless of how serious their illness is?"

"No, but that doesn't surprise me, the death toll is higher everyday."

Claire walked in with the laundry. "What will be next? The new rules and blackout practices are bad enough, but they now have closed the soap shop!"

"The library and the rodent control have been shut down too," Cora said.

"And what about the searches, unannounced searches," Betsy added.

"How much more can we take?" Claire asked.

"As much as the Imperial Japanese Army wants to give us, that's how much!" Betsy said. "We're Americans and we won't give up!"

The new prison commandant, Colonel Yoshie, ordered the internees to sign a revised oath. This differed from the original oath, which stated that the prisoners would not attempt an escape. The new oath stated that the prisoner would comply with all Japanese orders and it had to be signed by the end of April. The internees signed it under duress and added their protests under their signatures.

This was followed by many of the men being placed in labor gangs and working under the eyes of armed Japanese guards. The nurses were forced to practice with few medicines and supplies and the hospital had no plaster of paris; however, the nurses were experts at improvising. During their time at Santo Tomas, they had made cough syrup from boiling onion juice and sugar. The elixir taken from mango leaves was used to treat diabetes, and tea from guava leaves helped dysentery. As a last resort they were ripping old pieces of clothing into triangular bandages to hold set bones.

A new emergency clinic opened, but due to the rush of patients and few nurses, bowls of common medicines that were still available were placed on tables and patients helped themselves.

Food rations were cut again in the spring, and the Executive Committee took the money they had before they were disbanded and bought hogs and bananas, but that did not provide enough for the four thousand internees. Milk delivery was cut again and only ninety-five gallons a day were received.

With sunken eyes and stooped shoulders, the internees walked with a slow shuffle appearing older than their years. By spring most women had lost their hair and many were losing their teeth.

Unscheduled roll calls were in place by the end of May and the internees were not permitted to move during these exercises. The Japanese counted and recounted until they were satisfied everyone was present and exhausted from long periods of standing. Cora first experienced the effects of a prolonged roll call as she was climbing the stairs to her room. She had to freeze with one foot on one step and one on another for two hours in the hot humid stench. With a backache and weakness from hunger, she thought she would faint before the roll call ended.

"I was really disgusted when they reduced our toilet tissue the last time, but now there is none to ration!" Claire commented to Cora as she waited for her children to join her to hear a story. Whispering, she asked, "How much worse can it get?"

"Don't think about it," Cora answered.

The internees did celebrate Decoration Day with a service ending with the reading of the names of the two hundred and forty-nine internees that died while being held at Santo Tomas Internment Camp. Cora and the children attended. At the end of the list of names, a man stepped up to the microphone and began quoting the words to the "Star Spangled Banner." Everyone stood and joined him as the guards stood watch, not realizing the internees were saying their national anthem.

Cora's little garden planted by the shanty was not large enough to supply the food needed for the twins and the three nurses, but it did supplement some meals. They were receiving bananas in the chow line; they ate the peeling as well as the meaty fruit inside attempting to fill their shrinking stomachs.

The worry of starving to death became secondary when the nurses learned they were to inoculate everyone in camp against the plague. Cora, Betsy and Claire learned of their new orders before they met in the chow line.

"That could only mean that cases of the plague are in the vicinity," Cora said. "Or the Japanese are planning to kill everyone with the injection," she whispered so only Claire and Betsy could hear her concerns.

"Yes, and we will be doing it for them," Claire said as they reached the vats of gruel.

"But we have no control over their actions; we have to do as we're told," Betsy said.

"We can't let Patrick and Peggy hear us discuss this or detect our concern, I don't want them to worry" Cora paused. "Oh, how I wish they could have a normal childhood."

The day arrived when the nurses were to give the injections. Under the watchful eyes of the Japanese, the women cheerfully greeted each internee and administered the drug. After the entire camp had been inoculated, with few side effects, the nurses were thankful that it had not been the Japanese's plan to kill them.

News received over a radio hidden in camp reported that the Allies had invaded France. The song, "Over There," blared over the loud speakers and cheers broke out among the internees. Soon after the news the guards began practice drills and Zeros could be seen performing maneuvers over Manila.

The prison guards conducted several searches trying to locate the radio reported to be in the camp. The internees had the contraband in a bucket covered with rags, which they handed to prisoners that had already had their areas searched. It was never found and the internees continued to receive news from outside the camp.

A few days after the internees learned of the invasion of France, the labor gang was ordered to construct a barbed wire fence on top of the new security fence. The order was inhumane considering the men were starving and too ill to work.

* * *

With no cooking oil or fat available, all of the nurses were now using their cold cream to fry tops of plants. "This wouldn't taste too bad if we had some salt to put over it," Cora remarked one evening as they dined on fried grass.

"Well, there is none anywhere at any price," Betsy said.

When summer arrived the internees decided to celebrate the 4th of July in their hearts after the commandant rejected their request for a public celebration. He did, however, permit the children to celebrate by having a costume parade and party.

"Look at me!" Patrick called out to Peggy. "I'm an American cowboy!"

Spencer had found an old mop handle for a horse and Patrick's new mother made him a costume.

"Peggy, you look just like Betsy Ross with your needle and thread," Claire said. "Here is a piece of blue and white material I found, you can use it to represent the American flag you're pretending to make."

During the parade in front of the Main Building, a small child waved an American Flag. The internees held their breath as she passed by the guards. All flags were to have been surrendered and destroyed. As the child continued past the crowd all Americans stood quietly with their hand over their heart. It had been years since they had seen Old Glory. There was not a dry eye in the crowd, and to everyone's surprise the guards did not confiscate the flag.

Later that month, the internee's camp leaders began to use the canned meat and vegetable reserves in hopes of building up strength to aid in survival until the Americans came. It was a last resort, knowing the supplies would only last three months.

\* \* \*

August proved to be worse than July as the internees were ordered to surrender all of their money including the camp funds. Yet during this time of degradation and boredom the internees did not lose faith in the United States. They continually spoke of the Americans arriving any day to rescue them.

"I only have a little borrowed cash left and there is no way I'm going to give it to the Japanese! I will still have to pay off the loan when I get home," Betsy said.

"I agree," Cora said, and Claire nodded.

"It's like we agreed before we got here, cash could be the difference between death and survival," Betsy added.

"And we were right," Claire added.

The food rations were cut twice in September. Domestic animals, pigeons, the camp ducks and all other starving creatures where eaten by the internees. The nurses, like everyone else in camp, became weaker until they could no longer climb the stairs to the second floor of the Main Building without several periods of rest. Cora, Claire and Betsy shared their food with Patrick and Peggy, but the children were listless and couldn't sleep as long as their bodies needed for normal growth development.

During a cloudy morning on September 21, the internees went about their normal routine. Cora, Betsy and Claire finished their shifts and were resting in the shanty.

"I wish those planes would go away so I can get some sleep," Betsy remarked.

"Me too, it's too noisy and crowded in the dormitory and out here we have to put up with the constant roar of those engines," Claire complained.

In a state of drowsiness, Cora opened her eyes and shielded the sun with her hand. "Oh my Goodness!

They're ours! They're ours!" Jumping up and down she continued, "See the white stars and blue circles on the wings! They are ours!"

They heard and saw other prisoners jumping, waving and yelling as the hopes of liberation escalated. Guards quickly herded the jubilant internees into the buildings. Cries of joy and fear burst from the internees. Dancing, hugging and kissing were only a few outward signs of fulfilled dreams.

Inside the buildings the sounds of aircraft could be heard in the distance. When the planes flew over the camp at low altitude, the Japanese were thrown into chaos. Celebrations continued in the dorms.

*The twins, I've got to get to the children!* Cora's heart raced. *No, they will be safe at the school, but I will have to find them if we leave. They must be frightened.* Her bony hands trembled. Cora's thoughts were swirling when the man standing next to her said, "We're so close to getting home that I can smell hotdogs and apple pie!" Comments were being shouted with a new excitement.

The children were returned to their parents and guardians that evening before a curfew with tightened security was put in place for eighteen hundred hours. While confined to the dormitory, Cora, Betsy, Claire, the twins and others sang along with the last three songs playing over the loud speaker, thankful the disc jockey was permitted to continue broadcasting. Appropriately he played, "Pennies from Heaven," "I Cover the Waterfront" and last, "It Looks Like Rain in Cherry Blossom Lane."

The Japanese began to practice their bayonet skills in the middle of STIC, where the internees could witness their expertise. Sirens accompanied the smoke rising above the city from the bombings. Then abruptly, the raids stopped at which time the Japanese set up additional defenses by the education building.

Many Japanese soldiers arrived and firewood was removed from the west pavilion to provide space for additional housing. Tents appeared instantly over the grounds to house the added troops.

"Do you think they plan to use us as body shields or kill us?" Claire asked Spencer during one of the rare times that the four friends were permitted to be together.

"Let's not give up so quickly on the skills of the USA," he answered. "Those Japs are only staying here because they know our military will never bomb a prisoner of war camp."

"I just know they are coming to get us and take us home," Cora said, then added. "I would feel better if I could keep the children with me at night."

"Maybe you can. The Japanese are beginning to get sloppy with the inspections and roll calls," Spencer said.

* * *

The raids and bombings continued for several days in the Manila area. On 15 October American planes were spotted again by the residents of STIC. The Japanese cut the supply of food again that day, but the internees had a renewed hope and began preparations to be rescued. They had air-raid drills and took precautions as they would on the battlefield. The men and women dug trenches for shelter during the bombing and the nurses set up first aid stations with the few supplies available from the Red Cross kits.

"One thing we know for sure is that the Imperial Japanese Army does not care if we live or die," Cora said to Betsy. "And they will not surrender, it would be a disgrace, they would commit suicide before surrendering."

The days passed quickly as all the activity outside of the camp could be heard and inside everyone was talking and trying to predict what would happen next. Many wondered if they had survived only to be killed.

By the end of October, the excitement died down and the deaths the hospital reported had risen from an average of two a month to seven. Disposing of the bodies became a problem, since the corpsmen were too weak to push the camp gurney carrying the bodies, and weakening conditions of the carpenters and the gravediggers prevented them from building coffins and digging graves for the deceased.

Cora, Claire and Betsy did not spend much time talking, they were always tired and hungry. Cora fell several times on her way to and from the hospital due to dizziness caused by lack of food, but she did not give up. She was all the family Patrick and Peggy had and she refused to think of what would become of them if she died.

"My hands shook so bad today I couldn't change a dressing," Betsy said to Cora when they were waiting for Claire to join them in the dorm. "Have you noticed that Claire looks like a skeleton, her beautiful hair is thin and dark circles outline her sunken, dull eyes."

"Yes, she looks a lot like a baby raccoon I rescued when it's mother was killed. It was hungry and frightened just like we are," Cora's voice trailed off.

"I guess we all look like that."

When Claire joined Cora and Betsy, the three watched

from their dormitory room as another cruel order was being carried out. "I would never imagined that the guards would force the male internees to cut down the papaya trees. The fruit is almost ready to be picked!" Claire said. "That would be food for us. That is not fair!"

"This is war and there is nothing fair about war," Betsy reminded them.

By December 1944 there were six or seven internees dying each day and eighty percent of the camp had beriberi. The suffering children begged from the Japanese soldiers until they were ordered to stay away from the office and kitchen.

Cora, Betsy and Claire spent every free minute they had caring for the twins and sharing their food with them. During many of their meals, Cora taught the children nursery rhymes to help take their minds off their hunger.

\* \* \*

"I'm not sure Patrick and Peggy know when the seventh is with all of the confusion in camp but I want to have a birthday party, without gifts and food of course. We can invite their friends and Grandma Sanchez. We can play games and sing songs. What do you think?" Cora asked Betsy, Claire and Spencer while they stood in the chow line.

"It sounds great," Spencer said. "If I can be there, I'll help organize a ballgame if Betsy will help." He glanced at Betsy.

"Swell, I'll do what I can," she answered.

"I'll help you invite the guests," Claire said.

"So it's agreed, the twins will have a birthday party!"

Cora said. "We don't have much time so we had better get started by choosing a time and rounding up their friends."

Three days later a party was held for the five-year old twins. The adults' hopes of being liberated had carried over to the children and they all enjoyed the party.

It soon became obvious that there would be no Christmas celebration this year. Five days before Christmas the rice rations were cut again, this time by ten grams per day.

The internees continued to watch for the allies to rescue them as the days slipped by, and on 23 December the women were confined to their quarters.

"Did you hear who arrived in camp today?" Betsy asked her companions.

"No," they answered.

"The Kempeitia."

"The Kempeitia? Are you sure?"

"Who's that?" Claire asked.

They both looked at her, "You don't know?" Betsy asked.

Claire shook her head.

"They're the equivalent of the Nazi Gestapo, that's who!"

"Oh no! Why are they here?"

Betsy glanced at Cora, "You want to answer that?"

Just then one of the nurses returned to the dormitory from the hospital and announced, "The Kempeitia is searching the hospital right now!"

"What are they looking for?" Several women asked.

"No one seems to know."

"What are we going to do?" Claire asked in a trembling whisper.

Cora and Betsy hunched their slumped shoulders.

"Just wait and pray," Cora said. "I'm going to go find Patrick and Peggy and bring them here."

While she was gone, the Kempeitai searched the Main Building and arrested four men for no apparent reason. When Cora returned with the twins, the nurses' somber mood was obvious. She sat with her arms around the children while telling them stories of America.

On Christmas Eve the residents of STIC received a Christmas greeting, on leaflets dropped on the camp from allied planes. The message was a Christmas blessing for everyone and for the realization of hope in the New Year. The internees gathered the leaflets but were forced to hand them over to the Japanese or spend seven days in jail. Later that day the internees were given bread, a spoonful of jam and some chocolate. No one questioned the motive.

Betsy savored the sweets, but joined Cora and Claire to share with Patrick and Peggy. The children were ecstatic with the treat and the thrill of Christmas.

"This Christmas is going to be different from the others," Cora explained to them. "We will not have any gifts to give each other but we still have love to share."

"That's okay, Mama Cora. We're older now and we don't need presents," Patrick informed her.

Peggy held on to Lulu and lowered her gaze, then reluctantly nodded in agreement with her brother.

Betsy was busy cutting up the cigars the adults received to make cigarettes. She glanced at Cora and raised her brow but made no comment.

Cora continued talking as the children enjoyed their treat.

"We're going to sing Christmas carols and make plans to celebrate our next Christmas in the United States.

How's that sound?"

"Yea!" both children yelled.

"Will we have snow?" Patrick asked.

"I hope so." Cora smiled. "When you finish eating, you may go play with your friends," Cora said. "But if you see planes flying over, you must come to my dormitory quickly and if Aunt Betsy, Aunt Claire or I am not here I want you to wait for us. Do you understand?"

"Yes Mama Cora," they answered and sauntered away.

Cora turned her attention to Betsy and Claire.

"This blue paper is from the last shipment of bandages," Betsy said as she worked rolling a thin wobbly cigarette.

"We don't have any matches!" Claire exclaimed.

Cora produced three matches hidden in her pocket.

On New Years day the Japanese, intent on starving their prisoners to death, cut the rice ration to about four ounces per person and that included the worms and mold. Even the cup of vegetable gruel served every twenty-four hours did not dampen the internees' hopes of soon being liberated.

Cora looked out of a window from the second floor of the Main Building and witnessed the Japanese running around in a disorganized fashion tossing boxes and bundles of papers onto a roaring fire.

"Quick, over here. Look," she called out to Betsy and Claire who were trying to sleep.

Both women arrived at the window and didn't understand what they were seeing. "The Japs are burning their records; that means they are expecting company and *they* will become the prisoners," Cora said.

"You're right!" Betsy said.

Claire yawned, "I'm afraid to go back to sleep, I want to be alert when our guys arrive." She yawned again and falling onto her cot she hummed, "When Johnny Comes Marching Home Again."

The end of January found everyone starving and one of the hospital's physicians was placed in the camp jail because he refused to change the cause of death from starvation to natural causes on the death certificates of eight internees. He was told it was an insult to the Japanese Army, but he stood firm.

Exploding bombs were constant as the starving internees were gasping for their last breath. Many died everyday, there was nothing the nurses or anyone could do. Cora checked every morning to make sure Grandma Sanchez was alive and able to watch Patrick and Peggy.

On the first day of February a group of male internees were ordered to kill the last of the two remaining water buffalo for the Japanese to have meat. They were given no guns. They were forced to beat them to death with clubs, which was cruel and nearly impossible for the weak emaciated men.

"Thanks, Claire," Cora said learning that Claire happened onto a group of children watching the event. Claire had quickly removed the twins from the group and took them to the dormitory where she put them on empty cots for a nap.

"So many horrible incidents are embedded in their little minds, I hope someday they will be able to forget all of the bad things that happened here," Cora said looking down at the sleeping children.

"I wonder what the Japs will do next," Cora said.

She did not have to wait long for an answer. The following day they further humiliated the starving internees by destroying the few remaining vegetables in the camp garden and the small amount of remaining fruit.

Cora continued giving hope and care to the ill, but each day she found it harder to answer their questions about being rescued.

Back in her room on 3 February the twins sat on a cot playing a game they had made up. Cora watched and appreciated their good behavior and the fact they came to the dormitory to wait for her and their two aunts like she had told them to do after the water buffalo experience.

"Let's all go out and get some fresh air," she said to Patrick and Peggy.

"Okay," they answered. Cora hoped the fresh air would give them more energy. There was constant noise from fighting going on north of the camp. Cora needed to be with her friends to get her mind off the sounds.

"Want to go to the shanty and see if anyone is there?" she asked.

All she received was a nod, and they held her hands as they made the short trip to where they found Betsy and Claire resting. Patrick had his ball with him and Peggy was clinging to her doll. She sat Lulu up so she could watch her play catch with her brother.

"They are normal five year olds in less than normal surroundings," Claire said watching them play.

At seventeen hundred hours, the three women heard a roar overhead and ran outside the shanty, looking up in time to see ten American planes flying over the camp. As they looked up, one of the planes broke formation and dipped down barely clearing the buildings. They watched as the pilot extended his arm out of the cockpit and dropped something. Men on a clean-up detail ran to retrieve it before the guards knew what was happening. They found the pilot's goggles with a note attached. The message quickly spread through camp. It read, **"Roll out the barrel, Santa Claus is coming."**

# Chapter Seventeen

## 3 February 1945

Again the internees were ordered to their rooms. Cora took the twins with her as she, Claire and Betsy rushed to the Main Building. That night Patrick slept with her and Peggy slept with Claire. The medical staff working in the hospitals were not permitted to leave and the people scheduled to relieve them were told to stay in their quarters.

"Spencer isn't on duty, so he is in his dormitory too," Claire informed Cora and Betsy before she slept.

Darkness came, "Where are they? How will we know when they get here? It is so dark I can't see anything," Betsy said pressing her nose against the dormitory window.

"Get away from there! You know the guards said they would shoot anyone they caught looking out of the windows!" Cora said.

"I want to know what's going on and when they get here," Betsy said.

"We'll know, but you need to come to bed and get some sleep before they come," Cora said and drifted off to sleep.

"Cora, wake up!" Betsy whispered shaking her shoulders.

"What is it? Are they here?"

"No, but I saw a Japanese soldier placing a barrel under the stairway leading to the second floor. To our quarters!" Her voiced raised slightly.

"You left the room?" Cora sat up. "What were you thinking! You could have been killed!"

"But I wasn't. After he left I checked the barrel and found it filled with rags and gasoline! I came back as soon as I could. I think the Japs are planing to burn us up in this building."

"Slow down Betsy," Cora said taking hold of Betsy's trembling arms. "We will keep a watch on the stairs and if they do try to light it we will get everyone out, they can't stop all of us. Wake Claire and we'll go around and quietly wake everyone else and tell them what you saw."

"But there is no water," Betsy reminded her. "We'll have to beat the flames with our mattresses."

"We'll worry about that later, right now we need to awaken everyone and warn them," Cora said.

After all of the nurses were alerted, fumes began drifting into their dormitory. Before they could react a loud rumble coming from outside of the gates shook the Main Building. At first no one would speculate, but one brave nurse said, "I bet that is our troops coming after us." They agreed but fear forced them to remain quiet.

"Just listen to that rumble, that's the sound of heavy equipment," Cora whispered. "Those fumes are coming from outside! It's gasoline fumes!" At that moment flames engulfing Manila lit the sky.

"But whose equipment?" Claire whispered. Betsy and Cora looked at her and said nothing.

"Is it time to get up?" Patrick asked rubbing his eyes.

Cora said, "Yes honey it is. Will you get your sister up and tell her to be very quiet?"

"Yes ma'am."

The nurses heard the Japanese shouting, then they heard gunfire, "I think it's coming from inside the walls," Betsy said.

"Stay away from that window!" Cora shouted pulling her from the guard's view. The three stood like statues and the twins squeezed tighter against Cora; her arms protected them like a mother hen's wings as the gates came down with a great thunderous crash.

"They are going to kill us, I just know they are," Claire said under her breath.

"Don't talk like that, we've got to be brave," Cora whispered.

"Listen, they are coming across the field toward us," Betsy said as searchlights flashed across the camp. She peeked out the window, "There's a man walking in front of a big tank." She leaned out the window. "The whole camp is lit up! It looks like it is daylight. The tank stopped at our front door!" The nurses held their breath thinking it would be their last. Not a sound came from inside the structure. The silence was maddening.

"Hi folks! Are there any Americans in there?" A booming voice called out.

A stampede erupted as the prisoners raced outside, some praying, others singing "God Bless America" and all with tears in their eyes and smiles on their faces.

The men lit up the camp with flares then asked for

help for the wounded that they brought with them. Cora, Betsy and Claire stayed together making sure the twins were not trampled.

"Is this really happening?" Claire asked.

The twins had been quiet, but Patrick tugged on Cora's skirt, "Mama Cora, are they giants?"

Cora could not hold back her tears and laughter. "No Patrick, those are tall healthy American soldiers." Cora heard the call for medics and started to look through the crowd. A wife of one of the American missionaries appeared and said, "Cora they need you. I'll watch the children." Betsy, Claire and Cora rushed toward the truck of wounded Americans. Suddenly it was Bataan and Corregidor all over again. They worked alongside the only Army doctor with the unit and several medics.

Meanwhile, the Japanese stayed in the Education building with hostages, cutting off the main route to the hospital. Rather than take the wounded through the line of crossfire, a temporary hospital was set up in the Main Building lobby. Cora became faint as she tried to work fast, but her strict discipline got her through the moment and she did the job she had joined the army to do.

Cora helped support a wounded soldier as he hobbled to a bed in a dormitory they had quickly transformed into a ward.

"When you get him into bed give him an injection of penicillin," the army doctor ordered.

Cora's sunken eyes stared at him. "What?"

"Penicillin."

She didn't move.

"Oh my God, you don't know what penicillin is do you?"

She shook her head.

"It's a new drug, I'll tell you about it later." He took a bottle from his bag, filled a syringe and gave the injection himself. "Do you have sulfa powder?"

"Yes, but it's in the hospital." A medic helping her with the casualties confused her as he kept referring to each soldier as a GI

"Why are you calling him a GI? What does it mean?" Cora asked the young man.

"You don't know?"

She shook her head.

"It means Government Issue. That's what we are, so we shortened it and call ourselves GIs." He stopped working and studied her face. "You've been here a long time, haven't you?"

"Yes sir, we all have."

"There's a chocolate bar in my shirt pocket," he said. "I'd be pleased if you would eat it ma'am." He smiled. She took it thanking him. After two bites Cora placed the remainder in her pocket for the children. Like all of the nurses and doctors, she pushed her exhausted body until the job was finished.

When the sun rose Cora saw Betsy eating from a can. "What's that?"

"It's K-rations, all of the soldiers carry their meals with them." She offered Cora a bite, "Here try it, it's really good."

"You mean they take their food into battle with them?"

"Yes." Betsy handed Cora a bite.

"Wow that is good!" Cora said.

A passing soldier heard her and responded, "Boy, you

272

must be starved if you think that's good!" Then realizing that she was starving, he cleared his throat and apologetically said, "Here, you can have mine too and here are two chocolate bars."

Betsy glanced at Cora, "The woman is still watching the twins up in our dormitory, why don't you take this to them. You need a break; Patrick and Peggy need to know that you are okay?"

"Thanks, they will be so thrilled to see this food, and maybe they will sleep better after they eat."

The Japanese surrendered that morning and were taken out of camp and the internees held a flag raising ceremony. The American Flag brought reassurance to the prisoners that they really were liberated as they watched new troops, food, equipment and medical supplies arriving through the broken down main gate.

The wounded patients were moved to the hospital and the new medical personnel cared for them and the internees.

While the children napped, Cora went for a walk to survey the changes taking place.

"Cora! Cora!"

Turning, she tried to focus on the large man wearing khaki clothes and hiding behind a bushy beard. He ran towards her and took her in his arms. Neither spoke as he kept a gentle grip on her debilitating body. "Brice, is it really you or am I dreaming?" She said when she gathered her strength.

"It sure is, darling." He stared at her, and through his expression she realized how terrible she looked. Embarrassed for him she began to back away and his grip on her arms relaxed as he asked, "Are my other two darlings okay too?" His voice cracked.

"They sure are and so is Spencer!"

"Spencer! Here?"

"Yes, we're all here but Flint. Come with me, I think they are all at the hospital," she said placing her frail hand in his strong rough hand. "How did you hear about the invasion? We thought you were out in the jungle with a guerrilla outfit."

"I was. We made contact with the 1st Calvary Division and they needed our help." He stopped and looked at her. "How did you know where I was?"

"Who do you think got messages out to you?" She grinned. "Our Claire!"

"Betsy will explain it all to you," she smiled and they walked toward the hospital. *This feels right. No more bowing or starving. God Bless America.*

"You women never cease to amaze me."

"I didn't see any other guerrillas here, was your unit small?"

"No, but after we helped free the Bataan Death March survivors I heard Santo Tomas was going to be liberated, so I found out what outfit would be coming in and when they would be coming."

"Bataan Death March? Is that what they call the march Spencer escaped from?"

"Oh, I guess you wouldn't know about that since you came here straight from Corregidor." He lowered his head and shook it. "Yes, that's what Spencer escaped from before he arrived on Corregidor, but we'll talk about it another time." He glanced around his surroundings. "Hey don't look so gloomy, this is a time to celebrate!"

Cora looked up at him and smiled as they continued

toward the hospital past an army detail making caskets for those that had died during the liberation. Neither spoke of what they were witnessing.

* * *

"Look!" Spencer called to Claire, motioning for her to join him at the window.

"What is it?" Claire arrived at the window. "I don't believe it! It looks like Brice."

"Let's go see," grabbing her arm they hurried outside in time to meet Brice and Cora on the marble steps.

As soon as the excitement began to let up, Cora said, "I'm going to go look for Betsy."

In the surgical wing she was informed that Betsy had been given orders to get some rest. Cora assumed that she would go to the shanty, so after reporting to the others they walked to Hometown Avenue. From a distance they could see her sitting in a chair with her back to them.

"Brice, you go first and then we will be along," Spencer suggested.

The trio stood eagerly watching him run to the shanty. He knocked on the side and yelled, "Anybody home?"

Betsy jumped knocking over the lawn chair and flew into his open arms in one uninterrupted move.

"Shall we join them?" Spencer asked.

Cora and Claire nodded as Brice waved for them to come and join in the reunion. Five of the six friends enjoyed each other's company again.

An hour later, Cora jumped up, "Oh my, I forgot about the twins, they will be wondering what happened to me."

Brice's mouth opened, then after several seconds he asked, "What twins?"

"You'll see," Cora answered and left.

"Bring them here to meet Uncle Brice," Spencer called out as Cora hurried toward the Main Building.

Cora turned and yelled, "I will. You three explain it to him."

She was right; the twins had awakened from their nap and were worrying about her. Cora hugged each of them. "I have a surprise for you."

"More chocolate?" Patrick asked.

"No, it is a very special someone that I want you to meet."

"Who?" Two sets of big brown eyes widened.

"Uncle Brice. He is a real live cowboy from the United States," she answered.

Cora detected a slight sparkle she had not seen in months. "Are you ready?"

"Yes," they sang.

Cora thanked the lady that had stayed with them, and with a child holding each of her hands Cora proceeded toward her friends.

Both children appeared shy when they reached the shanty, but Uncle Brice soon took care of that. He took each child for a ride on his strong shoulders. They giggled and squealed and didn't want to stop when Cora told them Brice needed to rest.

"Does Flint know about your new family?" Brice asked Cora.

"Yes. Or at least I hope he does. I've written several letters to him, but I couldn't tell him much in case the letters didn't make it out of camp. I couldn't put the children in danger."

"Speaking of letters," Betsy said, "I was told that we can write letters to our families now and the army will send them for us."

"How many words are they allowing us to write?" Claire asked.

"As many as we want! We're free!" Cora exclaimed.

"Oh that is great, but I don't know where to begin."

"I think we need to write to our families and let them know we are alive and hope to be home soon," Spencer said. "We want their torture to end too."

The Red Cross contingent arrived on 6 February with forty-four hundred airmail letters for the internees, and later that day fourteen truckloads of food and supplies arrived from Lingayen.

The army took over the kitchens as the internees were receiving their mail. Cora received several letters from her mother and Doc. She had twelve letters from Flint and she anxiously arranged all of her mail by date. When she arrived at the shanty she found Betsy and Claire quietly reading their mail.

Cora started with Flint's letters. *There are none after June of last year.* She sorted through the stack of mail again. Nothing. *Did he learn that we were not getting mail? Yes that's it, I must have written it in one of my letters.* She released a sigh of relief. *That has to be it.*

Flint wrote of his work and the future, but Cora began to sense a tired worn spirit in him as she progressed through the letters, something she had never seen in him.

Claire was the first to break the silence. "Look, a picture of Courtney," she held it up for the others to see. "She has grown so much since I last saw her. I hope I never have to leave her again," she said holding the picture close to her chest.

"I'm an aunt, twice!" Betsy exclaimed. "Wow! Now I have two nieces and two nephews." She went back to reading her mail.

Doc's letters to Cora were pep talks and health reports. He included information on everyone in the mining community he treated or talked with and always included a detailed report on her mother's condition. He mentioned people she had not thought of since she had left home.

Cora finished reading the mail and realized that the only good news from Flint was that he loved her and looked forward to seeing her.

"What did Flint say?" Claire asked when she finished her last piece of mail.

"His last letter was not upbeat like the others, he sounded tired and discouraged."

"When was it written?"

Cora burst into tears. "Eight months ago," she sobbed.

Claire went to her and put her arms around her. Betsy stopped reading and said, "That doesn't mean anything Cora, he probably knows we weren't getting mail."

"Yeah, or maybe there is mail that hasn't caught up with you yet," Claire added.

"I know, you are probably right, but still I'm worried about him."

After Cora had stopped sobbing, the women saw Brice and Spencer walking toward them. Cora smiled; it was good to have her friends with her.

"We came to escort you ladies to a spectacular dinner," Brice announced. He looked around, "Where are your kids, Cora?"

"Over there," she pointed to a small group playing a game that was being supervised by a young sergeant.

Brice spotted the children and left to get them.

"He hasn't changed has he?" Spencer remarked.

"He doesn't appear to have," Betsy answered then quickly added, "But I'm sure he has. We all have."

"Yes, I suppose we all have our nightmares to live with," Spencer said as Brice returned with a giggling child dangling under each arm.

"Come on, let's go to the mess area," Brice said. "I hear the army is serving good old American food."

"What's that Mama Cora?" Patrick asked.

"You'll see. It's the best food in the whole world!"

They followed the aroma of real food. The meal was an American feast of hot dogs, bake beans and several green vegetables. Seeing Patrick and Peggy drinking milk brought a smile to Cora and their aunts and uncles. Apple pie was served for the desert and not a crumb was left on their plates.

Cora hated to ration the children's food, but did not want them becoming ill. "We'll take the leftover food to the shanty and you can have it after your nap."

Four sad eyes questioned her until she said, "Uncle Brice and Uncle Spencer will not allow anyone to take your food. I promise."

Then they nodded their approval.

That night after Cora tucked her children into bed, she sat with them until they were asleep. Her thoughts returned to the events of the last few days, *I have much to be thankful for and a future with these two lovely children.*

*I can't lose faith; I've got to believe that Flint is alive.*

During the next few days the internees became stronger and were pleased when more help arrived on 9 February. One hundred army nurses came to care for the internees, including the imprisoned nurses. The internee nurses were relieved of their duties and ordered to eat and rest.

"Do you think we ever looked as healthy and happy as they do?" Claire asked Betsy and Cora as they watched healthy nurses jumping off the army trucks.

"I'm not sure, but it's amazing how much better I feel since I've been eating bread and meat," Cora said.

"Well, I know the chocolate has helped my strength and attitude," Betsy said.

"Especially your attitude," Cora and Claire said in unison.

The next day Cora, Betsy and Claire heard that the nurses were going to be the first to leave Santo Tomas. The Sullivan twins were approved to travel to the United States in the care of 2$^{nd}$ Lieutenant Cora L. Adams.

The nurses began saying their good-byes to friends, and Cora took Patrick and Peggy to visit their friends before leaving. Cora made sure the children said good-bye to their teachers and their mother's friends, before she sought out a special few she wanted to see.

"We're going to America!" Patrick shouted to some of the older children.

"Stop showing off Patrick!" Peggy said. "It's not polite." Cora smiled realizing she was caught up in the twins' excitement.

They eagerly prepared for the trip but Cora continued to worry about Flint. She wrote letters to her mother, Flint and Doc informing them of her return to the United States.

Cora held on to the bundle of her children's few possessions and the special mementos Zennie had given her plus her own belongings. Clutching a ball and Lulu, Patrick and Peggy anxiously stood by Cora waiting. The news that the nurses were being taken out of Santo Tomas in ten minutes came over the loud speaker. Claire and Betsy dropped their bags by Cora.

"We're going to say good-bye to Brice and Spencer and review our plans to meet back in the States," Betsy said darting toward the men's dormitory.

The anxious group waited for the open trucks to pull up in front of the Main Building. *We're leaving the same way we entered.* Cora could not help but think of how her life had changed since August 1942.

Soldiers helped the female medical personnel and the twins onto the trucks. No one looked back as they were driven to Dewey Boulevard where the U.S. aircraft had landed. Patrick and Peggy held tightly to Cora's hands as they walked toward the plane. "I didn't know it would be so big," Peggy said.

"I did," Patrick told her. "Our Daddy flew one of these. He could fly anything because he was an American."

"We're going to be fine Peggy," Cora said sensing the child's fears. "There is no need to be frightened, all planes are noisy when you are close to them but inside they are quiet."

After a difficult take-off due to antiaircraft fire, the nurses were on the first leg of their trip home. Later the plane was forced to make an unscheduled landing due to engine trouble. Two planes were then secured for the women to continue on to Leyte where those in need of medical care would be admitted to the hospital.

When they arrived at Lyete, the nurses and twins were given physical examinations. Cora, Betsy, Claire and the twins were found to need rest and nutritious meals, which they received during the eight-day stay.

"Look, Mama Cora!" the twins shouted as they climbed onto real beds in their temporary quarters.

Cora realized the children did not remember real beds. "Yes, aren't they lovely?" *I wish Zennie could be here to see her children's reactions to their new surroundings and experiences.*

Before leaving Leyte the nurses were given Army Class A dress uniforms flown in from Australia. The winter uniform was dark olive-green wool and the summer uniform was white seersucker. This change of dress had occurred while the women were in captivity.

"Once we fill them out properly they will look much better," Betsy said as the three met wearing new uniforms. "I'll accept them as a late birthday gift from Uncle Sam," Betsy said admiring her uniform in a mirror.

"Oh no, in all of the excitement we forgot your birthday! Can you ever forgive us?" Claire asked.

"Are you kidding. You all have given me the best gift possible," Betsy's voice quivered. "You helped me survive to see another birthday. I can never thank you enough."

The three hugged before rushing out to join the other nurses for a special awards ceremony. Having disposed of their lethal dose of morphine, the women had their hair curled and applied makeup. They looked and felt feminine again as they stood on stage to accept their promotions. Cora, Claire and Betsy all received the Presidential Citation and a Bronze Star with two clusters of oak leaves, and they each were promoted one grade.

"I can't believe how tiring all of these interviews are," Claire said to her friends after several hours of debriefing and talking with reporters.

"I know, every time I try to take the twins someplace there is a photographer snapping our pictures," Cora said.

"Privacy is all any of us want," Betsy said. "Is that so difficult for the reporters to understand?"

"Apparently so; I do not want my picture turning up in newspapers or magazines! I'm trying to avoid having my picture taken but it isn't easy," Claire said.

"You don't look so bad Claire, and I'm sure you would look better than most of us in the papers," Cora said.

"Maybe, but I cannot have my face showing up in papers across the country. I just want to be left alone! The reporters could ruin my life!"

Betsy looked at Cora and shrugged her shoulders and Cora rolled her eyes letting Betsy know that she did not understand Claire's anger either. This was a side of Claire they had never seen.

Out of desperation the nurses requested they be isolated from the press. Their request was granted and they were moved to a secluded area, the 1st Convalescent Hospital located on the beach. The private beach provided the atmosphere they desired and they were able to get the relaxation they had dreamed of for years. Patrick and Peggy enjoyed playing in the sand and ocean, as normal children should.

While enjoying their last meal before boarding the C-54E to fly to Honolulu, Claire asked, "Cora, have you noticed how healthy the twins are looking?"

"Yes, and they are happy all the time, but I do think that Patrick could become a little butterball if I don't watch his diet." They laughed.

Hearing the conversation, Betsy said, "I understand you have begun rationing the Coca-Colas."

"Yes, I had to, I don't know how many he would drink if I didn't. The dentist also told him not to drink to many or eat too many sweets, but I don't think the dentist made a very lasting impression on either of them," Cora said with a glint in her eye.

Later, Cora held the twins' hands and said, "Come on children, let's go." She guided them up the steep steps onto a C-54 for the next stint of their trip home. Patrick clutched his new toy car and Peggy held Lulu close to her chest. After stowing their meager belongings, they shared a window seat with Cora next to them in the isle seat. The engines roared causing the plane to shake before gaining altitude; the wide-eyed children peered out the window. The cheering passengers were on their way to Honolulu, a flight that would take twenty-four hours.

"Our daddy flew a plane with a blue star on it just like this one," Peggy informed Cora.

"Yes, he did. He was a very brave American." Cora leaned back and tried to put the past where it belonged and focus on her future with hopes of Flint being a part of it. The plane soared above the clouds over the Pacific Ocean as she dreamed and the children slept.

Seated across the aisle, Betsy leaned over to Cora, "When do you think Spencer and Brice will get home?"

She shrugged her shoulders, "Soon I hope. When we get to Honolulu, I hope I will find out were Flint is too."

"Claire and I will help."

"Thanks. If I can't get information there when I get to the States, I'll contact the Ohio Valley Hospital like we planned."

## Chapter Eighteen

Arriving at Hickam Field in Honolulu, the nurses were met in much the same way they were when they arrived in Manila in 1941 – A cheering crowd and an army band playing the "Star Spangled Banner." The nurses stepped off the plane again to face ill-mannered photographers and reporters. After two days of being pampered and interviewed in Honolulu, they were flown to San Francisco on two C-54's.

"I don't want to talk to anyone, especially the Army officers with all of their questions and insinuations. I just want to get to a room and get some rest," Claire said as the plane descended off the California coast.

"So do I and these two sleepy children need to get some sleep." Cora responded.

"Me too," Betsy said from where she was standing for a better view of the Golden Gate bridge. "And a big chocolate milkshake!" Cora smiled remembering only a few days ago how she and Claire tried to keep her from looking out the window and getting shot.

A large gathering of fifteen hundred people, including the press, friends and families were bobbing up and down hoping for a glimpse of the nurses as the plane taxied up the runway. From the windows many of the nurses recognized relatives and friends frantically waving to them.

As they exited the plane the army band played "Stars and Stripes Forever." Ignoring orders to remain together for a ceremony, the nurses bolted into the crowd and into the arms of mothers, fathers, brothers, sisters, fiancés, husbands, loved ones and friends. The reporters and photographers were like vultures attacking their victims; only these buzzards had plans to exploit their prey – the war heroines.

Claire bolted into the crowd, but Cora and Betsy knew there was no one to greet them so they remained with the few other nurses waiting for the ceremony to begin.

"Betsy! Betsy!" Cora turned toward the voice and watched her friend being swept up into the arms of a handsome Marine.

Minutes later he set her down and Betsy motioned to Cora and the children, "Come here, I want you to meet my youngest brother Robert." Before Cora could respond Robert, swept her off her feet and whirled her around, then he did the same with the twins. When he set them down, Cora put her hands out for the children sensing their fear; they took hold of her hands immediately and held tightly. Cora pulled them close to her and backed up to get them out of the jubilant crowd; that is when she spotted Claire fighting her way through the mob.

Tears flooded Cora's eyes as she watched Claire embrace Courtney, then her Aunt and Uncle. *I could have picked that child out in any crowd,* Cora thought. *She is a miniature Claire.*

A couple of minutes later Claire dragged them toward Cora and Betsy. Cora explained to Patrick and Peggy who they were about to meet and they smiled as the three strangers approached. After a brief reunion the nurses assembled for the "Welcome Home" ceremony.

The tired nurses, in oversized uniforms and lips covered with red lipstick, stood while endless speeches were given with no respect to their physical or mental condition. Brigadier General Raymond W. Bliss thanked God for their safe return during his speech, then the mayor of San Francisco spoke followed by a representative of the San Francisco Chamber of Commerce.

When the ceremony ended, the nurses, Patrick and Peggy were loaded onto army trucks and taken to Letterman General Army Hospital for more medical exams and debriefings.

With an arm around each child Cora said, "This is a fun ride isn't it?"

They reluctantly nodded.

"Look at all of the automobiles! Aren't they beautiful?"

"I like that one," Patrick said pointing to a shiny black police car. Cora explained what it was and how the policemen were nice and if they ever needed help they should look for a policeman. She knew they didn't understand now, but hoped they soon would adjust to their new surroundings.

Peggy held Lulu as she watched the people walking on the streets in bright stylish clothes. "Pretty, aren't they?" Cora asked.

"Yes ma'am."

"Soon I will take you shopping and buy nice clothes for both of you and Lulu."

They arrived at Letterman and found the accommodations to be better than expected for an army facility. Their rooms contained vases of flowers, boxes of candy and best of all boxes of Kleenex. Patrick spotted the box of candy before they were inside the room. Cora opened the box and all three enjoyed one piece of rich chocolate cream. "We will have another piece tomorrow. There will be plenty of candy so we don't have to eat it all now and I don't want you to hide it." She looked into their faces and when she smiled they giggled.

Cora showed the children what the tissues were for and when they kept insisting their noses were runny, Cora allowed them to use all of the Kleenex they wanted. "Are there Kleenex in Aunt Claire and Aunt Betsy's rooms too?" Peggy asked.

"Yes, and we girls use them to remove our make-up." Cora took a tissue and removed her lipstick; later she saw Peggy pretending to do the same.

"Look Peggy, Lulu's nose is runny too." Patrick pulled out a tissue and wiped the doll's nose.

*They have so much to learn and so many fears to get over and forget.* Cora thought while watching them play with the new toys they received in Lyete and the few things she brought from STIC.

With no family of their own to visit them, Claire and Betsy shared their relatives with Cora, Patrick and Peggy. Patrick liked Betsy's brother Robert and loved listening to stories about Aunt Betsy. "Aunt Betsy told us about your dog Fluffy," Patrick said and Robert grinned as he told stories that included the pet.

Courtney and the twins became instant friends and she read them stories from one of their new books.

"She sounds so much like Claire, except her New England accent is much stronger," Betsy said to Cora as they listened to the story too. "She acts like a big sister to the twins doesn't she?"

"She has a good model to follow," Cora said glancing at Claire. Their gaze locked for a second before Claire turned away.

Aunt Irene and Uncle Jake were as nice as Claire had described and they insisted everyone call them Aunt and Uncle. Cora was pleased to see that the twins were comfortable with them.

"I feel like we are all family now," Aunt Irene said.

"We feel the same, we've heard so much about you all," Betsy said. "Especially Courtney."

"You must all come to Maine for a reunion after you are settled," Aunt Irene insisted.

"That's a great idea, I'll be there for sure," Betsy answered looking at Cora.

"We'll be there too but lets make it in the summer. Claire's descriptions of Maine summers sound fantastic," Cora said, as the children attempted to contain their excitement.

The nurses began exploring their new temporary quarters after two days of visiting and debriefing. "Cora! Cora!" Betsy shouted while pounding on the door to Cora's room.

"What?" Cora frantically opened the door.

"I found three of our patients from Bataan here," Betsy said before stopping to catch her breath. "They want you to come and visit them."

"Is Claire in her room?"

"I think so."

"I can go right now if she'll watch the twins," Cora said.

"Hi guys," Betsy said to the twins as they looked up from their coloring books. They stared at her with their big round eyes that had regained their sparkle.

Cora explained to them that Betsy had found friends of theirs that had been hurt and she was going to visit them." Cora knelt to hug the twins, "Don't worry I'll be back soon. You can play with Courtney while I'm gone."

After the children were placed in Claire's care, Betsy and Cora rushed to the patients they had abandoned on Bataan.

"Oh, here come the tears again," Cora said as she approached the first man. "I am so sorry we left you there. We didn't want to go but we were ordered to and . . ."

The wounded soldier attempted to put them at ease, "We understood and we all wanted you to get out before the Japs came. Who knows what they would have done to you," he lowered his gaze. "Don't feel guilty, you did the right thing. No one blames you for going."

"Thank you," they both said before moving on to the next Bataan casualty.

Each patient they visited expressed gratitude for what the nurses had done in the jungle. The words, "We'll never forget you," were repeated over and over.

* * *

When Cora returned to her room she had a telegram from the Red Cross telling her Major Flint Taylor was at Fletcher General Army Hospital in Cambridge, Ohio. "I found him! "I found him!" she shouted running down the hall waving the telegram in the air.

Before she reached Claire's room, Betsy stepped out

into the hall and Claire was in the doorway when they arrived. Cora rushed to her children, "I've found where Uncle Flint is and we will go visit him." The twins joined in the excitement and listened to the stories repeated about the prewar days in Manila.

The next day Betsy told her brother good-bye before joining Cora and the children for a shopping trip. The first store window they came to displayed fashionable hats. The two women reminisced about the day in Manila when they had toured a hat factory. "These hats are quite different, aren't they?" Betsy remarked.

Cora laughed, "Yes the styles have changed. I can't imagine wearing one of those."

With the one hundred fifty dollars they each received in Leyte, Cora shopped at a department store for children's clothing. After purchasing matching sailor outfits and hats, she bought each a winter coat and two play outfits. She and Betsy bought new dresses, a winter coat, hat and soft undergarments that in no way resembled Government Issue.

Cora enjoyed the thrill of shopping again, especially watching the wide-eyed children's reaction.

"Yes, they are yours to keep. No one is going to take them from you." She paused and grinned. "Of course when you outgrow them we'll have to give them away and buy you new clothes."

"Really?" They asked.

"That's right. You are in America now."

Peggy clutched Lulu and looked at Patrick; both of them were sporting large smiles. Cora handed each child a small parcel to carry and they guarded it as though it were a bag of gold. Cora arranged for the remaining purchases to be delivered to the hotel.

"I'm not sure I'll be comfortable wearing this," Betsy said holding up a dress. "The styles are so different now; I'm not even comfortable using the ration books yet." She held the dress next to her body and glanced around. "It's like we've stepped onto another planet."

"Yes, the planet earth," Cora answered. "I've been thumbing through magazines and my mind is having trouble absorbing the new styles. I think it will take quite a while to understand all that has taken place while we were away." *I can't make myself say 'when I was in prison.'*

"Speaking of adjusting, are the twins doing any better using silverware?" Betsy asked.

"I'm not sure. They are so afraid they won't get enough to eat. They start out eating with their forks or spoons, but when they think I'm not watching they eat with their hands," Cora said. "But silverware felt awkward to me too for a while, so it must be very difficult for them. They never really learned how to use a fork or spoon."

"Zennie would be so pleased with how you are caring for them," Betsy said.

"I hope so but I worry about them. They look so much like Japanese children that I'm afraid when they go to school the other children will be mean to them." Cora cleared her throat. "One arrogant reporter has already insinuated that I am their mother and their father was a prison guard."

"How could he? I hope you told him off!" Betsy said.

"After a few choice words, I told him they were war orphans; their father was a U.S. pilot and their mother a Filipino."

"Still, he must be very stupid! The twins were born in 1939, you were still in the states," Betsy said.

"I know, but how many other people will not stop to think about it before they make insulting remarks?"

"You have to learn to ignore them." Betsy paused. "That's why you have been refusing to allow the photographers to photograph the children isn't it?"

"Yes, it also frightens them," Cora said as they left the department store. The children enjoyed riding a cable car to the hotel.

By early March the nurses were cleared to travel home. Claire and her family and Betsy and Cora agreed to travel to Chicago together where Betsy's family would meet the train. After an hour layover they would go their separate ways. Courtney sat with Patrick and Peggy on the train and Aunt Irene and Uncle Jake sat across the isle. Claire, Cora and Betsy sat together sharing plans.

"Can you believe the Brass! Who do they think they are telling us to tell no one what happened to us? Already the reporters are making up their own stories," Betsy said. "And they are all wrong!"

"I just wish they would leave us alone and allow us to forget," Claire answered.

"It took a lot nerve for the army to ask us to recruit for them," Cora said then added, "Especially since they just told us to keep our mouths shut about what happened."

"They treat us like heroes then tell us to never speak of our internment. Well, when I get my back pay and I am a civilian again they can't control me!" Betsy said and lit a Chesterfield.

"Doesn't anyone understand that we just want to be left alone and get on with our lives," Claire said quietly.

* * *

The nurses and the twins had exhausted their supply of nervous energy by the time the train arrived in Chicago. The focus now was on getting home. The children needed to settle someplace they could feel secure and Cora was sure that would happen when she got home. *I must get them settled before I meet with Flint,* Cora thought while projecting how the children would be accepted.

Betsy's parents met the train at the station in Chicago, which was overflowing with military, mostly sailors greeting or saying good-bye to their families. After a brief visit with the Browns', the trio checked again making sure they had each other's home address. Promises were made to contact each other with their plans when their military leave ended.

Betsy explained the situation to her parent's while the others stood by. "After our sixty-day leave we can request additional time for rest and relaxation at a redistribution station before our reassignment," she paused. "Or we can get out."

"Where is the redistribution station," Betsy's father asked. "Or is there more than one?"

Cora, Claire and Betsy all answered, "Yes."

Betsy continued. "They are located at resorts in Florida, North Carolina and California. There may be more, we're not sure."

"Of course the transportation is free so we will probably go to Florida or California where it is not cold like it is here," Cora said shivering.

"They are also giving us the opportunity to get out of the army which looks like a good idea right now," Claire said and the others agreed.

Betsy's dad knelt down so he was eye level with Patrick and Peggy. "Do you know what snow is?" He asked.

"Yes sir, it's white rain," Patrick answered.

"And it is fluffy, just like the dog Aunt Betsy used to have," Peggy added.

"That's right and I think you will see snow on the train ride to West Virginia."

"Yea!" they shouted then looked at Cora. "Really?"

"Yes," she laughed, "I imagine we will. Before our train leaves tomorrow we will buy boots and mittens so we can play in the snow when we get there."

"Like Aunt Claire is wearing?"

"Yes, her family brought her winter clothes."

Their little faces glowed as they listened to the talk about snow. They were gaining weight and looking happy.

After the good-byes were said, Cora and the children got into a taxi. Claire, Courtney, Aunt Irene and Uncle Jake boarded another train traveling east. Betsy left in her father's Oldsmobile.

"Where are we going now, Mama Cora?" Peggy asked in a drowsy tone.

"To a hotel and then shopping. We are going to spend the night here in Chicago, then very early in the morning we will go back to the train station, get on a train and go visit my family."

"Aren't we your family?" Patrick asked.

"You sure are, but you have other family you have not met. While we are on the train I will tell you about all of them. Some are about your age too."

* * *

The children were not disappointed. The long trip provided mountains covered with snow. Cora read to them and they played games to pass the time. Other passengers, especially military men, talked with them, and Patrick told them where they had been and where they were going and everything else he could think of at the time. He told everyone about his father.

Cora didn't know who would meet them at the train station, but it was Doc Warner in his large LaSalle. After a hug and introductions to the twins he explained, "I had the rations for gasoline so I volunteered, but others were going to pool their rations if necessary to get you and these lovely children home. Everyone is excited." Doc rarely showed his emotions, but today he could not conceal them.

Patrick and Peggy beamed with eagerness to meet their new relatives.

Cora hoped Doc was right. *I don't know what I'll do if the twins are not accepted or if anyone mistreats them.*

Both children slept on the trip through the mountains to the coal-mining town. Doc carried Patrick and Cora carried Peggy up the steep steps to the company house where Cora had been raised. Her brother Charlie ran out on the porch to meet them and hugged Cora and the children. When the hugs were completed Cora told him to carry their luggage inside.

"You are still as bossy as ever! If the army couldn't correct that then I guess no one can," he muttered, stumbling down the steps to Doc's car.

Cora's excitement escalated when she saw how healthy her mother appeared. "Everyone come into the

297

kitchen for a snack," she insisted and lead the way. While Peggy and Patrick were enjoying chocolate Hostess Cupcakes and drinking a glass of fresh milk, Cora moved about the house studying each piece of furniture as if it were the first time she had seen it, then she slipped off to her bedroom. A piece of paper partially hidden under a hand embroidered dresser scarf caught her attention. Walking over to the worn walnut chest she slid two pieces of paper from under the scarf.

With a gasp, Cora covered her mouth and read the notice from the War Department to her mother. The first simply stated, "2$^{nd}$ Lieutenant Cora Leigh Adams, US Army Nurse Corps, stationed in the Philippines is missing in action." The second notice, dated more than a year later, informed Mrs. Adams that her daughter was a prisoner of war held by the Japanese at Santo Tomas, The Philippines.

Tears gushed from Cora's eyes and ran down her cheeks. *How horrible, Mother suffered as much as I did only in a different way.* Cora sat at her dressing table until the redness and swelling disappeared from her eyes. After wiping her nose she powdered her face and rejoined the festivities around the familiar oak kitchen table. All evening friends and family stopped by to welcome Cora and her children home.

"Mama Cora, some kid asked us to play with them in the snow tomorrow. Can we?" Patrick asked, with Peggy standing beside him.

"Of course you can, those new boots need broken in, don't they?"

He grinned, and turning to his sister said, "See I told you she would say yes."

"But now I need to get you two into bed, it's late.

Say goodnight to everyone," Cora instructed her children. Their new family insisted on hugs and goodnight kisses from the twins. With Patrick and Peggy holding onto her hands, Cora ushered them upstairs and after a bath tucked them into bed.

"We have a real family now, don't we Mama Cora?" Patrick asked.

"Yes we do" Cora answered.

"They're real nice too. I think they like me and Patrick," Peggy said.

"Yes they do. In fact I'm sure they already love you both very much. Cora kissed each child and turned out the light, leaving the door ajar.

Lying in her own bed listening to the coal being dumped into the train cars, Cora's mind shifted to the anticipation of seeing Flint.

* * *

Two weeks later Cora and the children stepped off the Greyhound bus in front of the Fletcher General Hospital. Sunshine warmed the April day and the three stopped to admire the American Flag blowing high above their heads before entering the hospital.

The one floor hospital with many wings reminded Cora of the tunnel hospital on Corregidor with all of the laterals. She was glad the twins were good travelers and comfortable in hospitals. The odors and uniformed personnel would frighten most five-year olds, but this was a natural environment for Patrick and Peggy.

Cora stood tall in her new army uniform that almost fit. Her hair had been cut into a bob and with the aid of make-up she appeared healthy and attractive. Nervously she walked up to the homely receptionist. "We're here to see Major Flint Taylor. Will you tell him 1$^{st}$ Lieutenant Adams is here to see him."

Through piercing eyes the woman studied Cora, then the children. She stood, clicked her tongue and said, "Excuse me," and disappeared into a small room off to her left.

Cora stood firm in front of the reception desk observing the twins as they sat quietly on heavy oak chairs playing with their toys. *They are adorable in their little wool sailor outfits.* She smiled, but neither looked up from their toys.

Moments later a nurse appeared. "Lieutenant, Major Taylor will be out shortly. He asked me to get you any-· thing you need while you wait," the nurse said.

"We're fine, thank you. I thought he might be in surgery so we came prepared to wait."

"Surgery? Oh no, that was over some time ago." The nurse turned and whisked through double doors leading into what appeared to be a long wide corridor.

The receptionist returned to her desk, and ignoring Cora and the children she continued her typing which the children found fascinating.

Cora sat for a while then paced the floor. *What if he has changed his mind? No, if he had he would have answered my telegram telling me not to come. No, he wouldn't have, even if he is married he would want to tell me in person. He would want to know about Spencer, Brice, Betsy and Claire too.* Cora's thoughts raced, as did her heart. *I still look thin, he'll think I'm ugly. Maybe I can get an assignment here and work with him.* Thirty minutes later she was sitting again and the children were engrossed with their new toys when the double doors leading into the waiting area burst open.

Cora gasped! She was speechless. Patrick and Peggy looked up at her with their big round eyes, then to the man in the wheelchair.

Cora temporarily froze, and then rushed to him, "Flint, I—," she stammered, searching for words.

"I know, I should have written." He took her hand in his and lowered his gaze. I was afraid you wouldn't come if you knew."

"How could you think that? I would come no matter what has happened." After a kiss she looked at the wide-eyed twins. "Children come here. This – this is Uncle Flint. You remember Uncle Spencer and Uncle Brice telling you stories about him, don't you?"

They stood close to her and nodded.

"Spencer and Brice? You've seen them?" Flint asked. Cora nodded and he spoke to the children. "You must be Peggy and Patrick, Cora has written about you and I am glad to have the chance to meet you."

Patrick held out his right hand, "I'm pleased to meet you, Mr. Flint, I mean Uncle Flint."

Flint smiled and shook the young man's hand. He looked at Peggy, "Hello, Peggy."

"Hello, Uncle Flint." He ran his hand over her smooth black hair.

"You two must tell me all about Uncle Spencer and Uncle Brice sometime. Is there an Aunt Claire and an Aunt Betsy too?"

"Yes sir," Patrick said then looked at Cora. "Mama Cora, would it be alright to ask Uncle Flint what's wrong

301

with him?"

"Oh, I'm sure Mama Cora wouldn't mind," Flint said smiling at her. "I was on a ship that was blown up by a bomb and I didn't run fast enough. I bet you two can run fast, can't you?"

"Yeah," they answered.

"Well the explosion blew my foot and part of my leg off."

Cora held her hand over her mouth willing herself not to be sick.

"Can you walk?"

"A little with crutches, but I'm not very good at it yet. An artificial foot and ankle is being made for me. When I learn to walk with it I will be as good as new." He looked serious. "Maybe you two will help me learn."

"We'd be pleased to, Uncle Flint," Patrick said as Peggy nodded.

At last Cora smiled. He still had a great attitude, and seeing him eased any doubts about her love for him.

"I have a question for the three of you. I'll be leaving here in about a month and going into the mountains of West Virginia to work at a home for children. My two brothers, their wives and I have started a home for orphans and children whose families cannot properly care for them." He looked up at Cora and flashed the smile she remembered so well. The smile she was afraid she would never see again.

"We also have a school and a large playground, and one of my brothers and both of my sisters-in-law are teachers. There are five children ranging from age two to six in my brother's families.

"I'm going to open a clinic and I need a nurse to help

me." He paused and looked at Cora then back to the twins. Patrick and Peggy smiled at each other attempting to contain their excitement.

"Here is my problem." Again he paused and rubbed his chin. "My other brother is a carpenter, and he built a big house for me; but I need a wife and children to live in it with me."

Cora was speechless.

"Now you take Mama Cora over by the chairs and decide if you would like to be my family and go with me."

The three looked at each other and all shouted, "Yes!"

Brenda Jones has a thirty-year career in the medical profession. The author's interest in WWII is a result of her father's service in the South Pacific and her mother's work on the home front as a private duty nurse.

Although this is Brenda's first novel she has published numerous short works. She and her husband, a retired university professor, live in Dover, Delaware.

You may contact the author at P.O. Box 980, Dover, DE 19903

NURSES UNDER FIRE
A World War II Novel

Brenda Jones

*Books may be purchased from Cherokee Books, your favorite bookstores or from the author. When ordering from the publisher or the author, please include $3.95 for shipping and handling.*